SECRET MURDER

by

J.C. Quinn

Cover Designed by Telemachus Press, LLC

Cover Art:
Copyright © Colorbox/2282002/ArenaCreative

Published by Telemachus Press, LLC
http://www.telemachuspress.com

ISBN: 978-1-941536-00-1 (eBook)
ISBN: 978-1-941536-24-7 (Paperback)

Version 2014.08.10

Printed in the United States of America

10 9 8 7 6 5 4 3 2 1

OTHER BOOKS BY J.C. QUINN

Dead Priest at Gator's Pond

To Kill a Fox

Triple Murder

Heroes: Stories, Letters, and Thoughts of A Catholic Man

ACKNOWLEDGEMENTS

I would like to thank my good friends—Mary Cassidy, John Stout, and Tom McGreal—for their assistance in the writing of this book. They continued to read *Secret Murder* as it progressed from chapter to chapter sharing with me their valuable insight along way. Thanks so much. And I cannot forget to thank the people at Telemachus Press for their assistance, especially the unflappable and competent Steve Himes. And to Karen Lieberman, my editor at Telemachus Press goes a special thanks. Karen, you did it again. You made another one of my books that much better. Finally, I save my greatest appreciation for my wife, Kathy, who has made writing books become a reality for me.

"Cain said to his brother Abel, 'Let us go out in the field.' When they were in the field, Cain attacked his brother Abel and killed him."

(Genesis 4: 8–9)

This book is dedicated to:

Our Lady of Perpetual Help

SECRET MURDER

CHAPTER ONE

FOURTEEN-YEAR-OLD Billy Turlop could not believe what lay at his feet. The Burmese python had to be fifteen feet long. Stretched out in the shade of a bent-over sycamore tree, the snake stared up at Billy. Black, beady eyes seemed to be saying, *Leave me alone, can't you see that I can't move with this calf inside my belly?*

"I got it. Down by the river. It's a big one. Hurry up and get over here."

Billy's best friend, Josh Kincaid, came running. The boy was holding a two-foot long machete in his right hand. Josh stopped just short of the big snake. Wide-eyed, he let loose with a loud gasp.

"So that's where all of Roscoe Tanner's newborn calves have been goin'. Fillin' up that big sucker's belly. How did it ever swallow that calf whole like it done? Billy, sure as I'm standing here that newborn calf is inside that snake's belly. Look how swollen it is."

Josh took a step toward the snake. Tan in color with dark patches covering a scaly skin, the python's huge head came off the ground. Its mouth opened wide. A hissing sound came out. The snake was ready to strike. Two black eyes stayed fixated on the threat no more than a few feet away. Josh raised the machete.

"Don't miss its head or it'll bite ya," Billy yelled just as Josh brought down the machete blade.

"Josh, you cut the sucker's head clean off. Look at the rest of it squirming around. Ain't that a sight? Open up its belly and let's see the calf. We got to be sure before we go and tell Mr. Tanner."

Josh slit the snake's underbelly with the machete. A dead, brown-colored, newborn calf slid out onto the sandy grass. Both boys looked at one another. Duplicate smiles lit up their faces. Roscoe Tanner would be happy. And he would reward them well. The two friends shook hands.

Billy Turlop said, "Let's take the head up to the big house to show Mr. Tanner. Then we'll bring him back here and show him the calf."

Billy bent down to pick-up the severed snakehead.

"What's that?" he asked Josh after seeing something that caught his eye. "Sticking out there under the snake's body." Billy kicked the python to move it out of the way. "That there, where the ground caved in, something's sticking out."

Josh dropped down to his knees to look. He pushed at the sand and dirt. There was something. The boy's face took on a queer expression.

"It sure looks like the finger bones on a human hand. And that there big bone could be a person's arm. I think it's part of a body. It sure looks like one. And don't that look like clumps of blond hair?"

"What would a body be doing buried out here?"

"I don't know. But we better tell Mr. Tanner right away," Josh said, standing. "And you can leave the snakehead, Billy. I don't think Mr. Tanner will want to be seein' that snakehead right about now."

****

Roscoe Tanner was inside his barn checking on a four-year-old Morgan mare about to give foal when he heard his name being called. Tanner's foreman, Jimmy Burke, was squatting down next to him. Both men looked up to see Billy Turlop and Josh Kincaid come running into the barn.

"Mr. Tanner, we killed that snake that's been eatin' your calves and found a body stickin' up out of the ground. It's just bones, but it sure looks like human bones to us."

"You found what?" Tanner said coming to a standing position.

"Let me tell him," Josh said shoving Billy Turlop out of the way. "Mr. Tanner I killed that python with my machete, and Billy went to get its head so that we could show it to you, that's when we saw the body. It was buried in the ground, but that big snake caved in the sand when it started squirmin' around."

"What are two talking about? What kind of a body? Are you talking about a dead snake or a person?"

"Both," Billy Turlop answered. "There's a dead python and what sure looks like a human body underneath it."

"Take me to it," Roscoe Tanner said while motioning for Burke to accompany him.

****

The Tanner ranch comprised five thousand acres of the best land in Southwest Florida. Roscoe Tanner and his sister, Mary Jo, received equal title to the ranch three years ago after their mother's death. But it was Roscoe who ran the day-to-day operations. He controlled the money and everything else relating to the Tanner ranch. Mary Jo received a check for seven-thousand-dollars every month. She along with her Wall Street broker husband chose the New York City lifestyle and had not laid eyes on the ranch since the mother's funeral.

Tall and square-shouldered, thirty-nine-year-old Roscoe Tanner looked every bit cattleman and horse rancher. He had a reputation for being ruthless and unmerciful whenever it came to a business deal. The accumulation of wealth was what drove Tanner. How he came by it did not matter. Stolen cattle, narcotics dealing, organized crime ties, all went into the man's make-up. Making money and supporting his lavish lifestyle was what preoccupied Tanner's every waking moment. So what he came to observe on the ground beneath the bent-over Sycamore tree did not sit well with him.

The tufts of blond hair and what looked like a human hand and arm bone sent his mind railing. The Pelican's Landing Police would have to be called. And that meant Lieutenant Jackson Stone would be coming out. Questions would be asked of Tanner and everyone else who worked for him. The surrounding property would be searched and the mobile meth lab down by the river discovered. The lab was stocked full of white crystal with shipment to Miami scheduled in another month. Hundreds of thousands of dollars were at stake, not to mention the promise he had made to Big Al Ruggiero for prompt delivery. Jackson Stone. The mere thought of dealing once again with the police lieutenant sent Tanner's stomach jumping. He hated the man. Last year Stone and two of his deputies while armed with a search warrant raided Tanner's barn. They had confiscated hundreds of pounds of marijuana inside a panel truck that was only hours away from leaving for Miami. Someone had to have given Stone the heads-up on the marijuana. Roscoe Tanner tried but had never been able to identify Stone's informant. Tanner knew that it had to be someone who worked for him. Someone he trusted. But who? The thought of seeing Jackson Stone again brought it all back for Tanner. He had promised himself a long time ago that one day he would kill Stone. Perhaps it would be sooner than he thought.

"Move that meth lab trailer down by the river over to that piece of property at Cattail Marsh. The piece I bought last month." Tanner said to his foreman, Jimmy Burke, well out of earshot of the two boys. "And after it's moved telephone the Pelican's Landing police. Tell them that there are the remains of what looks like a human body buried on the Tanner Ranch, and if they want to talk to me about it I'll be in the barn taking care of the mare."

"What kind of heat do you think this is going to bring down on us?" Burke asked while not taking his eyes off the protruding bone sticking out of the ground.

"I don't know," a grim-faced Roscoe Tanner said before walking away.

CHAPTER TWO

KERI MARTIN'S FLIGHT was more than an hour late in taking off from Chicago's Midway Airport. Heavy rain and high winds comprised Chicago's weather leaving planes backed up nose to tail on the tarmac. Frustrated passengers waited for their plane to rev its engines and begin takeoff. Keri's plane inched along behind all the others in line. She knew it would be quite some time before her plane reached the takeoff point. But the unexpected delay was of no consequence to the thirty-four-year-old former Deputy Chief of the Chicago Police Department. Her life the past few months had been moving at a snail's pace anyway. So why should things change now? Besides, arriving an hour or more late at Fort Myers International Airport was of no real consequence. It would give her extra time to read over the personnel files that she had brought with her. For the past week, Keri had been putting off the task using one lame excuse after another. But there was no time left for excuses. The reading of the files had to be done. Pelican Landing's new police chief knew all too well the imperativeness of completing the background work. She had to be familiar with the police personnel under her command prior to her arrival in Florida.

The flight was not fully booked, which allowed for several empty seats on the plane. Keri took advantage of the empty seat next to her having covered it with a stack of brown folders. She would do her best to get to know each department member before her arrival. Hopefully, the personnel files were up to date. Keri reached over and took the top folder. It bore the name Clifford Potts in the upper left corner. Flipping the outside jacket, she started to read Potts's file.

Clifford Potts: Male White, 5.10, 190 lbs., DOB: 22 Oct 1948, unmarried, present rank: sergeant. Joined the Pelican's Landing Police Department on 10 June 1979. Prior to joining the department served four years in the U.S. Marine Corp with two years deployment in Viet Nam. Sustained shrapnel wounds in both legs; underwent several surgeries. Both legs were left impaired, but did not limit his ability to serve on the police department. Keri noted the several letters of commendation from citizens and the dozens of past supervisor notations praising Potts for his police service. Potts obtained the rank of sergeant on 16 April 2010. Keri further noted that he was recommended for the sergeant's rank by Lieutenant Jackson Stone. She paged through the file looking for anything that could give more insight into the man. Aside from Keri and Lieutenant Stone, Potts was the only other supervisor.

The Pelican's Landing Police Department was a small department. It utilized three supervisors along with three full-time police officers and five civilian personnel. During the winter months when the tourists from up north flocked to Pelican's Landing, four part-time officers were added. Keri felt it was important to know as much as possible about Sergeant Clifford Potts. A police supervisor's job could be a demanding one. And Potts was advanced in age. Was he still up to the job? Would she be able to count on him in a tough situation? In viewing Potts's file, Keri found nothing that addressed her concerns. She was about to close the file when something caught her attention. It was inside the back folder, nearly covered over by a blank sheet of paper.

During the past year two written reprimands had been issued to Sergeant Clifford Potts for consumption of alcohol while on duty. Citizens in separate incidents had complained of having smelled alcohol on Potts's breath. Both complaints had been lodged with a civilian desk person at the Pelican's Landing Police Department. The complaints were then given to a supervisor for an internal investigation. Sergeant Potts received a written reprimand in each incident for the drinking of alcohol while on duty. Lieutenant Jackson Stone's signature appeared at the bottom of each reprimand. Accompanying Stone's signatures were notations indicating that no further disciplinary action would be taken. And that was it? Keri thought. Two written reprimands for drinking alcohol while on duty and no further disciplinary action? Maybe for the first citizen's complaint Stone could get away with giving a written reprimand. But surely not after Potts had received a second one. And why wasn't Potts given a breathalyzer to determine the amount of alcohol in his blood? Keri placed the two written reprimands back behind the blank sheet of paper. She closed Potts' file before placing it on the floor. Reaching for the next brown folder, Keri observed the name Lisa Moore on the outside cover. She opened it and started reading.

Lisa Moore: Female White, DOB: 10 March 1987, 5.04, 115 lbs., unmarried, rank: police officer. Joined the Pelican's Landing Police Department on 15 May 2010. Prior to joining the department worked as a restaurant waitress for three years. Education: high school in addition to some college computer classes. Keri noted four letters from citizens commending Moore on her thoughtfulness and dedication to duty. One was from a woman whose six-year-old daughter had been separated from her while at a music fair on the beach. Police Officer Moore found the lost girl alone in a park area four blocks from where she was last seen. Another letter commended Officer Moore for aiding an elderly man who suffered a heart attack on the street. Moore administered emergency CPR and saved the man's life according to the responding ambulance personnel. The other two letters were from citizens who received assistance from Officer Moore after their cars had broken down. They were also full of gratitude and praise for Moore.

Keri noted no disciplinary problems relative to Moore. But one item perked the new police chief's interest. Shortly after Lisa Moore joined the police department, she was allowed a three month paid maternity leave. The paid leave had been approved by Lieutenant Jackson Stone. There was no written summary detailing as to why the leave had been granted to a probationary officer. It seemed highly unusual. Keri Martin's mind raced. What was going on here? Moore had to have been pregnant on the day she joined the police department. Stone at some point should have come to realize it. The personnel file indicated Moore was unmarried. Procedurally, the woman's pregnancy should have been disclosed prior to her employment. Keri searched the file for some explanation. All she found were several notations scribbled along the file margins complimenting Moore on her work performance. The notations were signed by none other than Lieutenant Jackson Stone. Could Stone possibly be the father of Moore's child? Keri asked herself before closing the file. Had she made a mistake in accepting the new police chief's job at Pelican's Landing? And what exactly was she walking into? Keri dropped the brown folder onto the floor and reached for the next file. The name Robert Garcia appeared in the upper left hand corner. Please, no more surprises, Keri thought. She opened Garcia's file.

Robert Garcia, Male Hispanic, DOB 11 Nov 1988, 6.0, 185 lbs., unmarried, rank: police officer, education: two years of college, speaks fluent Spanish, joined the Pelican's Landing Police Department on 27 October 2012. Prior to his joining the department Garcia spent four years in the U.S. Marine Corp serving one year in Afghanistan. There were no letters of commendation except for a letter submitted by Lieutenant Jackson Stone to the Pelican's Landing

Town Council. It recommended that Robert Garcia be hired to fill the vacancy for police officer. In the letter Stone stated that he had known Garcia's father for several years and had served with the elder Garcia in the Marine Corp. He had also witnessed the younger Garcia growing up through the years, and found him to be of outstanding character while also possessing the necessary good judgment required of every police officer.

Stone again, Keri thought. The Pelican's Landing Town Council hired Robert Garcia on Lieutenant Jackson Stone's recommendation. Here was yet another member of the Pelican's Landing Police Department who owed their allegiance to Jackson Stone. Keri was aware that she and Stone had been the two finalists for the police chief's job. And the Pelican's Landing Town Council had awarded it to her. But why? She asked herself. Why did they pass over a man who had already been working for them? Yes, she was highly qualified for the job and had given a great interview before the town council. Keri could still recall watching Mayor Zach Worthington's face as she detailed the graduate work she had completed at the University of Chicago. The mayor also mentioned her work experience as a deputy chief for the Chicago Police Department.

"You have two masters' degrees and gained valuable experience while heading the Evidence and Recovered Property Section of the Chicago Police Department. More than two hundred personnel were under your command. Ms. Martin your education and experience are what we are looking for in our next police chief. Thank you for coming to Pelican's Landing for this interview."

Keri felt it had to have been her qualifications and the great interview she gave to the town council that landed her the police chief's job. Closing the Garcia file, she set it on the floor. Keri looked down at the next file in line. The name Jackson Stone appeared in the upper left hand corner. Hesitating, she picked it up with both hands. Why does it bother me to open his file? She asked herself. What could be in Stone's file to cause me concern? Did it contain the reason she had been given the job over him? Stone had been Pelican Landing's acting police chief for more than a year. It would seem logical that he would have been the obvious replacement for the outgoing chief of police. Most town councils prefer to pick someone from their own department. Instead, Stone was passed over by the mayor and town council. Why? What was the reason for him not getting the job? Open up the file and find out, Keri Martin found herself thinking. What are you afraid of? The answer is probably right there in front of you. Keri opened the file.

Jackson Stone, Male White, DOB 19 March 1975, 6.2, 210 lbs., unmarried, rank: lieutenant, education: law degree from Fordham University, joined the Pelican's Landing Police Department on 20 Feb 2004, previously worked nine years for the New York City Police Department, and achieved the rank of detective sergeant. Four years in the U.S. Marine Corp, while serving a full tour of duty in Iraq. Attended night school where he obtained a B.A. degree in English and a law degree from Fordham University in New York City. Several letters of commendation from both the New York City Police Department and the Pelican's Landing Police Department. Keri noted one letter of commendation from the FBI where Stone was praised for working undercover. It resulted in the arrest and conviction of several top organized crime figures in New York City. The arrests and convictions were for narcotics trafficking, extortion, and murder. A New York Times article was part of the file. In the article Jackson Stone was asked by a reporter as to why he would work undercover and place himself in such a dangerous position. His answer to the reporter was, "Because I detest narcotics dealers and murderers almost as much as I do journalists."

Evidently not someone who likes to mince words, Keri thought. He could easily become a public relations nightmare in a highly sensitive case. That is probably why he was passed over for the police chief's job. The mayor and town council must have come to realize it over the past year. Stone could be a loose cannon around the news media.

Keri came across a letter from the mayor in Stone's file. It was addressed to Acting Police Chief Jackson Stone. It concerned a charge of harassment leveled against Stone by someone identified as Roscoe Tanner. A year ago Jackson Stone had arrested Tanner for the cultivation and distribution of marijuana. But in a criminal court hearing the felony charges were dismissed. Judge Wilson allowed Tanner to plead guilty to one misdemeanor charge of possession and ended up sentencing him to two years of court supervision. In his letter Mayor Worthington took Stone to task, "You will not harass Mr. Tanner in any way, which includes entering upon his property without first obtaining a signed search warrant from a county judge. Mr. Tanner's previous criminal case involving the possession of marijuana has been adjudicated in a court of law. You, Lieutenant Stone, are not above the law and will in the future act responsibly while working for the Pelican's Landing Police Department."

Keri Martin closed the file. So that's it, she thought. Mayor Worthington has some sort of tie to this man Roscoe Tanner who deals in marijuana. And Stone would not let well enough alone. He did not care for Tanner's case getting fixed in court so he stayed after him. It had resulted in Stone losing out on the police chief's job and the mayor getting someone from out of town to take it. Someone who did not know about the mayor's relationship with Tanner. Keri set Stone's file down on the floor. She sat back in her seat and tried to think. Pelican's Landing was to be a fresh start for her. Keri was hoping to leave Chicago and begin a new life for herself. She was running away from one kind of trouble and did not need another kind. It was as if she were jumping out of one frying pan into a different one. Something inside told her to get up and walk off the plane. Do it now before it's too late. Hurry. You will be sorry if you don't. Keri unbuckled her seat belt. She was preparing to exit the plane. The pilot announced that they were cleared for takeoff. Jet engines started to rev. The plane jerked forward. It began picking up speed. "Sit back and relax," Keri heard the pilot say over the plane's intercom. "We are heading to Florida. Enjoy your flight."

CHAPTER THREE

TRAFFIC WAS LIGHT on Interstate 75. Deputy Lisa Moore moved the unmarked squad car into the left lane and pressed down on its accelerator. The palm and hardwood trees lining the roadway soon became a blur. While a steamy haze rose from the road's asphalt surface. The late afternoon sun proved to be unmerciful in its attack, enclosing the Florida landscape in its fiery grip. Off to her right, Deputy Moore spotted movement. Turkey buzzards, large and black, were swarming a road kill. It looked like a raccoon carcass the birds were tearing apart, but Moore could not be sure. Her squad car was traveling too fast for the deputy to get a good enough look. Reaching over, she turned down the car's air-conditioner. Earlier Moore's gray uniform shirt had been soaked through with perspiration. Now it felt cold and damp.

Glancing into the rearview mirror, the deputy let her dark sunglasses drop down onto the bridge of her nose. Two pretty, hazel-colored eyes looked back while an open-mouthed smile produced a set of stainless white teeth. Breakfast that morning at the Crow's Nest had consisted of ham and eggs with a side order of grits. Such a combination often left unsightly particles showing. Today of all days Moore did not want that to happen. But she told herself that there was nothing to worry about. Her pearly whites were as clean as a whistle. The twenty-seven-year-old deputy fluffed her short, brown hair and turned her head from side to side in the mirror. Satisfied that no loose strands were showing she propped up her sunglasses and sat erect in the car seat. Lisa Moore was more than ready to meet the new police chief.

Two weeks ago after hearing that Keri Martin was to be Pelican Landing's new chief of police, Moore obtained a computer driven photo of Martin. The deputy took it off the Chicago Police Department's official website. The 12 by 12.5 color photo was now resting on the passenger seat next to her. Moore looked over at it. The photograph had been taken at Martin's promotional ceremony for the rank of deputy chief. It depicted a strikingly attractive woman in her early thirties with long, red hair, and light green eyes. Martin was smiling while standing at a podium. She wore a Chicago Police uniform with attached gold braids. After having viewed the photo on several occasions, Moore was still taken by Martin's beauty. Lisa thought Keri Martin to be one of the most beautiful women she had ever seen. But the Pelican's Landing deputy did not stop at Martin's photo.

Moore wanted to learn as much as possible about the new police chief. Using her computer skills, she did an in-depth background check on one Keri Lynn Martin. An anonymous blog called Cop Shop proved to be a great source of assistance. Every tidbit of information concerning anything to do with the Chicago Police Department was on the website. Any rumors, gossip, news events relating to police officers, but especially bosses, appeared on the blog. Deputy Chief Keri Martin was frequently mentioned. The blog also displayed several newspaper photographs of Martin while off duty. They were taken either in a restaurant, nightclub, or some other public place. The photographs showed Martin in the company of a Chicago commodities trader by the name of Rance Stapleton.

One blog headline read, "The Bad and the Beautiful Cruise Rush Street." Moore determined "The Bad and the Beautiful" to be a label

Chicago newspaper gossip columnists had pinned on Stapleton and Martin. Moore did some further digging to find the reason behind the label. It surprised her at what she found.

Keri Martin and Rance Stapleton had been romantically linked for several months. He was a multi-millionaire living in a Gold Coast mansion overlooking Chicago's Lake Shore Drive. He also owned elaborate houses in Northern England and Southern Italy. The handsome and well-built Stapleton liked Chicago's nightlife and frequently appeared in the newspaper society columns. His relationship with Keri Martin only added to his appeal. She was attractive and a rising star in the Chicago Police Department. Keri's late father, Jack Martin, had been a deputy chief. When Keri was eleven-years-old, Martin was gunned down after having responded to an armed robbery call at a south side gas station. Jack Martin became a police hero. Keri Martin was his daughter. The Chicago newspapers found the combination of Martin and Stapleton irresistible. It was something that they could not pass up. Especially after rumors started circulating that their relationship was not exactly a happy one. Then it came out that Rance Stapleton had been arrested for domestic battery. Keri Martin reportedly was the complainant. At the initial court hearing, the Michigan avenue courtroom was packed with reporters and a gawking public. A smug Rance Stapleton displayed himself to the cameras appearing to enjoy every minute of it. A rather demure-looking Martin entered the courtroom flanked by two of her brothers. She quickly dropped her complaint against Stapleton.

After that "The Bad the Beautiful" label was bandied about all the more. Lisa Moore was able to secure a recent photograph of Martin that had been highlighted on the Cop Shop blog. Martin's left eye appeared swollen, nearly shut. Rance Stapleton had apparently struck Martin once again after a late night quarrel. A judge issued a restraining order against Stapleton. In the order Stapleton was told to have no further contact with Keri Martin. So she must have applied for the police chief's job in Pelican's Landing to get away from Stapleton, Moore had surmised on the day she visited the Cop Shop website. Martin is leaving Chicago because things have gotten too hot for her. She's coming down to Florida to get away from everything.

Lisa Moore steered the squad car into the right lane. The thought of Martin being the new police chief was bothersome to Moore. Does she really think she can tell Jackson Stone anything about police work? Lisa wondered. The woman would have to be crazy if she did. No, she got the job because of Mayor Zach Worthington. The mayor and Roscoe Tanner have their cozy deal. That's why they want Martin to be the new chief of police. They couldn't take the chance on Jackson Stone getting the job. Everybody on the Pelican's Landing Police Department knows it. Worthington and Tanner are the best of friends. Tanner does Worthington's heavy work with the town council. And now Worthington is helping out Roscoe Tanner, keeping Jackson Stone from becoming the new police chief in Pelican's Landing. Tanner has to know that he would end up in prison if Stone were running the police department. Worthington would never be able to protect him.

The airport exit sign came into view. "Well here goes nothing," Lisa Moore said out loud to herself. "Try and make with the nice and hope for the best." Taking the exit ramp, Moore let up on the accelerator. She directed her squad car toward the airport terminal.

****

Keri Martin looked at herself in the airport restroom mirror. What a frightful sight, she thought. Long strands of red hair hung limply across both her shoulders, showing not a bit of bounce. Keri lashed out with her comb. The lashing changed nothing. The long strands remained limp across her shoulders. Martin hurriedly brushed away the loose hairs that had fallen onto her dark blue jacket. What am I to do? She asked herself. A good first impression is so important. And they will all be at the Pelican's Landing police station waiting for me.

Martin's flight from Chicago arrived an hour late at Fort Myers International Airport. By the time Keri had retrieved her suitcase from the baggage claim area, forty more minutes had passed. Now she was in the women's airport restroom attempting to make herself presentable. The makeup she had applied to her chin and cheeks along with the penciled in eye-shadow left her reasonably happy. But it was the look of her hair. Keri could do nothing with it. She had spent three hours the day before sitting in a Chicago downtown beauty salon getting her hair done. It turned out to be three hours of wasted time.

Martin reached into her handbag and removed the bottle of Jean Paton Joy perfume. It was a birthday gift from Rance Stapleton. An eight hundred dollars an ounce birthday gift. It was the only thing Rance had given her that Keri did not either give away or toss in the garbage. She generously dabbed behind the lobes of both ears before securing the top and placing the bottle back in her handbag. Martin looked once more in the mirror. Two green eyes stared back at her. Keri observed the sadness in both eyes. They reveal how I truly feel, she thought to herself, before picking up her suitcase and walking out the restroom door.

CHAPTER FOUR

THE CHANGE IN temperature nearly took Keri Martin's breath away. Dragging her pink floral suitcase behind her, Keri stepped out into Southwest Florida's heat and humidity. She could not remember experiencing anything like it. The temperature was close to 100 degrees with a heat index topping 120. It left the late afternoon air absolutely stifling. Keri blinked away the bright sunlight while searching her handbag for sunglasses. She found everything else but what she was looking for. Her frantic search failed to produce the much needed sunglasses. Florida and no sunglasses, she thought to herself. What else could I have forgotten? She closed the handbag and observed for the first time the long line of taxicabs parked in front of the terminal. The driver of the nearest taxi waved at Martin. Keri shook her head. Turning away, she dragged her suitcase toward the other end of the terminal.

Someone was supposed to be picking her up. At least that was what the e-mail from the Pelican's Landing Police Department had said. Seeking relief from the sun's glare, Keri moved beneath a terminal overhang. It was not only hot. It was suffocatingly hot. She opened the top button on her white blouse while reprimanding herself for having worn the blue jacket and matching long pants. The blouse along with a skirt would have been much better. And wearing the pantyhose and spike-heeled shoes did not help either. They left her legs and feet feeling like they were on fire. Keri was about to walk over to the nearest taxicab and ask the driver to take her to the Pelican's Landing police station when a car horn sounded. Turning in the direction of the sound, Martin observed a Pelican's Landing police car pulling up to the curb. She dragged herself and the pink floral suitcase over to it.

"Chief Martin, I sure hope you weren't waiting too long," Deputy Moore said before removing Keri's photo from the passenger seat. She then leaned over to open the passenger side door. "I'll get out and help you with your suitcase. We can put it in the back seat."

"Thank you, but don't bother. I can manage it myself," Keri said prior to opening the squad car's back door and placing her suitcase on the seat. She then got into the front and shut the passenger side door.

The cool temperature inside the police car brought instant relief. Keri could not recall appreciating air-conditioning more in her life. She turned up the knob on the car's air-conditioner and directed the side air vent toward her face. Martin felt Lisa Moore staring at her. Smiling, the new police chief looked over at her.

"Does it always get this hot? I know Chicago can get hot in the summertime, but nothing like this. I don't ever remember feeling this kind of heat. It's like someone turned on the barbeque grill and slid me next to the hamburgers."

"This time of year it usually gets this hot or hotter," Moore said not quite believing what she was seeing. "But then, Chief Martin, you didn't exactly dress for our July weather. That blue outfit you're wearing is pretty, but jackets and long pants don't fly too well down here when it gets this hot. By the way, I'm Deputy Lisa Moore. I recognized you right off from your photograph, which I got off the Internet. I hope you don't mind me saying that you take a beautiful photograph."

"Thank you, Lisa," Keri Martin responded while observing the deputy's friendly smile and easy manner. And what else about me did you get off the Internet? Keri found herself thinking. What other information did you download, Lisa Moore? You're the one who had the baby after joining the Pelican's Landing Police Department. You're the one Jackson Stone could not praise enough.

"I assume you will be taking me directly to the police station so that I can meet the other members of the department," Martin said after seeing Moore edging her squad car into traffic. "How long of a ride is it? Will everyone be there?"

Deputy Moore told her, "I thought you would first want to go to the Holiday Inn where you are registered and get yourself settled in before doing anything else."

"No, I want to go directly to the police station and meet everybody. The hotel can wait. This is my first day as chief of police and I want everything to be done right. It is important that I meet everyone as soon as possible. They are all waiting there for me, aren't they?"

Deputy Moore's face took on a frown. "I'm sorry, chief, but other than the police dispatcher and the civilian desk personnel there's nobody at the station."

"Where is Lieutenant Stone? I specifically requested that he and all police personnel be present upon my arrival."

"Chief, they're still at the scene where the dead body turned up. I was out there before I came to the airport to get you. That's why I was late coming for you. I have no idea how long Lieutenant Stone and Sergeant Potts are going to be there. The Pelican's Landing Police Department doesn't get too many reports of human bones buried in a shallow grave. It sure looks like a murder. And before I left the scene some of the television stations were there along with reporters from our local newspaper."

"A murder? Who was killed? How was the body discovered? Do we know anything about the victim?"

"No, not yet. When I left they were just trying to move the sand and dirt off the bones. If there's no wallet found, it'll take a while before we get an ID. Two kids found the body while they were out hunting snakes."

"Hunting snakes? Lisa, take me directly to the scene," Martin said while feeling her stomach tightening into a hard knot. It was her first day on the job and here she was with a murder case. It was not something any new police chief would want on their first day. And especially for a new police chief who never had to deal with a murder case before. "You better turn on your emergency equipment, Lisa. And use your siren. I want to get there before everyone is gone."

****

A cloud of white dust trailed the speeding squad car down the gravel road. Pot-holed and bumpy, the north back road of the Tanner ranch caused Deputy Moore's squad car to bounce and veer from side to side. Keri Martin held onto the dashboard in front of her with both hands. The sight of flashing police lights and people standing just off the road up ahead could not have come too soon for Martin. She removed both hands from the dashboard as Lisa Moore slowed the squad car and brought it to a stop.

"It looks like I got you here in time. Everybody's still here," Moore beamed before throwing her car into park and opening the driver's side door. "Chief, I'd leave that jacket of yours in the car if I were you. It's goin' to be hot enough without you wearing it."

"I think you're right," Keri said taking off her jacket and laying it on the front seat. She opened the passenger side door and got out of the car. Lisa Moore came around to meet her.

"That crowd over there that's looking at us is the press" Moore said staring at a group of about ten or twelve men and women who were standing behind a long line of yellow police tape. "Right now they're wondering who you are. Chief, I don't want to tell you what to do, but I wouldn't talk to them right about now. At least not until you get the chance to talk to Lieutenant Stone first."

"Where is Lieutenant Stone?" Keri asked looking beyond the crowd of reporters. She observed a group of men approximately seventy-five yards distance from the gravel road. "Is that where the body is at? Are one of those men Lieutenant Stone?"

"Yes," Lisa Moore responded taking hold of Keri Martin's right arm. "I'll take you over there. The uniformed guy is Sergeant Potts. Lieutenant Stone is the tall one with the black hair. He's wearing the white shirt and tie. The other three are county tech lab people. The county medical examiner was here earlier, but he must have left. Chief, why don't you follow me and I'll take you to them. But be careful. Those spiked high heels you're wearing aren't exactly made for walking on ground like this. And watch out for snakes. Step where I step."

Keri followed Lisa Moore ducking down under the yellow police tape before moving in the direction of the discovered body. A couple of the reporters called Lisa by name asking for information concerning the body, but the Pelican's Landing deputy only waved without looking back.

Chief Keri Martin did all she could to keep up with Deputy Moore. The sandy ground was difficult to navigate in spike heeled shoes. Several times Keri lost her footing and nearly fell. Both her ankles felt as though they were ready to snap off. She was just thankful for having gotten rid of the jacket. It would have been too much to bear in this stifling heat. The late afternoon sun was blazing hot leaving Martin perspiring heavily. She could feel the make-up running down her face. Repeatedly, she ran a right sleeve across her mouth and chin. It left the white sleeve of Martin's blouse stained with traces of lipstick and make-up. Keri could only guess as to what her eye shadow looked like.

“Almost there,” she heard Lisa yell back to her. And none too soon, Keri thought as she looked up to find five men no more than twenty yards away staring at her.

CHAPTER FIVE

LIEUTENANT JACKSON STONE did not know what to make of the new police chief. Glancing to his right, he observed Cliff Potts. The sergeant's face was showing an amused smile. Potts returned Jackson's look before shaking his head. The crime lab techs abruptly stopped their tedious job of collecting dirt and sand from the gravesite. Dressed in white nylon jumper suits, the three techs slowly came to their feet. The men at the gravesite remained fixated on the two women approaching. Deputy Lisa Moore waved, grinning from ear to ear. A struggling Keri Martin followed behind her.

"She doesn't look anything like her photo, now does she?" Potts said in a drawn out Southern drawl. "And with all that smeared eye shadow around her eyes it'd be easy at night to mistake her for a raccoon."

"I don't think our Florida weather agrees much with Chief Martin," Jackson Stone said while taking in Keri Martin's drooping red hair and sweat-stained face.

Cliff Potts laughed.

"Jackson, you can sure say that again. I'll bet if that gal stays out much longer in this sun, she'll melt down to nothing right before our eyes."

"You might be right about that," Stone said taking off his sunglasses for a better look. The two women were nearly at the gravesite. There was no mistaking the pain on Keri Martin's face.

Lisa Moore said, "Chief Martin wanted to come out to the scene so I brought her directly here. Jackson, those press people are mighty fidgety over there. You're going to have to give them something or they're going to scream to the high heaven."

"They can wait," Stone said before turning his attention to Keri Martin. "Chief Martin, I'm Lieutenant Jackson Stone. I was hoping that we could have met under better circumstances, not out here in this hot sun with a bag of human bones lying at our feet."

Keri found herself looking into the bluest pair of eyes she had ever seen. They were eyes possessing a hard glint. Martin could only guess as to how a suspect would feel under such a stare. It would be unnerving to say the least. She extended her right hand. Stone took it. The awkwardness of the moment was felt by both.

Spotting the open body bag containing human bones, Keri Martin said, "Lieutenant Stone, I can see what you mean by better circumstances. Do we have any idea as to how long the body was buried here? And have you been able to make an ID yet?"

"The medical examiner was here earlier. He said the body was probably buried several years ago. No clothes were buried with it and you can see the blond hair on the skull and the tufts of hair that fell off. The ME was able to tell by the pelvic area that it's female. After examining the teeth, he estimated somewhere between 18 to 23 years old. We're running a check on all Collier County missings for the past twenty years within a ten mile radius of here. But I'm sure there's going to be plenty of them, and undoubtedly it will take some time before we get anything back. With any luck the dental records will eventually help us make a positive ID."

Keri Martin leaned closer to the body. She wiped her face with her right sleeve. Martin had never been this close to a dead body. The skeleton appeared to be intact. A pair of empty eye sockets stared up at her. They once held a human being's eyes, Martin found herself thinking. These bones were actually a real person. "Do we have any idea as to how she might have been killed?"

"Not yet," Stone said. "The postmortem will be done tomorrow morning at nine a.m. Hopefully after it's done we'll have some idea as to what killed her. But it could be tough coming up with a cause of death after all these years. The evidence tech's have collected all the dirt and sand covering the body. They'll take it back to the crime lab and check it out for bullet fragments and whatever else they might find. The ME took hair samples with him and he's going to put a priority rush on them for testing."

"Are we done here then?" Martin asked while straightening up and looking into the faces of everyone around her. All had sunglasses covering their eyes. Keri was the only one without sun protection. The sun's glare seemed overwhelming. She attempted to shade her eyes with both hands.

"Yes, we are," Stone said handing his sunglasses to Martin. "Chief, take these I have another pair in the car. This sun can be brutal on the eyes."

"It certainly can," Keri said after taking the offered sunglasses and putting them on. "And thank you, Lieutenant Stone. I won't ever forget my sunglasses again. Now what kind of statement do you suggest we give to the news media?"

"If it were up to me I wouldn't give them one. I'd have Deputy Moore tell them that an official statement will be sent to their respective outlets within the hour and leave it at that."

"But then it isn't up to you now, is it Lieutenant Stone? It is up to me. And I don't want to be making enemies out of the press on my first day as police chief. I've seen what they can do to someone when they band together. I suggest that the two of us go over there and make ourselves available to the news media. I'll introduce myself as the new police chief and defer all questions concerning this investigation to you, my second in command and chief investigator."

"Pardon me, Chief Martin, but I think someone has beaten you to your news conference," Sergeant Potts said. He directed Keri's attention to the news reporters on the other side of the yellow police tape. The reporters were gathered around someone who was speaking to them.

"It's the mayor," Lisa Moore said while not attempting to hide her disdain. "The man could find a news camera within twenty miles from wherever he was standing. He doesn't know diddly about what happened here and look at him. He can't stop talkin'."

"Lieutenant Stone, perhaps you and I should go over and join Mayor Worthington?" Chief Martin said looking directly at Stone. She checked his face for a reaction but found nothing. Stone's gaze stayed on her. It made Keri Martin glad to be wearing sunglasses. The man's steady look caused her to feel uncomfortable.

Sergeant Potts tapped Martin on the right arm.

"Chief, you won't have to be going over there for your news conference. It looks like the mayor is bringing it to you."

Keri turned and observed Zach Worthington traversing the open ground toward the gravesite. A string of excited reporters filed behind him. A couple of them with video cameras were running ahead. Martin could not quite believe what she was seeing. It reminded her of an early morning special at Macy's with everything on sale.

"Sergeant Potts, you and Deputy Moore get those people back behind the police tape immediately," Chief Martin said while not attempting to conceal the anger in her voice.

"Does that include the mayor, too?" Potts asked with a smile on his face. He looked over at Jackson Stone.

"No, the mayor can come here. But only the mayor and no one else."

"He's not going to like being made a fool out of in front of the press," Stone said after moving closer to Martin. "Zach Worthington likes to have his own way with everything that takes place in Pelican's Landing. Be ready for him when he gets here."

"I will," Martin replied. "And thanks for the use of the sunglasses, Lieutenant Stone. I don't think I will be needing them anymore."

Keri handed Stone back his sunglasses. He took them and observed Martin's green eyes staring at him. Stone noted the determined look. He was surprised by it. Maybe, he thought, things might work out after all.

CHAPTER SIX

ZACH WORTHINGTON HAD been Ohio State University's starting center for three years before the Dallas Cowboys drafted him. He played two years for Dallas and then a knee injury put an end to his professional football career. The computer software business became his next endeavor. Worthington started up a small company called Diamond Systems, Inc. in Fort Lee, New Jersey, specializing in computer software programs. A businessman from Dallas who Worthington knew had introduced him to Ricky Palermo. Palermo was a cousin to Vinnie Palermo, the head of the New Jersey crime syndicate. The Conigliaro Crime Family had ties to New York City's Five Crime Families as well as the Philadelphia Crime Family and the Loprino Crime Family of New England. Worthington's computer software company soon took off with both syndicate money and influence behind it. The once professional football player for the Dallas Cowboys soon married Carla Montel, a niece of Vinnie Palermo. Worthington's marriage served to put him in solid with the Conigliaro Crime Family. Zach and Carla had one child together. They named their son Joseph Vincent Worthington and called him Joey.

It was not long before Zach Worthington became a wealthy man. He also became a powerful figure on the east coast and casted a long shadow in New Jersey state politics. There was even talk of him running for governor. But Worthington wanted a change of scenery. He knew that sooner or later his ties to the Conigliaro Crime Family would come back to haunt him. New Jersey was no longer the place for Zach Worthington. After first clearing it with Vinnie Palermo, Worthington moved his family and Diamond Systems, Inc. to Pelican's Landing, Florida. Rapidly, he became Pelican Landing's leading citizen, donating money to numerous charities and becoming the town's largest employer. A year later Zach Worthington ran for mayor. He won easily. That was thirty-seven years ago. And after thirty-seven years Worthington was still the mayor of Pelican's Landing. No one ever ran against him.

Sixty-four years old and pushing three hundred pounds, the massive bulk of Zach Worthington cut an impressive figure ambling across the open ground toward Keri Martin and Jackson Stone. Thick, wavy, blond hair with tinges of gray on the sides topped his huge head. A friendly smile formed his fleshy, suntanned face. He was wearing a white short-sleeve shirt opened at the collar and dark blue slacks. The mayor's suntanned arms contrasted nicely with his white shirt. Worthington pointed towards the gravesite where he wanted the reporters to follow him. He had always told them that they would get their story as long as he was mayor. About twenty-five feet from the gravesite, the procession came to a sudden stop. The once friendly smile no longer appeared on Zach Worthington's face.

"That's far enough for you reporters. You can all get back behind the yellow tape where you belong," Sergeant Cliff Potts said as if he were talking to a group of misbehaved children. "But Mayor, you can keep on comin'."

"I told these people that they could view the gravesite and see the body. I hope, Sergeant Potts, that you are not going to make a liar out of me."

"I don't have to do that, Mayor. You do a pretty good job all by yourself."

Worthington felt the hair on the back of his head rise up. His jaw muscles tightened. No one talked to him that way. The half-smile on Potts's unshaven face made it that much more infuriating. Potts had moved closer to where Worthington could smell the whiskey on his breath. It only served to fuel the fire raging inside him.

"Potts, you have no idea who you are talking to," Worthington said in a low tone while leaning forward to be out of earshot of the reporters.

"I know exactly who I am talkin' to," Potts said with the half-smile still on his face.

Worthington started to say something but stopped. He was going to tell Cliff Potts that he could have him fired for drinking on duty, and that he could have his pension taken away from him and have it fixed so that he never worked again. The mayor was going to say all those things, but he did not. The look in Sergeant Potts's eyes stopped him. They were dead eyes. Two of the deadest eyes Zach Worthington had ever seen. He could recall only one other man who had eyes similar to Potts. The man's name was Johnny Rocco. Worthington had met Rocco on more than one occasion back in New Jersey. Each time it had something to do with Vinnie Palermo and the Conigliaro Family business. Johnny Rocco was the number one hit man for the Conigliaro Crime Family.

An elongated grin spread across Zach Worthington's face. So that was how it was going to be. The message was plain in Potts's eyes. Potts was telling him that he had better watch out. Jackson Stone was his friend and Worthington had kept Stone from getting the police chief's job. He had messed with Stone. That meant he had messed with Sergeant Clifford Potts. 'And I am not afraid of you,' Potts's eyes were telling Worthington. 'I don't care about what you might try to do to me. I don't care about anything.' The message was clear. Worthington saw it.

"All right folks, you heard the sergeant. Let's get back behind the yellow police tape. I promised you a story and Zach Worthington always keeps his word. Just give me a couple a minutes with the new police chief, and you'll get your story. I promise you."

Worthington stepped around Potts. He ignored the whining and complaining going on around him from the news media. They would have to get back behind the yellow police tape and wait for their story. There was nothing more that he could do. Potts had won this one. But it was not over. Not by a long shot. Keri Martin and Jackson Stone became the mayor's new focus. Showing a confident smile Worthington strode forward. He caught the hard look on Jackson Stone's face. A smiling Chief Martin with an extended right hand stepped out to meet him.

"Mayor Worthington, what a pleasant surprise. I didn't expect you to be showing up at a police crime scene. I was planning on coming by your office tomorrow."

"Chief Martin, nice to see you again," Worthington said taking Keri Martin's extended hand. "I don't normally get involved in a police investigation but something like this is out of the ordinary. We don't get many bodies buried outside of cemeteries here in Pelican's Landing. So, when we do get one it creates quite a stir. You can see that by the number of news media people we have waiting over there for information. Do you have any idea as to who the girl is?"

"No, we don't. It is going to take time before a positive identification can be made. The medical examiner was here earlier and he …"

"Chief Martin, we have to give the news media something. They have been waiting for a long time and I promised them a story. Either you or Lieutenant Stone will have to give a news conference. I don't care which one does it, but it has to be done."

"Well, I certainly can't get before a news camera appearing the way I do. Look at my hair not to mention my makeup and eye shadow. I can only imagine what I must look like. Lieutenant Stone, I think you should give the news conference. As Mayor Worthington correctly pointed out, the news media has been waiting for a long time, and they should be given something concerning our buried body."

"They can wait until hell freezes as far as I am concerned," Jackson Stone said while looking at both Martin and Worthington. "I'm conducting a homicide investigation here, and I don't have time to placate a bunch of reporters who could care less about anything else other than their deadline. I'm going over to talk to Roscoe Tanner and see what he has to say about the body that was buried on his property."

Mayor Zach Worthington moved forward stepping between Stone and Martin. There was no mistaking the anger showing on the mayor's face.

"Stone, you will not be talking to Mr. Tanner. You are leaving here once this body is removed and not stepping foot on the Tanner ranch again unless you have a warrant in your hand signed by a judge. Do you understand me?"

"Wait a minute, Mayor," Keri Martin said edging her way in between Worthington and Stone. "You're forgetting yourself. Lieutenant Stone works for me, not you. And if my chief investigator feels it's necessary to conduct an interview relative to a homicide investigation then he will by all means do so."

"Ms. Martin, I made you the police chief and I can unmake you anytime I feel like it. Pelican's Landing is a small town and it has its small town politics. Don't involve yourself if you want to remain chief of police. Now Stone you heard what I said."

"Obviously, Mayor, I didn't make myself clear," Chief Martin said while wiping away the strands of red hair that had fallen across her eyes. She could feel the anger waiting to explode inside her. "In the next few minutes Lieutenant Stone is going right over to interview this Roscoe Tanner fellow, and I'm going with him. And if you don't like it then you can fire me. But I want to remind you of my four-year-contract signed by you last month when you swore me in as police chief for Pelican's Landing. I'd like to see you trying to explain to those reporters over there how you fired me on my first day, but still will be paying me for the next four years."

"Chief Martin, wait one minute. You misunderstood me. I had no intention of firing you. This concerns Lieutenant Stone in a previous charge of harassment relating to Mr. Tanner. You are unfamiliar with the complaint. I was only trying to …"

"Mayor Worthington, I am well aware of Mr. Tanner's complaint. And I can assure you that there will be no trouble between Lieutenant Stone and Mr. Tanner. I will be present for the interview."

"And what about the news conference?" Worthington asked while conceding the fact that he had been outmaneuvered by his newly appointed police chief.

Keri Martin told him, "There will be no news conference by the police department. I will have Deputy Moore send a statement concerning this investigation to all the news outlets. That should suffice for the time being." Turning to Stone, she asked, "Are you ready for your interview with Roscoe Tanner, Lieutenant Stone?"

"I think so," Jackson Stone said while appreciating the look on Zach Worthington's face.

CHAPTER SEVEN

ROSCOE TANNER WAS exiting the barn's side door when he spotted the unmarked police car. He immediately recognized the dark blue sedan as belonging to Jackson Stone. The sedan pulled up to the barn and parked. Tanner observed Stone getting out of the car on the driver's side and a woman in her early thirties with long, red hair was doing the same on the passenger side. She must be the new police chief, Tanner surmised, while assessing the slim figure in spike heeled shoes walking towards him.

"Mr. Tanner, can we have a few minutes of your time?" Chief Martin yelled to the rancher as she hurried to catch up to him. Jackson Stone stayed behind allowing Martin the lead. A questioning looked showed on his face. *Lady, don't hurry. Make him wait for us. You're giving him the advantage.*

"I was wondering when you people were going to be getting around to me," Tanner said while running his right hand through a head of thick, brown hair. Two gray eyes took in the woman walking briskly toward him. Smeared black mascara had formed dark rings around both of her eyes. A painful wince showed on her face whenever a spiked heel from one of her shoes caught a hard piece of ground. Tanner could not help but smile. It was not often that he had visitors, especially not a woman police chief. But the sight of Jackson Stone walking behind Martin took away Tanner's smile.

"Stone, I have a signed court order up at the house that says you're not to step foot on the Tanner ranch. Get off my property, or my lawyers will be in front of Judge Wilson tomorrow morning. I've had enough of your harassment."

"No one is harassing you, Mr. Tanner," Keri Martin said as she came to face the rancher. "I am Chief Martin with the Pelican's Landing Police Department. Lieutenant Stone and I want to ask you about the body that you and your employees found. My understanding is that it was found buried on your property. Do you have any idea as to how it got there?"

"No, I don't. I'm not in the habit of allowing people to bury bodies on my ranch. Whoever buried that body did it without my knowledge, I can assure you of that. There is no way I can keep an eye on every inch of my land twenty-four hours a day. Now what do you want out of me? I didn't see anything and I don't know anything. I've got work to do, so if you don't have any more questions to ask me, get going."

Stone moved around Keri Martin to face Tanner. Taking off his sunglasses, he came close enough to force Tanner to take a step back.

"I have a question for you," Stone said looking into the gray eyes only inches away from him. "When was the last time you were on that section of the ranch?"

"I don't remember. It could have been last week or last year for all I know. What difference does it make? The body was buried and nobody could have seen it anyway. So what are you getting at Stone?"

"Tanner, who is going to kill someone and bring the body all the way out here to your ranch to bury? Who would take the chance unless they knew no one would see them doing it? Unless they killed whoever it was close by. So close there was nothing to worry about. For instance, here in this barn or up in your house. Then they would only have to move the body a short distance. That's what I'm getting at, Tanner. I'm saying you're my number one suspect. I'm looking at you for murder."

"I want a lawyer. I'm not saying another word until I talk to my lawyer. Stone either arrest me or get off my ranch."

Keri Martin observed the burning resentment spewing out of both men's eyes. Obviously, whatever was between Stone and Tanner had to have been brewing for a long time. The look on both their faces sent chills through her. As Stone's commanding officer Martin felt compelled to step in.

"Lieutenant Stone, we are leaving now. Mr. Tanner, I suggest you speak to your attorney. Any future interviews involving you and this investigation will be conducted in the presence of your attorney. Let's go, Lieutenant Stone."

"Stone, don't come back here if you know what's good for you. I'm not going to warn you again," Roscoe Tanner said as the police lieutenant turned to walk away. But instead of walking away Stone stopped. The suddenness of his action caught Tanner by surprise. Especially after Stone had come back around to face him once again.

"You're through, Tanner. The next time I come here it will be to take you to jail. We've known each other for a long time. You know when I say something, I mean it."

Stone walked away. Martin hurried after him trying to catch up. Roscoe Tanner stood watching. He observed Stone and Martin get into the blue sedan and drive off toward the gravel road.

CHAPTER EIGHT

THE SUN WAS almost down by the time Stone returned to the gravesite. He had dropped Martin off at her hotel suite and headed back. Parking the sedan, Stone got out and leaned against the driver's side door. He took in the surrounding terrain. It was mostly grassy with several patches of white sand along with some hardwood trees. A hint of rain was in the air. Stone knew a storm was brewing somewhere far off in the Gulf of Mexico. By morning it would make land and drop its heavy wetness on Southwest Florida. Overhead, a flock of White Ibis came into view. The birds looked graceful and stately against the early evening sky. Stone's gaze followed the soaring birds until the flock disappeared behind a high ridge running along the river.

Who killed her? And why was she buried in this desolate place? Stone asked himself. And when did it happen? Was Tanner involved? The man was certainly capable of murder. He could have picked her up in town and brought her back to his ranch. An argument could have started up between them. Or she could have found out something that she shouldn't have. Either way Tanner ends up killing her. But why would he have buried her so close to his own ranch house? And in a grave where there would always be the chance of the body one day being discovered? Down a sinkhole or dumped in some far out of the way place would have been better. Somewhere where the body could not have been traced back to him. But maybe Tanner had made a mistake. He could have presumed that no one would find the woman's remains in such a remote section. After all, the body had been buried for years and no one had found it until today. Two boys out hunting snakes. Who could have figured on that?

Stone moved away from the car and took a few steps in the direction of the gravesite. Then he stopped. His mind was racing. If not Tanner, then who? It had to have been someone who knew the area. No stranger to Pelican's Landing would have buried a body out here. Whoever did it had to have known about the gravel road and this isolated spot. Zach Worthington. The man's smiling face appeared. How did Worthington know that the body was female? *"Do you have any idea as to who the girl is?"* That's what he had asked Chief Martin. Worthington said girl. He didn't say woman. Worthington knew it was a young female's body. But how? Stone had asked Clifford Potts if he mentioned the body's age or sex while confronting Worthington and the news media. Potts said he hadn't. And Stone had telephoned the medical examiner asking him if he had told the mayor anything concerning the age or sex of the body found. The medical examiner said he hadn't been in contact with the mayor or anyone else from the mayor's office.

It could all be nothing. Worthington could have seen the blond hair and small frame and assumed it was a girl. Stone had assumed the same after seeing the skeletal remains for the first time. No, he couldn't read too much into what Worthington had said. But what else was there about the mayor? Something else that he had said. Stone tried to remember. Maybe it wasn't what he had said but more of what he didn't say. Chief Martin's first question after seeing the body was, *"Do we have any idea as to how long the body was buried here?"* Worthington never asked that question. Most people would have asked it. After having seen the skeletal remains they would have wondered how long the body was in the ground. Worthington apparently did not think it was important. But why not? Why did the mayor fail to ask the obvious question? Was there a reason for him not doing so? Again Stone had to ask himself if he was reading too much into it.

Stone stared out in the direction of the gravesite. Off to his right was the river. Roscoe Tanner's mobile meth lab had been there earlier. Stone's informant had told him that it was there that very morning. Tanner must have moved it, probably sometime prior to the arrival of the police at the gravesite. But where did he move it to? Stone had told Deputy Bob Garcia to check out every conceivable place the meth lab could be hidden on the Tanner ranch. The Pelican's Landing deputy found nothing. Where could Tanner have hidden the meth lab?

Syndicate money and power were behind the manufacturing of the white crystal. Once crystalized the meth could be worth millions to Big Al Ruggerio in Miami who took his marching orders from the Conigliaro Crime Family. That meant Vinnie Palermo. Ruggerio, Roscoe Tanner, and Zach Worthington all took their orders from Vinnie. Together, they made it possible for meth crystal to be sold on the streets of New York City and the countless other American cities where the Conigliaro Crime Family sold their illicit drugs. Killing people faster than any disease could ever do. Was the woman murdered over something to do with narcotics? Did she get too close to Tanner's operation? Tanner could have killed her to keep her mouth shut. Stone considered the possible connection between the dead body and the Conigliaro Crime Family. It did not seem likely. But there was always the possibility. The young woman could have been involved with the crime organization in some way.

Stone walked over to the sedan's driver's side door and opened it. Prior to getting in, he thought of Chief Keri Martin. The woman had no idea what she had gotten herself into by taking the police chief's job. The Conigliaro Crime Family wanted an easy time of it at Pelican's Landing. They had big plans for the small town on the west coast of Florida. Stone knew that Diamond Systems, Inc. had been quietly buying up land in and around Pelican's Landing. The Conigliaro Crime Family was prepared to bring gambling and prostitution on a large scale to the tourist town of only twenty-five thousand people. Through Mayor Zach Worthington the Conigliaro Crime Family had reached out across the country looking for a police chief that they could control. Someone who did not know police work, but who could still pass the muster test with the right kind of credentials.

Keri Martin footed the bill perfectly. She was an administrator with little if any actual police experience. The Conigliaro Crime Family had to be ecstatic over having just such a person running the Pelican's Landing Police Department. But maybe Vinnie Palermo and Zach Worthington had made a mistake this time. Stone recalled the determined look in Martin's eyes during the confrontation with the mayor over who was in charge. There was no backing down in her. But could she hold out against the money and power behind organized crime? Stone was not so sure. It would be difficult for her. He of all people knew the pressure that the mob could put on someone. If they could not buy or threaten to get their way, they killed you. It was as simple as that. And Keri Martin, by taking the police chief's job, was in the middle of it. Stone wondered if Martin had any idea of the danger that she was in. Probably not, he told himself. She most likely felt that she had earned the police chief's job. That she was highly qualified and suited for the position. Stone could not blame her for feeling that way. If their roles were reversed, he would probably feel the same. From past experience Stone knew that it was often difficult to see past one's own ego, especially after you have left a bad situation in an attempt to start over again. And that was what Martin was doing by leaving Chicago. She was trying to start over again. No, Stone could not blame her at all.

Jackson Stone got into the sedan and closed the door. He started up the car putting it in gear. A westerly wind entered the sedan's open window. It left little doubt about the scent of rain in the air. Stone could almost reach out and touch it. A storm was brewing. And the police lieutenant knew that it would not be long before it arrived in Pelican's Landing.

****

Roscoe Tanner put down the AR-15 rifle. He slowly came to his feet. Tanner watched Jackson Stone drive away down the gravel road toward Pelican's Landing. For fifteen minutes he had been lying in the high grass observing Stone through the AR-15's scope. On two separate occasions, Tanner had been all set to pull the trigger. The first time was when Stone leaned against the car door. Tanner was zeroed in on the lieutenant's face. It would have been an easy shot. Tanner could hardly have missed from two hundred yards. On the second occasion Stone had moved away from the car. Tanner observed Stone looking toward the river where earlier that day the meth lab was located. The shot would have struck the left side of Stone's head. Tanner almost pulled the AR-15's trigger. He certainly wanted to pull it. But each time the thought of Stone's dead body being discovered on his ranch stopped Tanner. The Florida rancher told himself that he would have to wait for a better time and place. It would have to be a location where Stone's murder could not be traced back to Tanner.

Tanner watched the dust cloud left by Stone's car trailing off in the distance. He could not help but wonder why Stone had come back? What was he looking for? What exactly did he know? Worthington was supposed to keep Stone away. He was also supposed to control the new police chief. But both Stone and the woman had come to Tanner's barn to interview him. Tanner had telephoned Worthington telling him that the girl's body had been found. And for him to get to the gravesite right away. But Worthington's showing up accomplished nothing. Tanner still had to submit to an interview. And in Stone's eyes he was the killer. Stone was looking at him for the girl's murder. Tanner knew that Stone would never give up. It was the same with the meth lab. Sooner or later he would find it. That Garcia kid searched the entire Tanner ranch looking for the mobile meth lab. The deputy had been out there for hours checking along the river and everywhere else. Jimmy Burke, Tanner's foreman, told Tanner that Garcia took in every part of the ranch. Who was Stone's informant? It had to be someone working for Tanner who was feeding Stone information? But who could it be? Tanner and Burke had gone over the list of twenty-two names, all people who worked for Tanner. They could not come up with anyone who might be supplying information to Stone.

Roscoe Tanner bent down to pick up the AR-15 rifle. Dust from Stone's car could no longer be seen in the distance. The police lieutenant was gone for the time being, but Tanner knew that he would be coming back. Holding the rifle tightly in both hands, Tanner walked in the direction of his ranch house. He stopped momentarily to look over where the girl's body had been buried all these years. Tanner could not help but feel he had made a mistake. He should have pulled the trigger on the AR-15. The Florida rancher told himself that he should have killed Jackson Stone. And one day he would regret not doing it.

CHAPTER NINE

THE WARM WATER left Keri Martin's entire body feeling relaxed. Leaning back in the bathtub, she closed her eyes. The bubble bath had been on Keri's mind ever since she and Stone had left the Tanner ranch. Stone dropped her off an hour ago outside the Holiday Inn. The hotel would serve as her residence until she could find suitable housing. After checking into her suite, Keri wasted no time in getting out of the dirty, sweaty clothes that had been clinging to her for what seemed like a lifetime. Earlier Deputy Moore had brought over Martin's suitcase.

A pink, flowered bathrobe now hung from the back of the bathroom door. After her bath Keri would put on the bathrobe and settle in for the night. And it would be a short night for sure. She was more than ready for a good night's sleep. The throbbing in her ankles and legs had finally subsided. There was no more of the sharp, pulsating pain that she had experienced earlier. But the achiness in her back and shoulders was still there. The soreness did not seem to want to leave her. Trekking across hard, uneven ground in spike heeled shoes had taken its toll; and she was paying the price for it. Keri reached for the glass of red wine on the footstool next to her. She took a long sip before setting it back down. Reclining once more, Keri experienced the wet warmth of the bubble bath across her aching back and shoulders.

It had been a day like no other. Her first day as police chief. Besides the searing heat and humidity, and the inappropriate clothing she had been wearing, along with the spiked high heels, which were presently in the hotel suite trash bin, it was not too bad of a first day. Especially not with a murder case greeting her first thing upon her arrival at Pelican's Landing. Who could have expected that? Certainly not her. And then there was the mayor. What was Worthington doing showing up at a police crime scene anyway? He said that it was because of the rarity of a body being found buried in Pelican's Landing. Keri was not accepting Zach Worthington's explanation. She felt that it had more to do with the body being found on Roscoe Tanner's ranch. The mayor had been quick to intercede on Tanner's behalf when Stone mentioned that he was going to interview Tanner. And then Worthington turned on her after she had asserted her authority as chief of police. What is going on in Pelican's Landing? Martin asked herself. Before coming here, she thought Pelican's Landing would be a nice quiet seaside town with no real problems. Take care of the speeders and keep watch over the drunks coming out of the bars at closing time. That would be the extent of what she had to be concerned about. She couldn't have been more wrong. Keri felt something was going on in Pelican's Landing that she did not fully understand. There was more hidden under the surface and undetected. It was there but she could not yet see it. Keri Martin's survival instincts were telling her to use the utmost care and proceed with caution.

And then there was the confrontation between Stone and Tanner. The hatred between the two men was obvious. Keri had been close enough to not only witness it but to feel it as well. Both men were tall and appeared to be physically strong. Neither showed any real fear of the other. But there was something in Tanner's eyes that she could not help but notice. It became apparent after Jackson Stone had turned around to face Tanner. The rancher showed caution at that moment. Apprehension might better describe what she had seen. It told Keri that Tanner was not someone Stone could ever show his back to. Roscoe Tanner was the type who played by his own rules. And he would stoop to almost anything to get over on an adversary, no matter how despicable the action. Keri Martin knew first hand that kind of a man. There were plenty of them out there. The cocksure smile and handsome face of Rance Stapleton came to her.

Keri had just received her promotion to deputy chief of the Chicago Police Department when she and a group of friends went down to Rush Street to celebrate her new promotion. There she met Stapleton inside one of the premier lounges on the strip. Tall and good-looking, Stapleton walked up to her at the bar. He was holding a gin and tonic in one hand and a gold-leaf necklace in the other. A confident smile adorned Rance Stapleton's suntanned face. Two loose strands of dark hair fell aimlessly across his forehead. Obviously, the man had too much to drink. It only made him that much more appealing to Keri.

Stapleton told her, "There isn't another woman in this place who could do justice to this necklace. That is why I am giving it to you."

She allowed him to place the necklace around her neck while at the same time kissing her on the cheek. They danced under the lounge's blue overhead lights until closing. He took her home and did not try to come inside. They shared a goodnight kiss on the front porch. Keri thought that she had finally found Mr. Right. He was handsome and rich and everything she had ever hoped for in a man. That took place nearly two years ago. Now, after several slaps to the face later, Rance Stapleton was still on her mind. Keri reached for the glass of wine resting on the footstool next to her. She took a sip, holding the glass in both hands.

Could she trust anyone ever again? Probably not, she thought. Rance had put an end to that for her. After all, most people were basically out for themselves. If you kept that in mind, you would be fine. Don't get too close. Keep everyone at arm's length. Take care of yourself because no one else will. That was the way Jackson Stone seemed to conduct himself. Keri found herself centering her thoughts on Stone. She remembered him thanking her in the car for backing him up with Zach Worthington at the gravesite. It was right after they had left Tanner's ranch on the way to the hotel. She told him that she would always back him up as long he was doing his job. He smiled right after she had said it. Keri remembered the smile on his face. *It was like 'sure you will lady. We'll see what you're made of as time goes by and the going gets tough.'*

She had sensed the doubt in him. After all she was a woman who had just taken his job. A job that he was more than capable of handling. Keri had to admit that Stone was far more qualified than she for the position. But it was not given to him. It was given to her. And he did not show any resentment whatsoever. He must have wanted the police chief's job terribly. Yet he displayed no animosity toward her. In fact he had told her about the autopsy on the skeletal remains scheduled for tomorrow at nine a.m. And that he would have Deputies Moore and Garcia drop a car off for her at the hotel in the morning. He was quite civil and polite. Detached as well. He kept his emotions well hidden. She would have to try and be more like him. Not to let people know what she was really feeling. That way they would never know that they had hurt her.

Jackson Stone. What kind of a man is he? Keri wondered. A good police officer for sure. Her father would have liked him. Jack Martin always showed a likeness for any police officer who did his job. Police work was everything to him. Keri knew that was why she had become a cop. Her four older brothers went into other professions. The boys wanted nothing to do with a profession that had cost them the life of their father. But Keri thought differently than her brothers.

Keri wanted to follow in her father's footsteps. And as long as she was around to carry on in his name, Jack Martin would still be doing police work. The job that he had loved would be his daughter's job. No junkie's bullet was going to end her father's memory. Keri would not let that happen. Not as long as she was a police officer giving honor to his name. Yes, her father would have liked Lieutenant Jackson Stone. Stone was a policeman's policeman. But would he have liked me? Keri asked herself. Would Jack Martin have liked his daughter? Would he have approved of the new police chief for Pelican's Landing? Would he have put his arms around her and told her that he was proud of her? Wiping the tears from her eyes, Keri Martin set the empty wine glass down. She reached for a towel and got out of the tub.

CHAPTER TEN

THE HEAVY STORM coming off the Gulf of Mexico had knocked out the beach house's electricity. After discovering there was no gas for the backup generator, Joe Worthington used a flashlight to search the kitchen cabinets for candles. Finding two, he brought the candles into the dining room where he set them down on the table. What to light the candles with presented a problem. No one seemed to smoke anymore. Worthington went back into the kitchen and started rummaging through the kitchen drawers. He discovered a number of odds and ends including his father's 38. caliber, five-shot, Smith & Wesson revolver. Zach Worthington kept the loaded gun at the beach house for protection. In addition to the Smith & Wesson, there was a hunting knife Joe had found years ago while hiking in Silver River State Park. He was with his grammar school Cub Scout pack on a weekend camping trip. But no matches showed up in the kitchen drawers. Worthington knew that he could not expect his friends to hold flashlights up to their faces. There had to be matches somewhere. After all his father did smoke cigars on occasion. Switching his search to the bedrooms, Worthington spotted a cigarette lighter resting on his mother's dresser top. He took the lighter into the dining room and used it to light the two candles on the table.

Jack Hardin and Sam Costello looked like two frightened boys. Worthington could not blame his friends for being scared. He was scared, too. How could any of them not be scared? After eighteen years the nightmare had come back to haunt them. Not that it had ever left. It would just be more real now, not something that they could pretend away as though it had never happened. It would be in every waking moment, consuming every thought. The events of the night so long ago had caught up to Joe Worthington, Jack Hardin, and Sam Costello. It was the reason behind their coming to the Worthington beach house so late at night. The secret they had shared with one another was no longer a secret. The girl's body had been found.

"Is that where you buried her, close to the gravel road that runs through Tanner's ranch?" Hardin asked while sounding very much like a lawyer in his questioning tone. "It couldn't be a different girl's body that they found, now could it? I mean it's a big area out there. And it would have been dark when you buried her. You could have put her somewhere else and not anywhere near where they found the body."

"No, it's her. Blond hair and small build. That's how the news accounts described the remains. They didn't give a cause of death, but it's her. I'm sure of it. It's Ginny's body."

"Do you have to say her name?" Sam Costello said wiping his right hand across his mouth. Worthington noticed the beads of perspiration on Costello's forehead. They appeared to glisten in the candlelight. There was also a visible shake to his friend's hands. Both of Costello's hands were resting on the table in front of him.

"I suppose not," Worthington said. "I don't know if there's much more that we can do at this point other than to wait and see what happens. If they identify her body, and it comes back that she's from Gainesville and the three of us were attending school there, the police might try to connect her to us."

"Connect her to us?" Hardin said. "You mean connect her to you. She was your girlfriend. She wrote you the letter wanting to come to Pelican's Landing to visit. It was your idea to invite her here to your parent's beach house and to slip the knockout drug into her drink. Sam and I just went along with it. What twenty-year-old guy wouldn't go along with getting laid? You set the whole thing up. We waited in the bedroom while you two were in the living room partying, and after the knockout drug took over Sam and I brought her back into the bedroom. I remember both of us taking turns with her. We drank some whiskey, smoked some weed, screwed her a couple of times and that was it."

Worthington could feel the hot flush coming to his face. He stared hard at Jack Hardin seated across the dining room table from him.

"Jack, she wasn't my girlfriend and you know it. She was a waitress working at Zimmy's bar who I happened to take out on occasion. If you recall, both you and Sam were with me when I first met her, so don't go saying that she was my girlfriend. I hadn't seen her for at least a year before getting the letter from her. During summer break from school, she wrote me saying that she wanted to come to Pelican's Landing to visit. I wrote her back and told her to come. I had the intention of putting her up here in the beach house for a weekend of sex, and that's all I planned on doing until I got the idea to share her with you guys. I still can't believe that I did it, put a knockout drug in her drink and turned her over to you two. And what happens to her? She ends up dead with neither of you knowing how it happened."

"Joe, don't go starting that bullshit all over again. Both of us told you on several occasions that we don't know what happened to her. My best guess is that after Sam and I left the room she came to and tried to stand up. She probably was still dizzy from the knockout drug you gave her and fell down. It had to have happened that way.

The back of her head had blood on it, so she must have hit her head on something. Isn't that right, Sam?"

Costello shook his head. "Jack, I don't know. I was really wasted that night. I don't know what happened to her. I'm just so sorry that I went along with it and got myself involved in the whole thing. All I remember is getting off her and leaving the bedroom. She was still lying on the bed when I left. I don't know what happened to her after that."

"And I followed you out of the bedroom," Hardin said shifting his gaze from Costello to Worthington across the table. "She must've stood up sometime after that and fell down. It was an accident, but the police sure as hell won't see it that way. I'm a lawyer, and I know how they'll see it. We brought her here to the beach house to rape her, and then afterward hit her over the head with a blunt instrument to kill her. We wanted to shut her up for good so she couldn't go to the police. And to conceal the crime we buried her body in a remote section on Tanner's ranch. They give out the death penalty for committing murder and rape in this state. In our case we'd be lucky if we got off with life in the penitentiary. The police must not connect any of us to the dead girl. Without making that connection, they got nothing."

Worthington thought he observed something odd in Jack Hardin. It might have been the look on his face or the inflection in the man's voice. Worthington could not be sure. But whatever it was it bothered him. Something about his friend did not seem quite right.

"Jack, I remember you coming out of the bedroom telling us that she was dead. And then Sam and me walking in, seeing her lying there on the floor with blood on the back of her head. But what I could never figure out is why you went back in the first place. It couldn't have been for more sex. You and Sam took turns with her for over an hour. So why did you go back into the bedroom again?"

Hardin's hazel eyes brightened. His upper body came over the table toward Worthington. There was the semblance of a grin tucked in at the corners of Jack Hardin's mouth. Worthington felt as though he were looking at a grinning cat.

"Why do you think I went back into the bedroom? When I left her she was naked on the bed. I expected to find her still lying there with her legs spread. I didn't expect to find her dead on the floor. Anyway what are you getting at? Joe, are you trying to say that I killed her?"

"Jack, take it easy, he's not saying that," Costello interjected while placing his right hand on Hardin's left arm. "He's just talking, that's all."

"Well, he better quit talking. I'm not going to sit here and listen to him accuse me of killing that girl. I don't know any more than you guys do about how she ended up dead."

Hardin unexpectedly stood up. Worthington and Costello immediately came to their feet. The three boyhood friends looked at one another in the shadowy light cast by the two candles on the table. A crash of thunder outside broke the silence between them. An unforeseen tension seemed to fill the room. Sam Costello gripped the table in front of him to keep his hands from shaking.

"I think we should call it a night," Costello said trying to play the role of peacemaker.

Hardin agreed. "Yeah Sam, I think you're right. But both of you better remember to keep your mouths shut about knowing the girl. Otherwise, we'll all find ourselves charged with murder and rape."

****

Joe Worthington took a bottle of whiskey from his father's liquor cabinet and with a glass from the kitchen brought it into the dining room. He sat down at the table and poured himself a large glass.

Worthington seldom drank, but this night would be the exception. Tonight he needed a drink. He needed lots of drinks. Jack Hardin and Sam Costello had just left. Before leaving Costello waited by the front door to say goodbye. Hardin did not bother to wait. He left without saying a word. Worthington knew that finding Ginny's body had driven a wedge between the three friends. Nothing would ever be the same again. Hardin had his wife and law practice to think of. And Costello had his wife and three kids along with a prosperous trucking business that he had built up from scratch. Worthington could think only of his wife, Janet, who was due any day with their first child. Janet had two previous miscarriages and this pregnancy had proven to be difficult. Both she and Joe were worried about something happening to the baby. Keep her away from stressful situations, the doctor had told him. Stressful situations? How much more stressful can it get than learning your husband gave a knockout drug to a nineteen-year-old girl so his two friends could rape her? And that she ended up falling down and hitting her head and dying.

Worthington took a long drink out of his glass. The whiskey burned his throat going down. It left a hot feeling in his stomach. How could he have been so callous to do what he did to Ginny? What kind of a man was he? To put a knockout drug in a girl's gin and tonic so she could be raped without her knowing it? What kind of a man would do such a thing? Certainly not the Joe Worthington who eight years ago married Janet Byrne in a church wedding; and most certainly not the Joe Worthington who was going to be a father for the first time. No, it had to have been some other Joe Worthington who placed that knockout drug in Ginny's drink. It couldn't have been him. It had to have been someone else. Because he was not that kind of a man. He could never do such a thing. Worthington raised the glass to his lips and emptied it. He immediately poured more whiskey out of the bottle into his glass.

Ginny's face appeared in Worthington's mind. Through the years he had been successful in blocking it out. But now it appeared more vivid than ever. He saw the round, blue eyes, and the small, thin nose along with the easy smile. Ginny had on a yellow dress and long, blond hair tied back in a ponytail. Smiling, she danced to the music on the radio, saying to him over and over again that she loved him. Then the knockout drug started to take effect. Worthington remembered Ginny sitting down on the sofa. She put her head against his shoulder. After a few minutes he could tell by her breathing that she was unconscious. He signaled to Jack Hardin and Sam Costello. They hurried out to take Ginny back into the bedroom. He saw the door close behind them.

Worthington buried his head in his two arms resting on the dining room table. After they found Ginny dead in the bedroom, Hardin and Costello told Worthington it would be up to him to get rid of the body. Alone with the dead girl's body, he panicked. He telephoned his father who immediately came to the beach house. His father told him to go home and tell no one what had happened. Joe Worthington had gotten into his car, but he could not go home. Instead he parked the car further down the beach and waited. It was not long before Roscoe Tanner and Jimmy Burke, Tanner's ranch foreman, pulled up to the beach house in a pickup truck. Zach Worthington came out to meet them. After a few minutes talking together, the three men went into the beach house. Tanner and Burke came out shortly afterward carrying Ginny's body wrapped in a bed sheet. They put the body in the back of the pickup truck and drove away. Worthington told Hardin and Costello the next day that he had buried her, not wanting to involve his father. He never knew what Tanner and Burke had done with Ginny's body until he heard it on the news. That human skeletal remains had been discovered on the Tanner ranch.

Worthington pushed himself up from the table. It was well past midnight. The storm outside was still raging. He decided to stay overnight at the beach house and go home in the morning. Staggering from side to side, Worthington made his way into the living room. He saw the sofa that he and Ginny had sat on eighteen years ago. Once more the music was playing. And Ginny was dancing with both arms raised above her head. She was saying over and over again that she loved him.

Then Worthington suddenly got the crazy notion that it never happened. That he never gave Ginny a knockout drug; he never signaled for Hardin and Costello to come out of the bedroom. Ginny did not die, but was still alive somewhere living out her life. The whole terrible night had never taken place. He could erase it from his mind.

"You didn't really die," Joe Worthington said before passing out on the living room floor.

CHAPTER ELEVEN

Chicago

FBI SPECIAL AGENT Patrick Carollo decided to park his car and walk the half block to Angelo's Barbershop. Chicago police personnel were keeping all vehicular traffic off of Taylor Street. It had rained earlier. The street and sidewalks were still wet while more dark clouds loomed overhead. Carollo remembered that he had an umbrella in the trunk of his car. He thought about going back for it but decided against it. There was not enough time. He was already late. An older policeman stopped Carollo at the barbershop door. The FBI Special Agent showed the officer his photo/identification card and moved past him. Entering the barbershop, Carollo spotted Detective Rick Santini bending over a dead body. Carollo and Santini had been friends since grammar school, but seldom crossed paths anymore. The FBI Special Agent was assigned to Washington D.C. and did few trips back to Chicago. Santini looked up to see Carollo coming through the barbershop's front door. Putting down his clipboard, Santini walked over to shake his friend's hand.

"Pat, I knew it wouldn't be long before you'd be showing up. We never get to see each other unless one of these gumbas ends up killing another gumba."

The two men had known each other since both attended St. Dominic's Grammar School on Chicago's Westside. Physically, they lent a Laurel and Hardy look. Carollo appeared tall and lanky while Santini emerged squat and heavy. Each wore a white shirt and tie along with a dark sport coat. Both men had black hair and an olive-complexion. There was no mistaking their Italian ancestry. Santini took Carollo by the arm and walked him over to the dead man seated in a barber's chair. A white sheet covered the man up to his chin. A bullet hole showed prominently above the man's left eyebrow. A second bullet hole was in the area of the man's heart.

"Meet Mickey Marsullo, one of the top capos in the Chicago Outfit," Santini said. "But Pat, I'm sure you knew him. He's got a criminal sheet a mile long, and off the top of my head, I can think of at least three murders he personally was involved in, and we could never prove a thing."

"Who are the other two guys?" Carollo asked staring at the dead man seated in the barber chair next to Marsullo. A bullet hole was showing just above the man's left eyebrow.

"That guy and the one lying on the floor over there by the back door were Marsullo's bodyguards. Some bodyguards, huh? They never even got their guns out. All we know is that some kid came into the barbershop and told the barber that the owner of the deli next door wanted to see him right away. After the barber left a bread delivery truck pulled up outside. Then a guy wearing a White Sox baseball cap and dark sunglasses got out of the truck and came into the barbershop. He was carrying loaves of Italian bread tucked under one arm. That's all we know. He must've shot Marsullo and his bodyguards using a silencer because nobody heard any gunshots. Whoever did it had to have had a hell of a lot of nerve coming into the Chicago Outfit's backyard to do a stunt like this. We found the bread truck about mile from here in an alley. It was stolen sometime earlier this morning from the Southside. Pat, I hope you can help us with this because right now we've got nothing. We don't know why Marsullo was targeted and we don't know who did the shooting."

"Your shooter is Johnny Rocco," Carollo told him. "He's the Conigliaro Crime Family's number one hit man. Vinnie Palermo must be making his move and he started with the Chicago Outfit. By killing Marsullo, he sends a message to the Chicago Outfit and the Five Families that they had better not get in his way. Vinnie wants to put the Conigliaro Family ahead of all the other families by demanding a larger percentage of the gambling in Florida. Rocco must have flown in a couple of days ago from New York City. He flies his own twin engine plane, and usually files a phony flight plan. He brings the plane down in some out of the way landing strip so it can't be traced back to him. Right now you can bet he's on his way back to New York and a long way from Taylor Street."

"How can you be so sure it's this guy, Rocco?" Santini asked while not totally buying that Vinnie Palermo would risk a war with the other crime families by killing Marsullo. "I'm looking at it being another member of the Chicago Outfit wanting Mickey out of the way and knocking him off here in the barbershop."

Carollo pointed to Marsullo's body. "How many bullet holes do you see? Two right? One to the head and the second one to the heart. That's Johnny Rocco's trademark whenever he does a hit on an intended target. Marsullo's bodyguards each got one to the head. That's the way Rocco usually kills, but he adds one more to the heart whenever he wants to send a message that he got his intended target. Another thing, Rick, you won't find any expended shell casings on the floor. Rocco never wastes time picking up shell casings. He uses a 38. caliber revolver with a silencer. I'll bet a year's salary against yours that the doctor doing the autopsy will dig 38. caliber rounds out of these guys. No, it's not the Chicago Outfit that's behind these murders. It's Vinnie Palermo. And Vinnie sent his number one hit man, Johnny Rocco, to do the job."

****

Carollo had just made it back to his car before the heavy rain started to fall. The special agent in charge immediately reached for his car phone. He only had to wait a few minutes before Randall Maxwell, the FBI's Assistant Director of the Criminal Investigation Division (CID), was on the other end of the line.

"Pat, is it as bad as we thought? Is this the start of a gang war between the Conigliaro Crime Family and the other crime families?"

Carollo could detect the anxiety in his boss's voice.

"Yes, sir, it's started. Vinnie Palermo has made his move. Mickey Marsullo and the Chicago Outfit have been the most outspoken against the Conigliaro Family. Now Mickey and two of his bodyguards are dead. And there's no question in my mind that Johnny Rocco was the shooter. But I don't think the Chicago Outfit and the Five Families want a shooting war right about now. Dead bodies piling up in New York City and Chicago, not to mention Boston and some other cities are not good for business. I think Vinnie Palermo knows that, and that's why he's pushing things by killing Marsullo here in Chicago. He's counting on the other crime families to back down. What Vinnie really wants is majority control of the gambling and prostitution in Florida. He's also looking for a larger percentage of the illegal drug trade, especially the sale of meth crystal. So sir, it is just like what we discussed two days ago in your office. The Conigliaro Crime Family is staking everything on Pelican's Landing becoming their town. Right now they have the mayor in their pocket and a lot of money tied up in land purchases. If we can stop them from taking over Pelican's Landing, then we can stop Vinnie Palermo and the Conigliaro Crime Family from taking over the rest of Florida as well."

"Pat, isn't that where your friend Jackson Stone comes into play? We both know that the FBI can't be seen getting involved in

Pelican's Landing at this time, not with our informant right underneath their noses supplying us with information on the Conigliaro Family. It would make things too dangerous. Vinnie Palermo would become suspicious, and we could lose one of the best inside tracts that we ever had on a major crime family. Stone and the new female police chief will have to run interference on their own for a while. Right now the FBI can't be seen getting involved in Pelican's Landing."

Carollo stared straight ahead at the rain striking the windshield in front of him. He knew that Maxwell was not going to change his mind. Protecting the informant's identity was paramount as far as Maxwell was concerned. Jackson Stone being Carollo's friend meant nothing to Maxwell. But Pat Carollo felt that he had to at least try and change Maxwell's mind. He felt that he owed Stone that much and a considerable bit more.

"Sir, I don't think that I ever told you that I was Stone's handler when he was on the New York City Police Department and working undercover for the FBI in New York. Back then the Bureau was going after the Giaccone Crime Family for murder and extortion. Stone penetrated the upper echelon to where he got the goods on a top capo in the Giaccone mob. He brought down more than a dozen of the scumbags. He didn't back away, even after I told him that it was too dangerous and he had to get out. Stone and I had a prearranged warning system where if he ever received a single red rose it meant that they were on to him and that he was to get out right away. Stone remained undercover for twelve more hours after receiving the rose I sent him. He was able to get the evidence that we needed for arrests and convictions on a dozen members of the Giaccone Crime Family. Sir, that's the Jackson Stone we will be turning our backs on by not going into Pelican's Landing."

"I'm sorry, Pat. You told me before that he was your friend, and that he once did a service for the Bureau. I fully understand that and am grateful, but I cannot jeopardize an ongoing operation out of sentiment. My loyalty and concern rests with the FBI and nowhere else."

"He lost his marriage and everything else in that operation," Carollo said while knowing that he was wasting his time in trying to sway Maxwell. "Stone came home and found his wife had left him and had moved to Los Angeles. She later divorced Stone claiming abandonment. Two years after the divorce was finalized the police found her dead in an Eastside apartment. She took too many sleeping pills and died. I know that Stone blames himself for her death. He told me once that a man can't be married to a job and a woman at the same time. The woman won't put up with it."

"Again, I'm sorry," Maxwell said. "But Lieutenant Stone and Police Chief Martin will have to take care of themselves. The FBI cannot do anything for them."

Carollo hung up the car phone and sat back in his seat. He thought about Stone and the sort of danger his friend would be facing in the coming days. The Conigliaro Crime Family was not going to let Stone or anyone else prevent them from taking over Pelican's Landing. Carollo turned the key in the car's ignition and switched on the windshield wipers. Before pulling out onto Taylor Street, the FBI special agent wondered what kind of a chance, if any, Stone would have. Keri Martin, Pelican's Landing's new police chief, was inexperienced. Stone could not count on her for much. He would basically be facing whatever Vinnie Palermo wanted to throw at him all alone. Carollo wished that there was something more that he could do, but his hands were tied. Stone would be facing the Conigliaro Crime Family by himself. Carollo knew the chance of his friend surviving the coming days was not good. Putting the car in drive, FBI Special Agent Pat Carollo pulled out onto Taylor Street and headed for the Eisenhower Expressway.

CHAPTER TWELVE

KERI MARTIN HAD just finished dressing when she heard the phone ring. Slipping into a pair of tan-colored, low-heeled shoes, she hurried over to answer it. A woman identifying herself as the hotel desk clerk was on the other end. The clerk told Martin that Deputies Moore and Garcia had dropped off the keys for an unmarked police car. They had also left a map of Pelican's Landing. After thanking the clerk, Martin hung up the phone and walked over to the hallway's full-length mirror. Keri had purchased the yellow blouse and olive-green skirt along with the blue earrings at the Macy's in downtown Chicago. Now turning every which way, she glanced in the hallway mirror. The blouse and skirt were an excellent choice. Their bright colors went well together and the earrings stood out nicely against her red hair. Her hair, Keri thought. She had nearly forgotten. Martin had made an appointment the night before to get her hair cut that morning at the hotel's salon. The appointment was in five minutes. She told herself that she would have to hurry if she ever hoped to make it to the salon on time. Keri had been wearing her hair long ever since high school. Having a shorter look would be quite a change for her. But the thought of yesterday and another day of having to deal with Florida's heat and humidity made the change a most welcome one.

Keri grabbed her handbag off the bed and was starting towards the door when she stopped halfway. The pink floral suitcase was on the floor next to the desk. Martin bent over to open it. The Glock 9mm handgun and two fully loaded magazines were exactly where she had packed them. Keri picked up the Glock and inserted one of the magazines into it. After placing the gun and extra magazine into her handbag, she continued towards the door.

An hour later sporting shorter hair and a brand new pair of sunglasses, Keri Martin walked out of the Holiday Inn's main entrance. It was a bright, sunny morning, not a cloud in the sky. The temperature seemed comfortable, but Keri knew that would soon change as the day wore on. A soft breeze was coming off the Gulf of Mexico. And with it came the salty scent of the ocean. Martin took a deep breath, finding it invigorating. She liked the freshness of the sea air and the closeness of the water. It was quite a change for someone coming from the Midwest.

The unmarked police car was parked in a restricted parking zone. Keri had no trouble finding it. It turned out to be a light gray sedan with less than 10,000 miles showing on the odometer. Taking a look at the map, Martin took in the contour of Pelican's Landing. The autopsy on the unidentified girl's remains was being performed at the Kendall Memorial Hospital, which was located at the south end of town. Normally all autopsies in Collier County were performed at the medical examiner's office in Naples. But the ME had made an exception in this case because only skeletal remains were being examined. And the close proximity of the hospital made it a convenient choice. The notoriety of the case also came into play. The news media was surely to be camped out at the ME's office in Naples wanting to find out whatever it could about the investigation. Both Martin and Stone had agreed that any autopsy results would be kept confidential for the time being. Stone was able to get the medical examiner to sign on to the agreement as well.

Looking at her watch, Keri saw that she had more than enough time to get to the hospital for the autopsy. She decided on a drive along Treasure Island Boulevard. It was not out of her way, and it would give her the opportunity to take in Pelican's Landing's ocean front business section. The majority of the town's high-priced hotels and fancy restaurants were located along Treasure Island Boulevard, not to mention the numerous beachfront bars. During the winter months people from up north came down to spend time and money in the many establishments dotting the coastal street. Starting up the light gray sedan, Martin pulled out of the hotel parking lot. She headed the unmarked squad car west in the direction of Treasure Island Boulevard.

The Blowfish, Pirate's Cove, The Caribbean Sunset, Thirsty Whale, The Crow's Nest, Mother's Pearl, The Drop Anchor were just some of the names Martin spotted along the boulevard. Even though it was not high season, a fair number of people populated the street. It was morning and some of them were already carrying open bottles of beer. Keri could only guess as to what nighttime would bring to the area. It had to be a street party for sure. White sand beaches and the blue water of the Gulf of Mexico were off to her right. Swimmers, sunbathers, and walkers on the beach dotted the white sand landscape while a bright sun shone down. Keri became enamored by it. It was so different from what she was used to seeing. She had always thought Chicago beaches along Lake Michigan were a sight to see. They could not even compare to the white sand beaches along the Gulf of Mexico. Keri drove the sedan while shifting her attention from the many restaurant and bars on her left to the endless panorama of sand and water off to her right. So taken with it she nearly missed her turnoff. Martin turned south on Maida Street and started looking for the hospital. Three-quarters of a mile down she saw the entrance sign for Kendall Memorial. Stone had told her to look for the two large glass doors on the hospital's west end. That was where the autopsy would be performed. Spying the two doors, Keri pulled into the lot. She found an empty parking spot close to the hospital entrance. The Pelican's Landing police chief parked her car and got out.

CHAPTER THIRTEEN

JACKSON STONE WAS seated with a cup of coffee in his right hand when he observed Keri Martin walking down the hallway toward him. At first glance he did not recognize her. Martin's red hair was a lot shorter. There was also the absence of black eye shadow around both her eyes. The yellow blouse and green-colored skirt lent an attractive look. It revealed the smooth curve of Martin's hips and her supple figure. But it was the low heel shoes that produced the most notable change. Keri Martin's gait was strong and steady. It portended a woman full of confidence. Someone who knew where she was going and not afraid to go there. Stone could not help but liking what he saw.

"I hope I'm not late," Martin said walking up to him. Stone came to his feet placing the coffee cup down on the table next to him. There was a steely look in Keri's eyes. It spoke volumes for Stone. She seemed to convey with her look—*The person you saw yesterday was not really me. It was only someone who looked like me. You are now seeing the real Keri Martin.*

"No, you're right on time. They are bringing the body out now and Dr. Snyder should be getting started any minute."

She caught the trace of a smile on his face. "What's so amusing?"

"Nothing really. It's just that you look different, that's all. I guess I wasn't expecting such a change in you. You got your hair cut."

"Lieutenant Stone how observant of you. And you must also have noticed that I got rid of the coat and pants as well. What do you think, Lieutenant? In your opinion does this outfit appear Florida enough for you? For Pelican Landing's new police chief to be wearing?"

"It sure does," Stone said laughing while appreciating a different side of Martin. He was hoping to get along with her. There was no question that he was going to need her help if he ever hoped to get Roscoe Tanner charged with narcotics trafficking. And the same for Zach Worthington and the members of the Palermo Crime Family, who he was hoping to get charged as well. "Please call me Jackson. Or, if you prefer, Stone. But if it is all right with you let's drop the lieutenant title. Pelican's Landing is a small police department and we try to keep things informal. But if you want me to refer to you as Chief, then I most certainly will."

Keri did not have time to respond. The door to her immediate right opened. A slightly built man in his early sixties with a bushy, gray mustache along with a head of ruffled, gray hair came out. He was holding a pair of black-colored frame eyeglasses in his right hand. A blue smock covered his long-sleeve white shirt and black dress pants. The sleeves of the shirt were rolled up to his elbows. Keri could not help but notice that the man was wearing white surgical gloves.

"You must be Chief Martin. I'm Dr. Snyder, the Collier County Medical Examiner," the man said before putting on his eyeglasses and holding up his right hand. "Excuse me for not shaking hands. But as you can see I have been working."

"Glad to meet you, Doctor," Martin said with a smile. "Are you ready to begin the autopsy?"

"Basically, it is already finished. I started last night with the hair samples that were taken from the scene before getting to work on the skeletal remains earlier this morning. But it was more of an inspection than a full blown autopsy because I didn't have the actual flesh and blood corpse to work on. Please come inside and I will explain everything."

Martin and Stone followed Dr. Snyder through the doorway. Upon entering the room, Keri was immediately taken by the compactness of it. A large stainless steel table occupied its middle while gray-colored countertops with metal sinks lined two of its walls. File cabinets and an assortment of white boxes labeled medical supplies filled the remaining space. A thoroughly washed human skeleton rested in plain sight on the stainless steel table. Dr. Snyder moved over to it and placed his right hand on the skull.

"After examining the teeth and bone structure, I put her about eighteen or nineteen years of age at the time of death. Three notable injuries were sustained on the body. The index finger on her right hand was fractured. It would be indicative of someone squeezing the finger tightly and then twisting it. But more notably, I discovered a linear fracture to the base of the skull area. If you look closely, you can see it. It runs right along here where my finger is touching."

Martin and Stone moved closer, bending down to see where Dr. Snyder's right forefinger lightly touched the base of the human skull.

"It is difficult to see because it is only a hairline fracture. The injury could have been inflicted by a blunt object or perhaps the result of a fall whereby the victim struck the back portion of her head."

"Would it have rendered her unconscious, Doctor?" Stone asked.

"Perhaps. But it would not have resulted in a serious injury. The victim would probably have regained consciousness and ended up with nothing more than a bump on the head."

Keri Martin said to him, "Earlier you said three injuries, Doctor. I take it that the third injury is the one that killed her."

Dr. Snyder smiled. His piercing brown eyes widened, magnified by his eyeglasses. He looked first to Martin before switching his gaze to Stone. Looking down, he focused his full attention on the skeletal remains in front of him.

"Her hyoid bone was crushed," Snyder said in a matter of fact manner. "That, Chief Martin, is your third sustained injury."

Stone felt his upper body flinch. "You mean somebody strangled her to death?"

"Yes."

"I'm sorry, Doctor, but could you explain how you happen to know this?" Keri Martin said, not fully grasping the doctor's findings.

"The hyoid bone is in the throat area. It aids in tongue movement and swallowing. I presently have my forefinger resting on her hyoid bone. If you look closely, you can see that the bone is severely damaged. A great deal of pressure must have been applied to her throat in order to cause that kind of damage to the hyoid bone. I would say that it was manual strangulation. A strong person used his or her hands to strangle her."

"So that means our victim was abducted and killed by strangulation," Martin interjected. "Someone grabbed her right hand, and in the process broke her index finger before striking her in the back of the head with something. Then while she was unconscious he strangled her to death."

"Maybe that's how it happened," Stone said looking at Martin. "But she could have been running away, fallen, and then hit her head. We don't know enough yet. We have to find out who she is and what she was doing in Pelican's Landing."

Turning to Stone, Dr. Snyder said, "Lieutenant, perhaps I might be able to shed some light on things for you in that regard. I tested her hair sample last night and it proved positive for Rohypnol, which is commonly known as a 'date rape drug.' It can be put in someone's drink without his or her knowledge. And once consumed, Rohypnol takes approximately 15 to 20 minutes to take full effect. The drug lowers a person's blood pressure causing sleepiness and slurred speech. If given the right dosage, an individual could be effected for up to 8 to 12 hours."

"A date rape drug?" Keri Martin exclaimed. "She could have been picked up in a bar in Pelican's Landing and taken to a house where she was raped and strangled to death."

"Are you thinking of a certain ranch house close to where the body was found?" Stone asked Martin while seeing in her eyes what each of them was thinking.

"Yes, I am. It certainly could have happened that way."

"One other thing," Dr. Snyder said lifting the bottom portion of the skeletal remains. "I want you to look at her pelvic area. And while doing so I am asking you to pay special attention to the pelvic inlet, which is right here." Snyder pointed to a particular spot for Martin and Stone to observe. "The pelvic inlet is widened. Can you see it? It has contracted somewhat, but it is still widened. This young woman at some point gave birth. That is why the pelvic inlet is extended."

"So, she had a baby," Keri Martin said while considering what this new information might mean to the investigation. "Do you think the baby was with her when she was killed? And if so, what happened to her baby? What do you think, Stone?"

"There was only one body in the grave. If the baby was killed at the same time as the mother, it would have been buried along with her. No, I don't think the baby was there when it happened."

"But that might be the reason why she was killed?" Martin said staring down at the human skull, trying to imagine a young woman's face attached to it. "She might have been murdered because of her baby."

"We won't know that," Stone said. "Until we find the father and sit down and talk to him."

CHAPTER FOURTEEN

Budapest, Hungary
Fall, 1956

THOUSANDS OF UNIVERSITY students had taken to Budapest's narrow streets to protest the Soviet Union's oppressive regime. Fredek Lantos, 20, and Ada Barna, 17, were among them. Ten days earlier Fredek and Ada had marched with their fellow students through central Budapest to the *Orszaghaz*, the official building of the city parliament. Once there, they stormed the front doors and seized the radio station. Bullets from the rifles of the State Security Police did not stop them. All of Hungary cheered the courage and patriotism of the Budapest University students. Freedom for the nation of Hungary had come at last. No longer would the sickle and hammer of the Soviet Union cast its dark shadow over the freedom-loving Hungarians. But the sudden influx of more Soviet troops and tanks changed everything. Thrown bricks and Molotov cocktails proved to be no match against machine guns and high-powered rifles. University students ended up being killed by the thousands.

"It is finished," Fredek said to Ada while the two huddled together in a bombed out church building in the center of Budapest. Both were exhausted and feeling the effects after three days of intense fighting. Dried, cached blood coated Fredek's black hair. A Soviet soldier's rifle butt had left a deep laceration. Both of their clothes were torn and dirty. Ada's long blond hair was covered by a brown men's cap. She took the cap off to shake loose her hair.

"Fredek, it can't be finished. We won. The *Orszaghaz* was ours and all of Hungary cheered it. We can't let the Soviets take back our country from us after we won it with our own blood. It can't be finished. There must be something that we can do."

"Yes, there is something. We can try for the Austrian border and get out of Hungary. The AVO will surely have our names by now. They will be searching everywhere for us. We must leave Budapest as soon as it gets dark. The freight yard is less than a mile away from here. We will look for a train that is heading west."

"But my mother and father. And my sister. I must say good bye to them. Fredek, I must."

"Ada, it would be too dangerous. I, too, would like to say good bye to my family. But the AVO will be watching our houses. It would only serve to bring danger to those we leave behind. You must realize that."

He took her into his arms. Ada's head fell against Fredek's right shoulder. She nodded her head to tell him that she understood. Her quiet sobs broke the stillness of the bombed out church. Fredek held Ada in his arms while his mind raced ahead. They would have to travel across Hungary and then make their way into Austria. Once across the Austrian border, they would go to the U.S. Embassy and find a way to get to America. The United States of America was their only hope. In America, he and Ada could find the freedom that they so desperately sought. They would not have to be afraid anymore.

Fredek brought Ada closer to him. He whispered into her ear, "Don't be afraid, Ada. I promise that I will take you to America. And after we get there, you will never be afraid again."

****

Jackson Stone and Keri Martin took a table in the back corner of the restaurant. The Crow's Nest was nearly empty except for the handful of occupied tables up front. Stone immediately recognized the occupants as being boatmen from the marina who, after an overnight of fishing, had stopped by the Crow's Nest for breakfast. The men were loud and boisterous and appeared happy. Stone deduced the overnight catch had been a good one.

The fishermen were seated beneath a large, black fishing net suspended from the ceiling. The net hovered over most of the restaurant including Stone and Martin's back corner table. It was decoratively spattered with brightly colored seashells, which was given a rainbow effect by the sunlight from the overhead skylight. Being late morning, most of the breakfast crowd had already gone. And those seeking lunch had yet to arrive. It was Stone's preferred time in coming to the Crow's Nest. It allowed for a quiet breakfast or lunch. Two people could talk without being overheard.

"This is a beautiful place," Martin said looking around. "I just love the way they did everything up. The sun reflecting off the net's colorful seashells and the different kinds of fish on the walls. It's absolutely beautiful. And over there, what's that? It looks like a pirate. He has a hook instead of a right hand. And in his other hand he's holding a sword. How delightful. I can't remember seeing anything like it. I bet the tourists just love it."

"Captain Hook," Stone said smiling while appreciating Keri Martin's liking the place he had taken her for breakfast. After the autopsy Stone had decided on the Crow's Nest. It would be a good place for him and the new police chief to have a serious talk regarding what was happening in Pelican's Landing. The Crow's Nest was familiar territory for Stone. It was the only restaurant and bar that he could actually say he felt comfortable in.

Stone told her, "Freddie and Ada Lantos are the owners, and they are good friends of mine. They escaped from Hungary during the revolution in 1956 and came to the United States. Both share a remarkable story. They ended up in San Francisco with hardly more than ten dollars between them. Freddie had studied music at the University of Budapest, so he began playing the piano in various bars along Fisherman's Warf. Ada had a good singing voice, so she took the stage name, Canary Martini, and joined him. While Freddie played Ada would sit on the top of the piano and sing. Throughout those early years the Lantoses were able to save enough money to buy a run-down shack here on the beach in Pelican's Landing." Stone held up both of his hands. "And here we are," he said, smiling. "Forty-five years later and look at what they have done. The Crow's Nest is the best restaurant and bar in Pelican's Landing. Nearly all of the locals are regular customers. The spiral staircase that you saw coming in leads to a deck on the roof that overlooks the Gulf of Mexico. At night Freddie plays the piano up there and Ada sings. On a clear, moonlit night you can relax with a drink in front of you while hearing the sound of the waves running up on the beach. Freddie plays his piano and Ada sits propped up in front of him with her legs crossed singing old-fashioned love songs. It makes for an enjoyable evening, I can assure you."

"It most definitely sounds like it," Keri said looking into the dark blue eyes staring at her from across the table. Was she seeing a different side of Stone? Keri Martin wondered. She had not seen this side of him until now. The man actually sounded like a romantic. "Do they have any children?" Keri asked wanting to change the subject.

"Six. Two boys and four girls. The four oldest are living out of state while Anna and Julie, the two youngest, help out with the restaurant. That's Anna coming over to our table now. She looks a lot like her mother."

Keri observed a pretty, dark-haired woman not much older than herself approaching the table. Anna was wearing a rose-colored blouse along with a light, beige skirt that seemed to cling to her; while a thin, black belt accentuated a narrow waist. An engaging smile lit up the woman's face. Martin noticed that Anna's eyes stayed fixated on Stone.

"Anna, this is Chief Martin, Pelican's Landings' new police chief. I was just telling her about your parents and how they came to America and eventually started up the Crow's Nest."

Anna turned to Keri Martin. "Yes, they came to this country with practically nothing and look what they have accomplished. They left Hungary to start a new life in America and ended up here in Pelican's Landing. They raised their family here and created a new life for themselves. It is so nice to meet you, Chief Martin. I hope that we will see you often here at the Crow's Nest."

"I am sure that you will, Anna," Keri answered while seeing that Anna's gaze had returned to Stone. She's taken with him, for sure, Martin found herself thinking. He does have that effect on women. The thought of Deputy Moore and her out of wedlock baby came to mind. Could Stone actually be the baby's father? And were he and Moore still involved?

"Chief Martin, would you like to see a menu?" Anna Lantos asked for the second time. Martin had not responded to her first request.

"No thank you, Anna," Keri said. "I'm not hungry. Just coffee for me." Martin saw that both Anna and Stone were staring at her. It made Keri feel somewhat uncomfortable. "But Lieutenant, don't let me stop you from having breakfast. Order whatever you want."

"No, coffee will be fine for me," Stone said. "Perhaps I'll be back later for dinner. Anna's mother's Chicken Paprikash is my favorite."

"Mine too, Lieutenant," Anna said before walking away.

****

Stone held the red coffee cup inside his two hands and stared across the table at Keri Martin. He could not decide on what approach to take. How was he going to explain to this woman staring back at him that the only reason she got the police chief's job was because the Conigliaro Crime Family thought her incompetent and no threat to them? And where would that then leave him? He could be making an enemy out of someone who he might need later as a friend. Without Martin's help, he could never hope to expose Tanner and Worthington as being the crooks that they were. And the Conigliaro Crime Family would be free to do whatever it wished in Pelican's Landing. Stone knew that he would have to tell her. Hopefully Martin would realize that there was no hidden agenda on his part. Stone could think of no other way. But how would Martin take it? Would she believe him?

Stone watched Keri take a sip of coffee before putting her cup down. He knew that she was not the brainless socialite the news media in Chicago had tried to make her out to be. *The Beauty and the Beast* tag they had pinned on her and the boyfriend was all wrong. The sensation-grabbing journalists had chosen to ignore the real Keri Martin. They had discounted the person behind the attractive face and striking figure. Yes, she was beautiful. At the moment Stone could not recall any woman quite as beautiful. But behind the pretty green eyes and delicately shaped face there existed a great deal more. A keen intelligence showed. It told Stone that a calculating mind was at work. Even now he felt as though he were under a microscope. Martin had to be tossing around something inside that pretty head of hers. But what was it? Stone moved back in his chair. He detected that Keri Martin was about to say something.

"All right, Lieutenant, let's clear up a couple things concerning you and me. It's been on my mind since I first arrived here in

Pelican's Landing. Now tell me the truth, why did I get the police chief's job over you? On the plane I had the chance to read your personnel file. It showed a law degree from Fordham University, not to mention the excellent undercover work you completed with the New York City Police Department. And you were the acting police chief here for the past year. Why didn't you get the job permanently? And why did they choose me? Did the mayor and other members of the town council want a woman for some reason to be heading the police department? Is that why they chose me and not you?"

Stone said to her, "Do you want the truth?"

"Nothing but. And don't leave anything out."

Stone observed the intense look on Keri Martin's face. Her green eyes seemed to have caught fire while an upturned chin jutted out. Stone found himself appreciating the woman's straightforwardness. He grasped the solidness about her.

"Okay, I will," Stone said. "But I don't think you're going to like what I have to say."

CHAPTER FIFTEEN

KERI MARTIN ATTEMPTED to keep pace with Stone. She estimated her unmarked police vehicle to be approximately ten car lengths behind Stone's sedan, while her dashboard speedometer was indicating a speed of seventy miles an hour. That was more than fast enough for Keri. The two-lane highway encompassing the outskirts of Pelican's Landing had enough vehicular traffic on it to cause her concern. Stone evidently did not feel the same. Keri watched as the speedometer increased to seventy-five miles an hour. And to her chagrin it did not stop there.

It all began with the phone call from Lisa Moore. So that Martin could hear what was being said, Stone had increased the volume on his cellphone. Moore was telling Stone that she had attempted to contact him on his police radio, but received no response. She sounded anxious and upset. Stone told her that he and Martin were at the Crow's Nest and his radio was in the car. There was no mistaking the tension in Moore's voice. Keri leaned closer to the phone. She heard Moore say that a motorcycle gang, known as *The Satan Ramblers,* was in a bar on the outskirts of town. A place called the Blue Marlin. The gang had supplied free drinks to one of the regulars at the bar and enticed the inebriated man to place his right hand inside a fishbowl of piranhas. The drunk ended up losing three of his fingers. The bartender telephoned the Pelican's Landing police who in turn called the county fire department. An ambulance took the injured man to the hospital. Lisa Moore along with Potts and Garcia were at the Blue Marlin. There was a virtual standoff going on between the deputies and the motorcycle gang. Moore said that it looked like things could blow up at any moment. Stone instructed Moore to tell Potts and Garcia not to do anything until he and Chief Martin arrived. They would be there in a matter of minutes.

Prior to the phone call from Moore, Stone had told Martin that Worthington and Tanner were associated with Conigliaro Crime Family. Gambling, prostitution, and the sale of illicit drugs were how the family made most of its money. He explained to her the concept behind Diamond Systems, Inc. whereby syndicate money kept the corporation afloat and served as a means for laundering the crime family's dirty money. And that there was a larger plan involving Pelican's Landing.

"What kind of plan?" Keri asked him while taken back by what he was telling her.

"Gambling on a large scale. Right now the Florida state legislature is close to approving statewide gambling on the same level as the state of Nevada. That could mean billions of dollars in revenue for the state of Florida, not to mention to whoever controls the gambling. And along with gambling comes prostitution and the sale of narcotics. The Palermo Crime Family is spearheading everything for the other crime families. They've bought up property in and around Pelican's Landing while using Diamond Systems, Inc. to do it. They've got a fortune sunk into this venture. Vinnie Palermo, the boss of the Conigliaro Family, sees Pelican's Landing as another Las Vegas with him as its king. He is not going to let anything or anyone get in his way."

"Is that why Worthington chose me as the new police chief?" Keri asked. Worthington had contacted her after she let it be known that she was seeking a police chief's appointment somewhere within the United States. She had been so blinded by everything going on around her that she had failed to become suspicious. At the time, Rance Stapleton and the Chicago news media had been consuming her every waking moment. The offer of the police chief's job in Florida was too good to pass up. It was a way out for her. A chance to get away from everything and start over again. How she happened to be the one chosen for the job out of everyone else in the country never came into play. She honestly felt that she had been the most qualified for the position.

"Yes, they think of you as nothing more than a pushover and not a problem for them. And that you won't get in anyone's way when it comes to their breaking the law and running roughshod over Pelican's Landing."

Stone witnessed the pain appearing in both of Martin's eyes along with the flush to her face.

"And what do you think?" she asked him. "Do you see me that way?"

"No, I don't. I think that they got you all wrong," Stone said while reaching into his jacket pocket to answer his cellphone. "And someday they're going to find out just how big of a mistake they've made."

CHAPTER SIXTEEN

THE BLUE MARLIN was nothing more than a white, wood frame building at a crossroads in the middle of nowhere. The shape of a blue marlin fish decorated its front, while a gravel parking lot surrounded the lounge. Parked outside were twenty-two Harley-Davidson motorcycles. Keri Martin had counted them before following Stone's blue sedan into the parking lot. Clouds of dust from Stone's car made it difficult for her to see clearly. But Keri was able to make out Stone in his white shirt, blue tie, and black pants. He was standing next to the blue sedan's driver's side door. She observed the 9mm Beretta in a black holster strapped to his right side. Martin parked her car next to Stone's sedan and got out. She walked over to him keeping her right hand inside her handbag.

"Where are the deputies' squad cars?" Keri asked.

"In the back. You never walk through the front door of this place if you can help it." Stone noticed Keri's right hand inside the handbag. "I sure hope that's a gun you are holding onto."

"It is."

"Are you any good with it?"

"Stone, I might be lacking in certain things, but shooting a firearm and hitting what I am aiming at is not one of them."

"Well, hopefully, you won't have to use it. I figure on us going through the front door this time. Me first and you right behind me. Once inside I want you to step immediately to your left and stay there. I want to know where you are at all times, so don't stray from that spot. Are we clear on that?"

"Very clear. I am not to move without first asking your permission. Now don't you think we better get in there and find out what's going on? Or do you have more orders for me?"

"No more orders," Stone said before heading for the Blue Marlin's front door.

****

The smell of marijuana along with a musty odor hit Stone the moment he walked through the front door. It left him with the feeling that a window had not been opened in the place for several years. The Blue Marlin's dinginess came next. Two overhead ceiling lights seemed to be the only light. But it was adequate enough for Stone to discern the long line of men standing at the bar. The police lieutenant could not recall ever seeing such a ragtag group. Sporting long hair, scraggly beards, and half-grins, the bikers reminded him of a pack of dogs sizing up prey. Various tattoos decorated well-muscled arms, while frayed blue jeans covered the tops of scuffed-over biker boots. The Blue Marlin's long bar stretched the entire length of the room. Stone spied Lisa Moore standing behind the bar near its middle. The deputy had a handgun clutched inside both her hands; Moore's wide-eyed stare was directed at Stone. To her left was Cliff Potts. The sergeant was standing at one end of the bar holding a 12 gauge shotgun. Potts had a smile on his face. The crazy bastard is actually enjoying this, Stone thought to himself. Bob Garcia stood at the other end of the bar. And like Potts, he, too, held a 12 gauge shotgun. The gun's barrel rested on the bar in front of him. Garcia looked at Stone before going back to the men at the bar.

"Stone, we were wondering if you were ever going to show up. And I see that you brought your bitch with you. Along with these three deputies, that's all the help you could get? You had to go home for your bitch to help you."

He was known by the name of Erik the Red. And he was the leader of *The Satan Ramblers*. Standing six-foot-five and weighing close to three hundred pounds with scraggly red hair and a matching beard, Red looked every bit the Viking. His real name was Billy Dollar. He had been *The Satan Ramblers* acknowledged leader for the past three years ever since his release from California's Solano Penitentiary. Dollar had done five years of a fifteen-year sentence for killing a rival biker member. Stepping away from the bar, Red walked to the center of the floor. He wanted to be closer to Stone. There was a smile on his face. Red's earlier comments had drawn laughter from the other bikers. It encouraged him to do more. Two weeks before, Stone and his deputies had ordered Red and four of his *Satan Ramblers* out of the Blue Marlin, telling them never to return. Well, Red had returned. And this time he had brought the rest of the outlaw gang with him.

Stone took in Red's matted, red hair and monstrous beard. The beard came down to cover most of Red's chest. Stone thought it looked like a shaggy red rug with a hole cut out to make room for the man's mouth. Devil tattoos decorated both massive arms. Stone appreciated the penitentiary muscles and overall bulk. Red was standing no more that fifteen feet away. But it was close enough to make Stone's six-foot-two, 220 pound frame appear small in comparison.

"Stone, we're not leaving this time. *The Satan Ramblers* are taking over this bar and making it their own. You can leave now or wait until we throw you out just like we did that bartender a little while ago."

"If anyone is going to be thrown out of here, it is going to be you, Red," Stone said before glancing back to see if Keri Martin was still by the door. He saw that she was. The three men sitting at a table in the far corner of the Blue Marlin bothered Stone. Undoubtedly, one of them had a gun in his belt underneath his tee-shirt. And where they were seated the deputies at the bar could not cover them. The location gave the three men an unobstructed view of Stone's back. Only Keri Martin had a bird's eye view of them. She alone was in position to see the corner table. Stone told her, "Chief Martin, the three yokels in the corner are yours. If any of them looks like he's going for a gun, shoot him."

"Stone, I got them covered," Keri said removing the Glock 9mm from her handbag and letting the bag drop to the floor. She immediately raised the Glock to eyelevel, pointing it toward the three men seated in the corner.

"Chief Martin? So Stone, you have a lady boss?" Red said, laughing. "What do you think of that, boys? The lady chief has her gun pointed at you. She's got you covered, so don't go making any false moves. Don't go pickin' your nose or scratchin' your ass or she might get all flustered and pull the trigger. Who knows who she might shoot? She could even end up shooting Stone in the back. The bitch looks like she's scared shitless. What's wrong lady? Aren't us *Satan Ramblers* pretty enough for a bitch like you?"

"No, you're not. And yes, I just might shoot," Keri said looking down the Glock's barrel at the three bikers seated at the table. "And you there in the middle. You had better put your hands back on the table where I can see them."

"And what if I don't?" He was wearing a red bandana wrapped around greasy black hair. The black mustache and beard served to make his light gray eyes show up that much more. There was a mocking grin on his fat face. And along with the mocking grin was an 'I-dare-you-look.' His name was Bart Cotter. *The Satan Ramblers* called him Lucifer. Keri could tell by just looking at him that he was not going to put his hands back on the table. Above Lucifer's head and nailed to the wall was a green dart board. Keri raised the Glock and fired the gun three times in rapid succession. The sound inside the Blue Marlin was near-deafening. Lucifer and his two companions dove for the floor. Stone quickly looked over at the dart board. He observed three bullet holes clustered together less than an inch apart in the dart board's center. Turning back, he saw the astonished look on Red's face. The bikers at the bar were staring at one another in disbelief. Lisa Moore laughed out loud. Potts let loose with a drawn out cackle. Garcia tapped the top of the bar with the shotgun's barrel. Not a sound came from any of *The Satan Ramblers*. The Blue Marlin became notably quiet.

"Get back in your chairs with your hands on the table. I will not say it again," Keri Martin yelled pointing the Glock's barrel at the three men on the floor.

"Just don't shoot, lady," Lucifer said while getting back into his chair and placing both hands on the table. The other two bikers got up from the floor to do the same. "That's better," Keri told them. "Next time, it won't be the dart board that I'll be shooting at."

Smiling, Stone said to Red, "What's wrong, big bad biker? Did the lady make your boys look like a bunch of pansies?"

Red came at Stone swinging both arms. The police lieutenant stepped to one side and grabbed Red's beard. Pulling downward, Stone ran *The Satan Ramblers'* leader across the room, ramming his head into the bottom of the bar. A hard sound followed. Red let out a groan. He ended up unconscious on the floor.

"Potts," Stone yelled. "Do you know which one of those bikes out there belongs to Red?"

Sergeant Cliff Potts, with shotgun in hand, walked over to Stone.

"Jackson, I sure do. He rides that big red one with the skull and crossbones on the front of it."

"Good. You know what to do then."

"I sure do. It'll only take me a minute."

Potts went directly to the front door and stepped outside. Four loud shotgun blasts immediately followed. Stone turned to face *The Satan Ramblers* who lined the bar.

"Take Red and carry him out of here. He rode in on a bike, but he won't be riding out on one. And the same goes for any one of you who decides to come back to Pelican's Landing. Now get going."

Keri Martin stood by the front door. She watched Red being carried out of the Blue Marlin. After the last of the bikers had walked through the door she went outside. The new Pelican's Landing police chief saw what was left of Red's motorcycle. Potts had destroyed it with the four shotgun blasts. She turned and observed Stone standing next to her.

"Stone was this necessary? How can I, as chief of police, explain in a police report that my sergeant destroyed a man's motorcycle by shooting it with a shotgun? Can you tell me that?"

"I'll take full responsibility for Potts. I just want to know how you ever learned to shoot the way that you did in there. You were a game changer. Things could have gone against us if you hadn't done what you did. Where did you learn to shoot like that?"

Keri told him, "I had four older brothers who my father taught how to shoot. They in turn taught me. While back in Chicago I was a member of the Illinois police officers national shooting team. Now, Stone, answer my question. How do I explain in my report about Sergeant Potts's destroying a motorcycle by shooting it with a shotgun? You are not the police chief, I am. And that makes me responsible."

"Don't leave a report," Stone said to her. "Then you won't have to explain anything."

Keri Martin's face turned red. Stone recognized the familiar fire coming alive in her green eyes. The police lieutenant knew it was time for him to leave. Stone hurried to his car and did not look back.

CHAPTER SEVENTEEN

ZACH WORTHINGTON WAS not even hungry. And that was after having had nothing to eat since breakfast. Now with a dinner plate set in front of him consisting of roast duck, garlic potatoes, baked squash, and Bermuda onions—all perfectly prepared in a steamy, hot duck sauce—Worthington still had no appetite. The mayor had come home to his Tudor mansion on Franklin Street in a bad frame of mind. Earlier, his contact at the Collier County Medical Examiner's Office told Worthington that the girl found buried on the Tanner ranch had been strangled, and the cause of the death was due to manual strangulation. Now it was officially a murder case. The mayor knew that meant Jackson Stone would be poking his nose around to get a lead on whoever killed her. And it was all because of Tanner. It was Tanner's fault. Worthington had specifically instructed the rancher to find a place to bury the girl's body where it never would be discovered. And what did he do? He buried it in a shallow grave not more than a half mile from his own ranch house. In a place where even two dumb kids could find it.

But Worthington's day got only worse. In the late afternoon he learned that Stone and the new police chief, Keri Martin, successfully ejected Erik the Red and his *Satan Ramblers* from the Blue Marlin. The motorcycle gang had left town and was not returning. Fifty thousand dollars of the Conigliaro Family's money had been wasted. That was what Erik the Red had demanded to have *The Satan Ramblers* make their new headquarters in Pelican's Landing. And now Red and his gang were fleeing back to California. The latest news caused Worthington to become boiling mad. How was he ever going to explain Red's disappearance and the missing fifty thousand to Vinnie Palermo? Vinnie had killed men for a lot less. But Worthington knew that it was not only the money. It could have been one dollar just as easily as fifty thousand. The amount of money really had nothing to do with it. Vinnie Palermo did not like to lose at anything. That was why the boss of the Conigliaro Family was so dangerous.

And now seeing his wife, Carla, seated across the dinner table from him did not make things any better. Worthington noted her gray-streaked black hair and plump cheeks along with the way she chewed her roast duck over and over again like some quarry grinder creating gravel out of stone. He pictured in his mind the sagging breasts and bulging hips covered over by the white top that she was wearing. And how they had replaced the firm, young body he once took so much pleasure in. *You disgust me,* Worthington was thinking to himself as he looked across the table into his wife's dark, brown eyes. Her menacing glare revealed the fact that she hated him as much as he did her.

"So how was your day?" she asked him through a mouthful of garlic mashed potatoes. "Did you get a chance to talk to Joey? I was just wondering how Janet was doing with the baby due any day now."

"No, I didn't talk to Joey and I don't know how Janet is doing. If you must know, my day was horseshit, and sitting down to dinner to watch you fill your fat face hasn't helped any."

Carla smiled before reaching for the bowl of baked squash.

"So you had a horseshit day and have no appetite. I suppose that it's my fault like everything else that goes wrong in your life is my fault. What's the matter, Zach? Doesn't that twenty-two-year-old whore you keep in your condo up in Tampa ever eat food? Or is it just my eating that bothers you?"

"I thought we agreed not to bring up that subject again."

"You are the one who agreed not to bring little miss hot pants with her curly blond hair and tight skinny ass up again. I just sat and listened like I always do. Zach, why don't you call up my Uncle Vinnie and tell him you're divorcing his favorite niece because her ass got too big and she eats too much? And while you're at it tell him about little miss hot pants. I'm sure Uncle Vinnie would love to hear all about her."

"Carla, that's enough. You don't want a divorce any more than I do," Worthington said hating the sight of her. "Ending our marriage would leave both of us with nothing. If I divorced you, Vinnie Palermo would take Diamond Systems Inc. away from me and give it to someone else. I'd be left out in the cold and so would you. So don't mention a divorce or my condo in Tampa again to me. Better yet don't talk to me at all."

Worthington picked up his untouched plate of food and walked over to Carla. He put the plate down in front of her. "This will help you keep from talking," he said to her. "You can eat my dinner, too." Carla shoved the plate of food off the table. There was the sound of breaking glass. Zach turned and walked away. Carla Worthington heard her husband's profane ranting followed by the sound of the front door's opening and closing. This, too, will soon come to an end, Carla thought to herself, as she got up from the table and walked out of the room.

CHAPTER EIGHTEEN

IT IS A short drive over the George Washington Bridge from Fort Lee, New Jersey, to New York City's Lower Manhattan. It was a drive Vinnie Palermo had made many times in his life. But without question, today's trip over the Hudson River had to be the most important of all. Because in less than an hour Palermo planned on meeting a representative of the Commission, which was comprised of New York City's Five Crime Families along with the Chicago Outfit. And there he would receive an answer to his set of demands. One demand was for the Conigliaro Family to be given ten percent of all profits stemming from illegal narcotic sales within New York City. It was a ridiculous demand. And Vinnie knew it as such. But he was hoping that his outlandish demand would mask what he really wanted.

The southern half of Florida was the prize Palermo truly sought along with the Conigliaro Family having a permanent seat on the Commission. If given those two concessions, the Conigliaro Family would come to dominate all future gambling in the state of Florida as well as influence any decisions made by the Commission. A gambling empire in the state of Florida could be created, easily dwarfing Las Vegas and the state of Nevada. It could mean millions of dollars and untold power to the family in control. Palermo knew that he was taking a huge gamble. He was playing with fire and could easily get burned. The odds of his succeeding were against him. But the boss of the Conigliaro Family told himself that he did not care. He was going ahead with his plan anyway.

Leaning back in the dark leather padded seat, Palermo stared out the limo's rear window at the sun reflecting off the Hudson River. It was such a beautiful day, not a cloud in the sky. The Conigliaro Family's patriarch spied the Hudson's sparkling water along with the grass and trees that lined the river bank. His mind ran in ten or more different directions. Vinnie knew that after today nothing would ever be the same. He would either be *capo ditutti capi*—"boss of all bosses"—or a man marked for death.

The killing of Mickey Marsullo and his two bodyguards in Chicago had set the wheels in motion. The Five Crime Families and the Chicago Outfit had received Palermo's message—*Give me what I want or there will be war.* The message might have come from Vinnie Palermo, but everyone knew that Johnny Rocco was the man who had delivered it. And Rocco was one hit man the crime families feared. He along with a group of assassins known as the "enforcers" made Vinnie Palermo, the boss of the Conigliaro Family, a thorn in the Commission's side. The realization of it brought a smile to Palermo's dark, olive-skinned face. *They will soon find me far more trouble-some than a mere thorn,* the seventy-one-year-old Sicilian-born Palermo thought. *I'll stick them like they've never been stuck before.*

Palermo was aware that the Commission had grown soft and lazy over the years. None of its members had the heart for an out and out gangland war. And especially not the kind of war Vinnie Palermo could wage. More than two hundred soldiers belonging to the Conigliaro Family were in safe houses throughout New York City, Chicago, Boston, Philadelphia, and other major cities waiting for or-ders to hit designated targets. The end result would be a gangland slaughter unprecedented in the United States. However, it would only be the start not the end of the Mafia war. Vinnie was nobody's fool. He knew that together the Five Families and the Chicago Outfit could crush him within a week. They had the Conigliaro Family outnumbered in soldiers by more than twenty-five to one. But Palermo was fairly confident that would not happen. He expected four out of the five New York City crime families along with the Chicago Outfit to stay out of the war. They would remain on the sidelines and watch the bloodbath without taking part in it. Palermo's plan was to hit the Giaccone Family, the largest of the Mafia families, with everything he had. If he could bring down such a formidable organization, it would produce fear and caution in the other families. Not one of them would dare challenge Vinnie Palermo ever again. Destruction of the Giaccone Family was the key to Palermo's taking control of the Commission.

Tommaso Cracchiolo, also known as Tommy the Barber, was the boss of the Giaccone Family. His younger brother, Antonio, also known as Fat Tony, was the Giaconne Family's underboss or second in command. Palermo planned to have both brothers assassinated should he not be given the southern half of Florida and a permanent seat on the Commission. Johnny Rocco would do the killing. Vinnie had learned that later in the week both Cracchiolo brothers planned on attending their father's ninetieth birthday party at their sister Carmen's house in Whitestone, a wealthy residential neighborhood in the northernmost part of New York City, in the borough of Queens. The party had been planned for months. A four-layered birthday cake was on order from the bakery down the street. Palermo had made arrangements with the owner of the bakery to have Johnny Rocco deliver the cake to the party.

The Giaccone Crime Family's tentacles reached far and wide across the United States. It had *capos* controlling designated cities and mapped out areas throughout the country. Once the Cracchiolo brothers were taken out, Palermo knew the *capos* would immediately begin looking among themselves for a new boss to head the family. Vinnie Palermo had no intention of allowing that to happen. His selected group of assassins, the "enforcers," was already in place to take out the Giaccone Family's *capos*. The "enforcers" were standing by waiting for word from Palermo to spring into action. The remaining soldiers belonging to the Conigliaro Family would remain sequestered in safe houses should one or more of the families on the Commission decide to come to the Giaccone Family's aid.

However Palermo did not expect anything out of the other crime families. He was confident that they would stay on the sidelines, closely watching in the hope of gaining new territory for themselves. But by then it would be too late. The Conigliaro Family would have already obtained enough new territory to dissuade any of the other crime families from joining the bloody war. While at the same time the feds would have answered the public outcry against gang warfare by putting on the heat. Scores of FBI agents assisted by local police would have come down hard on all organized crime. The change would be immediate. Paid off politicians would seek cover; mob-controlled union bosses would refuse all Mafioso requests. Illegal narcotic sources would quickly dry up; cartage thefts, juice loans, construction kickbacks, every illicit activity connected to organized crime would come to a sudden halt. The Five Families and the Chicago Outfit would be left with no other choice but to call for a sit down. They would ask the Conigliaro Family to end the bloodshed. And a smiling Vinnie Palermo would graciously comply with their request. *"La Guerra è finita,"* he would say to them, "The war is over."

"Pull over and park under that big oak tree," Palermo instructed Bobby Vaccaro, his driver and personal bodyguard. "We'll wait there for a while. I don't want to get to the meeting too early."

Palermo opened a gold-plated cigarette case and removed a cigarette. The unfiltered cigarettes were imported from Carini, Sicily, the town where Vinnie was born. Each had been hand-rolled and packaged especially for him in a small shop located on the edge of town. Before lighting one, Palermo liked to picture in his mind the face of the old woman who had rolled it. Hers was an ancient, leathery face—craggy and timeless—like the Sicilian countryside itself. One day Vinnie had sat for hours watching the old woman rolling shaved black tobacco into white papered cigarettes. Palermo promptly lit the cigarette using the limo's armrest lighter. Immediately, the strong scent of tobacco came to him accompanied by a bitter taste upon his tongue. Taking a deep drag on the cigarette, he drew the hot smoke into his lungs before exhaling it out the limo's open back window.

The rugged, barren hills of Sicily came to mind. It had been a long time since Vinnie had allowed himself to think of the twelve-year-old boy who once mourned the death of his father, or the mother who told him that he would have to go live with her brother in America because there was not enough money to take care of him along with his two older sisters. It all came back, and with it came the remembrance of saying goodbye while not knowing if he would never see his mother again. Vinnie remembered the pretty face, the dark eyes filled with tears. And with her memory came the loneliness that he had felt coming to a new country, not to mention the empty days and dark nights, the being afraid; and the not telling anyone lest they know his weakness. Because if they knew then they could hurt him. Survival was all that mattered. Trust no one but yourself. That is what Vinnie had learned upon coming to America while working twelve hour days, seven days a week, in his uncle's tavern off of Mulberry Street in Lower Manhattan's "Little Italy."

"You'll earn your keep as long as you eat my food and sleep under my roof," his Uncle Whitey Gallo had told the skinny runt of a boy over and over again through the years. And Vinnie listened to his uncle while slopping tables and mopping floors and doing countless other chores in the tavern. His adolescent years consisted of attending the local public high school during the day and working nights until well past closing time. And when Vinnie did not measure up, he felt the back of Whitey's hand striking him across the side of his face. It left the teenager hard and bitter inside. But Vinnie would not let anything defeat him, or cause him to cower like some whipped dog at the end of a rope. Each beating, each endless night of work, only made young Vinnie Palermo that much tougher, more determined to succeed in life. He watched and listened to whatever was going on around him. Like a human sponge Vinnie took it all in.

Whitey Gallo's tavern was a well-known hangout for Mafioso connected to the Conigliaro Crime Family. The *capos* and their crew members often came to Whitey's for meetings, which were routinely held in one of the tavern's back rooms. Afterward the men would drink and party long into the early morning hours. Vinnie soon became a fixture among them. He would clean their tables and bring them drinks and laugh at their crude, drunken jokes. It was not long before Palermo was doing errands during the day for the Conigliaro Family. He would cut school and deliver brown packages of heroin to wherever he was instructed to go. The pay was good, fifty dollars for each delivered package. Vinnie kept the money safely hidden from his Uncle Whitey who he knew would take it from him if given the opportunity. This was all happening about the time Palermo became acquainted with twenty-three-year-old Al Ruggiero, a *made man* in the Conigliaro Crime Family. Not caring for most people, Vinnie liked Al Ruggiero right from the start. The older Ruggiero likewise had been born in Sicily and always brought the feeling of home to Vinnie whenever the two of them sat down together. It was not long before Vinnie and Al became good friends. They would remain friends for the rest of their lives.

"So you want to be a *made man* in the Conigliaro Family?" Al Ruggerio said to Vinnie one day, laughing. "What are you seventeen or eighteen?"

"I'll be nineteen next month."

"Nobody's ever become a *made man* that young. Hell, I wasn't made until I was twenty-one, and that's only because my old man had been in the Conigliaro Family for years."

Vinnie refused to be deterred. "I know that I'm young, but I was thinking that maybe you could speak to your father. He's a *capo,* and if he put a good word in for me to Ernie Savino, it would go a long way. Al, I'd do anything to be a *made man* like you."

"Anything?"

"Yeah, anything. Tell me what I have to do and I'll do it. And I don't care what it is as long it gets me into the Conigliaro Family."

"All right then, listen up to what I'm going to tell you. And you better not breathe a word of it to anybody else, because if you do I'll be the one who will personally put a bullet in your head and dump your ass in a place where nobody will ever be able to find it."

Ruggerio wrapped his right arm around Vinnie before walking him over to a corner table in Whitey's tavern. The two sat down well out of earshot of the other patrons. Leaning forward, Al Ruggiero commenced to tell Vinnie about a job he had to do in Chicago and that he needed someone whom he could trust to help him do it. It was a hit on a union teamster official who had become a prosecution witness against the Chicago Outfit. As a personal favor to the Chicago Outfit, Ernie Savino, the boss of the Conigliaro Family, agreed to have one of his people do the hit. The Chicago Outfit did not want to use any of their own people, preferring an out of town person to do the killing. So they approached the Conigliaro Family for a hit man.

"So you want me to help you?" Vinnie asked, wide-eyed, staring hard into Al Ruggerio's dark face across the table from him.

Ruggerio told him, "Yeah, I do, Vinnie. A lot of planning has gone into getting this guy whacked. The feds have him covered day and night with at least two FBI agents watching him all the time. The Chicago Outfit says the only chance to get him is when he and his wife go downtown to a fancy restaurant. Every Friday night they go to the same restaurant while two FBI agents wait outside for them in a car. That means he has to get whacked inside the restaurant with his wife seeing it happen."

"Al, what would you want me to do?"

Al Ruggiero leaned back in his chair observing the jet black hair, the marble dark eyes, and the young, boyish face looking so intently at him from no more than an arm's length away. Could the kid do it? Ruggerio asked himself. Could he kill someone in a crowded restaurant and then walk away like nothing happened? Did he have the cajones to shoot the guy while the guy was looking at him? Ruggiero felt in his gut Vinnie could do it, but he was not absolutely sure. The uncertainty bothered him. Staring straight ahead, the Mafioso started talking in a low tone.

"There's a restaurant door off the alley that leads to the kitchen. It'll be unlocked and someone will be inside waiting for you. He'll hand you a busboy's uniform and a 38. caliber revolver that'll have a silencer attached to its barrel. You put on the uniform and place a bar towel over the gun before going into the restaurant's dining room. The guy and his wife will be sitting at a table to your immediate right as you walk in. You'll know him from the photograph that I'll show you beforehand. After you spot him walk over to his table and shoot him twice in the face. Do you got that? Twice in the face before getting the hell out of there. I'll be in a car waiting outside in the alley. Whatever you do, don't bring the gun with you. Drop it somewhere inside the restaurant before you leave. Do you think that you can handle it?"

"What do I get for killing him?" Vinnie asked staring back at Ruggiero with two dark, piercing eyes that never seemed to blink.

"You'll be a *made man* in the Conigliaro Family. I've already talked to Ernie Savino about you and he said you're in the family if you do this hit. I got his word on it, and that's as good as it gets. What do you say?"

Vinnie held out his right hand for Ruggiero to shake. "I say when do we leave for Chicago?"

Two weeks later Vinnie Palermo became the youngest ever *made man* in the history of the Conigliaro Family. The public, execution-style murder of the union teamster official in Chicago had been carried out without a hitch. After the murder Palermo and Ruggiero drove the hundred miles north to the city of Milwaukee where they boarded the first flight back to New York City. Ernie Savino, the boss of the Conigliaro Family, could not have been more pleased. The Chicago Outfit was now indebted to him for taking care of their legal problem with the U.S. Justice Department. And Savino's reputation for being someone who could get the tough jobs done grew precipitously in the eyes of the other crime family bosses.

After three more years, Al Ruggiero became a *capo* and Vinnie took over as his right hand man. The two worked well together bringing in lots of new money for the Conigliaro Family. Vinnie turned out to be quite adept at finding trucking outfits, construction companies, garbage haulers, and other types of businesses the mob could extort money from by threat and intimidation. Soon the dark-haired, thinly-built Palermo came to be looked upon as someone to keep an eye on in the Conigliaro Family. There was a swagger about him, a wise-guy look, a deadly stare that seemed to cut right through whoever made eye contact with him. Nothing had to be said. The message was all too clear: *Mess with me and you'll end up with a bullet in the back of your head.* And while he kept busy making the big money, Vinnie was never too busy not to watch out for an opportunity that might come his way.

Ernie Savino was nearly eighty years old. He had been talking about retirement for years. So it came as no surprise to anyone when the boss of the Conigliaro Family called a meeting and elevated Vinnie Palermo to *capo.* Most people at the time felt Savino was naming the man who eventually would succeed him as boss. And five years later it proved to be true. Ernie Savino was found dead on his bathroom floor from what appeared to be a heart attack. And two days later a smiling Vinnie was unanimously chosen boss of the Congliaro Family by the other *capos.*

Vinnie Palermo worked steadily to build up the Conigliaro Family into a fine-tuned army of killers. He personally had gone to Carini, Sicily, to recruit the young men who would become his "enforcers," trained assassins loyal only to him. One of the new recruits was Johnny Rocco. Vinnie discovered the sixteen-year-old living in a home for delinquent boys on the outskirts of Carini. The boy's jet black hair, dark insolent eyes, and contemptible sneer reminded Palermo of himself at that age. Vinnie quickly paid off the town magistrate before whisking Johnny Rocco away to America under a forged passport. The sixteen-year-old Rocco became one of Palermo's best pupils. All the Sicilian recruits were cold and ruthless, but Johnny Rocco turned out to be much more. He was intelligent as well. And that set him far above the others. It made Johnny Rocco an invaluable piece to Vinnie Palermo's plan. A plan Vinnie had formulated long ago while working in his uncle's tavern. It was something he had dreamed of every day since becoming acquainted with the Mafioso. The boss of the Conigliaro Family wanted it all; and he would not to be satisfied until he had it. Vinnie Palermo wanted to be *capo ditutti capi*—"boss of all bosses."

"Bobby, we've kept them waiting long enough," Palermo said tapping his limo driver on the left shoulder. "Let's get to the meeting and find out if there's going to be a war."

CHAPTER NINETEEN

"WE DON'T HAVE any other choice. It's either him or us. You should be thinking of your wife and kids not Joe Worthington. After all he's the reason why we're in this mess in the first place. He's the one who allowed the girl to stay at his parent's beach house and put the knockout drug in her drink. She wouldn't have fallen down and hit her head if he hadn't done it. Now she's dead and the two of us are looking at murder one. We can't just sit back and wait for the police to connect Joe Worthington to the girl's body. Because if they do we go down with him. You can see that, can't you?"

Jack Hardin had phoned Sam Costello earlier that morning requesting to meet with him. Both men had agreed on the Pelican's Landing pier. The pier was normally not crowded in the afternoon, which allowed for privacy. And that was what both men sought. They wanted no one to hear their conversation. Hardin was the first to arrive. Costello initially spotted him standing at the far end of the pier gazing out at a flock of seagulls diving toward the water.

"Jack, I don't believe you," Costello said after having heard Hardin's proposal that they kill Joe Worthington. "You're talking out of your head because you're scared just like I am. And sure I'm worried about my wife and kids. If it ever came out that I raped a girl who later died, I wouldn't be able to look my wife and kids in the face again. It's too awful to even think about."

"Well, you better start thinking about it," Hardin said moving closer to Costello who had his back against the pier's wooden railing. "Jackson Stone is about the best I've seen when it comes to police work, and if he connects that dead girl to a missing person report from Gainesville we're in deep shit. The girl's family must have reported her missing to the police. Stone will talk to them and eventually find out who she was dating and everything else they can tell him about the men she knew. Joe Worthington's name is sure to come up. And after it does Stone will know that we went to the University of Florida with him and were his friends. That the three of us were inseparable and did everything together. Before it's all over Stone will have come down on Worthington like a ton of bricks. Joe will puke his guts out and tell Stone everything, including how you and me raped the girl while she was knocked out. Don't forget Worthington didn't go into the bedroom until after the girl was already dead. He could blame the two of us for killing her."

"But we didn't kill her. She fell and hit her head."

"Try telling that to Stone after Worthington points the finger at us. We're the ones who will be looking at rape and murder. Worthington can say whatever he wants, and who is to say different? He could say that you and me raped and killed her. He could even deny putting the knockout drug in her drink while blaming us for that, too. Don't forget his old man is the mayor and Zach Worthington wields a lot of clout in this town."

"Joe wouldn't do that. He wouldn't blame us for putting the knockout drug in her drink."

"The hell he wouldn't. His father will tell him to, and Joe Worthington will lie to the high heaven to save his own ass. I've seen what people can do when they find themselves in a corner. Sam, we have to kill him. We have no other choice. Either Joe Worthington ends up dead, or you and I go down for murdering the girl."

Hardin's words tore into Costello. The possibility of the scenario Hardin just laid out proved overwhelming. Costello's entire body started to shake.

"I couldn't deal with Peggy finding out about this," Costello said. "It would kill her, I'm sure of it. And the thought of me going to prison for the rest of my life, especially over something that I barely had anything to do with. But to murder Joe Worthington, even if he is to blame for all this. I mean to actually kill him while he's watching us do it to him, I just don't think ..."

Hardin grabbed both of Costello's wrists and squeezed them.

"I got two Mexicans who will do it for us. They did a murder in Mexico and they're on the run. They crossed over the Arizona border illegally into this country five months ago, and I know they're desperate for money. They'll do almost anything to get some. I handled a robbery case in court for one of them up in Tampa. I'm sure for five hundred, they'd be happy to take care of Worthington for us."

Costello pulled his wrists out of Hardin's grasp. There was no mistaking the angry look showing on Costello's sweat-stained face. The look caught Jack Hardin by surprise. It caused him to take a step backward.

Costello said to him, "Then why don't you do it yourself if you've got two Mexicans to do the job for you? Why do you have to involve me? You call me up and have me come out here to meet you just to tell me this?"

Hardin shook his head. "Sam, you don't understand. I need you to telephone Worthington and arrange for the three of us to meet again at the beach house. Tell him we have to talk some more, tell him anything you want but just get him to meet us at the beach house. If I called him he would suspect something, but not if you made the call. You're his best friend. He trusts you. The two Mexicans will meet him at the beach house and that'll be the end of it. After it's all over you won't have to worry anymore about Peggy finding out about the dead girl, or you going to prison for the rest of your life."

Costello turned away from Hardin. He took hold of the pier's wooden railing with both hands. Joe Worthington had been his closest friend since grammar school. They were best man at each other's wedding. And now to take part in having him killed. Costello stared out at the blue-green water of the Gulf of Mexico. A pair of porpoises were playing together not far off the pier. Costello found himself wishing that he could trade places with one of them.

"When should I tell him to meet us at the beach house?" Costello said after turning to face Hardin.

Hardin told him, "Give me a day to arrange things. Then I'll call you with the exact time."

CHAPTER TWENTY

STONE'S INVITATION TO dinner at the Crow's Nest caught Keri Martin by surprise. She did not know what to say. After all it had been a long, trying day. It began with the autopsy on the murdered girl at the hospital; and later came Stone's informing her about the real reason she had been chosen as the new chief of police. Next was the ejection of Erik the Red and the *Satan Ramblers* from the Blue Marlin bar. But the day did not end there. After leaving the Blue Marlin, Keri drove down to Pelican's Landing beach to be alone. Stone had upset her with his cavalier attitude regarding Potts's shooting of Erik the Red's motorcycle. In her opinion, it had been an irresponsible thing to do. Keri wondered how she would ever be able to have a working relationship with such a man. But after an hour of watching the waves wash up on the shore, and observing flocks of seabirds fighting over their next meal, she was finally able to calm herself down. Keri decided to drive her unmarked squad car back to the Pelican's Landing police station.

A town square was comprised of the city hall and police station buildings along with a smaller building that served as the county tax office. The front of the square was beautifully arranged. It had a red brick motorway with towering rows of palm trees planted on either side, not to mention a spectacular water fountain that attracted hundreds of tropical birds throughout the day. The town square separated the government buildings from the rest of town. Keri parked the squad car at the rear of the police station in a parking space designated *Chief of Police Only*. One of the perks of the job, Martin thought to herself, as she exited her car and walked over to a tinted glass door. Keri opened the door and took a flight of stairs up to the second floor. There were a string of administrative offices on the second floor including the office for the chief of police.

Straightaway, Martin observed Jackson Stone's black hair and smiling face. Then she took note of the other people standing behind him in the open space at the top of the stairs. Lisa Moore, Cliff Potts, and Bob Garcia were there. And so were fifteen or more other people Keri did not know. Stone started clapping his hands together and the others joined in with him until Cliff Potts let loose with a high pitch rebel yell. That set everyone to laughing, and the whole group came rushing over to Keri to tell her how proud they were to be working for someone like her.

"I guess we surprised you," Lisa Moore said with the laughter still on her face. "It was Jackson's idea to get everybody together including the part-timers, dispatchers, and civilians to show you how much we appreciate what you did at the Blue Marlin today. I for one was scared shitless."

"Well, thank you," Keri said, quite taken aback by it all. "I want to thank every one of you."

Martin looked for Stone's face among the well-wishers. She quickly spotted him on the other side of the foyer. He was standing in front of a clear glass office with "Lieutenant" inscribed above its door. Keri saw that Stone was signaling for her to join him in his office. But in order to do so she would have to first deal with Cliff Potts. The police sergeant appeared set on talking to Keri. Instantly, Martin detected the strong scent of alcohol emanating from his entire being. It was obvious to her Potts had been drinking. His eyes were watery; a silly grin adorned his face. He began telling her how one day he would like to take Keri wild boar hunting with him and Stone in the Everglades.

"They got tusks that could rip you every which way just like that," Potts said snapping two fingers together. "They're the down-right onerous cusses …" Keri did not hear anything further. She abruptly walked away from Potts leaving the sergeant staring after her. Stone saw her coming. And the look on Martin's face told him that she was upset.

"Potts, what did you say to her?" Stone found himself asking. He opened his office door and watched Martin step inside. Stone observed the folded arms, red face, along with the simmering look. He thought of a red kettle waiting to boil over. He offered her a seat pointing to the brown padded chair behind his desk. Shaking her head, Keri said she preferred to stand.

Stone told her, "They don't normally cheer for a new boss around here like that, but what you did today at the Blue Marlin made a real impression on them. Because of you, they're proud to be a part of this department. And that goes for me, too."

He observed the light green eyes staring intently back at him. If she appreciated his words, it did not show. Keri Martin appeared to have her mind set on something else.

"Potts is presently on duty and reeking of alcohol," she said spitting out the words. "Earlier today he was waving a shotgun inside the Blue Marlin. A person could have been shot, not just a motorcycle. Stone, I will not stand for my people drinking on duty. Is that clear?"

"I'll talk to him."

"I want more than talk. On duty drinking cannot be tolerated. I won't stand for it."

"I agree. And I promise to talk to him," Stone said to her. "Potts can't go on any longer like this. It's bad for the police department and it's bad for him too. But I'll tell you something, Cliff Potts never used to be like this. If you knew him twenty-five years ago you'd know what I was talking about. Back then he was what every boy wanted to be when he grew up. He was a policeman's policeman, and by far the best man to ever walk the streets in this town. It's just that life changes some people more than it does others, and Potts is one of those that life changed a lot. But you don't have to worry about Sergeant Potts, I'll take care of him."

"I'm glad to hear that," Keri said while seeing something in Stone she had not seen prior. Sadness. Potts obviously meant a great deal to him. Martin appreciated Stone's feelings especially when they were for a friend who was in serious trouble. "Lieutenant, I'll leave Potts's drinking problem up to you," she said to him. "Now what did you call me into your office to discuss?"

"To ask you out for dinner at the Crow's Nest this evening," Stone said, smiling, appreciating the surprised look on Keri Martin's face. "Ada Lantos's chicken paprikash is out of this world. I know that you will absolutely love it. What would be a good time for me to come by the hotel to pick you up?"

Keri had planned on eating dinner alone in the hotel restaurant. The thought of having dinner with Stone at the Crow's Nest had never entered her mind. She observed his dark, blue eyes staring at her, waiting for an answer.

"How does seven o'clock sound?" Keri heard herself say while finding it hard to believe that she had actually agreed to have dinner with Jackson Stone.

CHAPTER TWENTY-ONE

"Rising moon shining down on me/ There is nothing you don't see/ Where's he gone?/ Where's he now?/ The man I love/ Tell me rising moon."

ADA LANTOS SANG a love song for the dining room patrons. She was wearing a black lace, side-slit dress, and no shoes while seated on top of an ivory white piano in the dining area on the Crow's Nest's roof. The blonde wig she wore contrasted nicely with the black dress, diamond necklace, and accompanying earrings. Ada's seventy-seven-year-old husband, Fredek, sat at the piano playing. He was dressed in a shiny black tuxedo, white shirt, and black bowtie. Fredek moved his fingers across the piano keyboard touching each key with an almost delicate reverence. Ada stayed seated on top of the piano looking down at him singing her sad song about a broken-hearted girl and a love gone by.

Jackson Stone and Keri Martin watched from a nearby table. They had just finished eating dinner and were having after dinner drinks. Stone held onto a dry manhattan while Martin sipped a glass of red wine. A flaming torch topping an ornate black metal pole flanked their table; and sets of red-clay flower pots overflowing with white and pink orchids lined the wall behind them. The torch's yellow light mixed nicely with the bluish glow from the moon overhead. It lent a certain intimacy to the evening. The cascading surf rolling across the beach below only added to the rooftop's ambience.

"She has such a lovely voice and he plays so beautifully," Keri Martin said after Ada had finished singing and the people around them began to applaud. "I was so glad to have met Ada and Fredek Lantos earlier. Lieutenant, I have to thank you again for introducing them to me."

"I was glad to do it," Stone said appreciating how the torch's light reflected off Keri Martin's beautifully formed face. It caused her green eyes to brighten, and her parted lips and smooth cheeks to appear radiant. The arrival of a night breeze only added to her appeal. It stirred Martin's red hair producing fiery wisps in the torch's light. Stone wanted to tell her how beautiful she was, but decided against it. Instead he brought up the unidentified girl's murder.

"Before Ada began her song you were asking about the Jane Doe investigation. So far we haven't even come close in getting a match. Lisa Moore checked out NamUS (National Missing and Unidentified Persons system) and found nothing. She also did a six county radius for every missing girl in the past twenty years that fits Jane Doe's age group along with her slim build, blond hair, and having had a baby. Again nothing close to our girl. Moore said that she's going to broaden the search statewide and see if anything pops. Meanwhile the medical examiner, Dr. Snyder, has contacted someone in New York who is an expert on facial reconstruction. Hopefully, we'll be able to put a face on our Jane Doe. Maybe that'll help get something going."

"You still feel that whoever killed her is from Pelican's Landing?" Keri asked, staying focused on Stone seated across the table from her. The black hair resting on his forehead along with the dark blue eyes brought an unsettling feeling to Keri. She attempted to ignore it, but the feeling did not leave her.

"Yes, I do. Whoever buried Jane Doe on that remote section of Tanner's ranch didn't just happen to come by and decide to bury her there. He knew about the place beforehand, and knew it would be unlikely for anyone to find a body buried out there. If some stranger was the one who killed her, he would have just tossed her body off to the side of some road and kept on going. No, the one we're looking for never wanted Jane Doe's body to be found. He knew that finding her body would enable the police to trace the girl's murder back to him. That tells me our killer lives in Pelican's Landing. And after we identify Jane Doe we're going to know who he is."

"I have been feeling more and more that it's Tanner who killed her," Keri said remembering how the rancher had reacted after being confronted by Stone outside his barn. "He strikes me as the type of man who could kill someone without it bothering him in the least."

Stone nodded. "You read Roscoe Tanner pretty well. I've known him nearly all my life. We both grew up in Pelican's Landing, and he's never been any good. I can remember back in grammar school when he would push the other kids around to get his own way. I never liked him, and he never liked me. And now that I'm the police and he deals in meth crystal for the Conigliaro Crime Family, things have only gotten worse between us. There's no doubt in my mind that one day we are going to have it out once and for all."

"So do you think he killed the girl and buried her on his ranch?"

"I don't know. Like you said, Tanner is definitely capable of committing murder, but I don't get the feeling in my gut that tells me that he killed Jane Doe. I didn't see it in his eyes yesterday after I accused him of being a murderer. Most guilty people show you something. All I saw in Tanner's eyes was hate for me. But I can't rule him out because the girl's body was discovered on his property."

"So you grew up in Pelican's Landing, I didn't know that," Keri said to him. "I read your personnel file and it showed you at one time working for the New York City Police Department. I just assumed that you came to Pelican's Landing to get away from the big city, not that you were actually born and raised here."

Stone told Martin how he had joined the NYPD after getting out of the Marine Corp, but always felt that Pelican's Landing was his home. It was where his mother still lived until three years ago when she had passed away. And it was the only place he ever really cared about settling down for good. He also told her that Cliff Potts was his mother's brother and had always been more than a just an uncle to him. Potts was actually more like a surrogate father. Especially after Stone's real father had died in a boating accident when Stone was five years old. Keri caught the instant change in him after the mention of Potts's name. Stone's affection for his uncle was obvious. He told her that Cliff Potts had been his role model while growing up and the reason for his joining the NYPD. Stone said that after he had returned to Pelican's Landing it was Potts who helped him get on the town's police force.

"The rest is history," he told her. "I left New York City a pretty beaten up guy. Working undercover for an extended period of time takes its toll on a person. It can also wreck a marriage and that's what happened in my case. I came home one night after being gone for three days and found the place empty. My wife had taken everything—car, furniture, money in the bank, even the mongrel mutt I had found half-starved on the street three years before. She took off for California and I never saw her again. About four years ago I got a phone call from some sergeant on the Los Angeles Police Department telling me that they had found her dead in a transient hotel. My name and phone number were written on the note that she had left. She ended up taking a vial of sleeping pills to kill herself and wanted me to know about it."

"I'm sorry," Keri said to him while witnessing the troubled look in Stone's eyes. "I hope you don't blame yourself for her wanting to commit suicide. After all, she's the one who walked out on you and took everything of value. People have to make their own choices in this world and she made hers."

"You're right, we do have to make our own choices. And I made mine by spending months working undercover to get the goods on the Giaccone Crime Family while all the time knowing that I had a wife waiting at home who needed me to be there with her."

Keri watched Stone finish his drink and set the glass down on the table. He smiled back at her. "Thanks for lending me your ear. I don't tell that story to too many people. It must have been that last manhattan I had along with my staring into your pretty face for the past two hours. You have the kind of face a man likes to tell things to. Did anyone ever tell you that?"

"No, not at least anyone lately," Keri said finding herself liking the man seated across the table from her. Stone was different than most of the men she had met in her life. There was no pretense about him. What you saw was what you got. Her father would have called him a man's kind of a man. But a woman's kind, too, Keri thought. She liked the way Stone had taken over the biker gang in the Blue Marlin by slamming Erik the Red's head into the bar. And for what he did afterward as well. He came back to the police station and set up a welcoming committee for her. He did not have to do that. Especially not after she was given the police chief's job when by rights it should have been given to him. But that's the kind of man he happens to be, Keri thought. A much different kind than Rance Stapleton, or any of the other men she had known in her life.

"It looks like we're the last ones to be leaving," Stone said before rising up out of his chair. Keri grabbed her handbag from under the table and came to her feet. Together, they walked to the stairwell taking the stairs down to the first floor. Fredek Lantos waved goodnight from behind the bar. Stone and Martin waved back before walking out the Crow's Nest's front door. Two minutes later they were in Stone's blue Mustang convertible driving down Treasure Island Boulevard in the direction of the Holiday Inn.

The convertible's top was down. Clusters of stars lit up the sky overhead. Keri could not remember the last time she felt so relaxed. The evening was absolutely beautiful. She told Stone that she would have to start looking for a condo or townhouse to rent or buy. The Holiday Inn suite was satisfactory for the time being, but she would be glad to have her own place. She asked him where he lived. Stone told her down by the marina on his boat, a 32-foot Sportcraft cabin cruiser. It had all the comforts of home including satellite television and a fully stocked liquor cabinet. Keri stared at him while not quite believing Stone actually lived on a boat.

"I've never known anyone who lived on a boat before," she said, smiling. "You actually spend your nights sleeping on a boat?"

Laughing, he told her, "Yes, I do. And one of these days I'll have to take you out on the Gulf of Mexico. You'll absolutely love it."

Stone went on to explain how he had named his boat the *Roll of the Dice* because after leaving New York and coming to Pelican's Landing he was not exactly sure how long he was going to stay.

"Well, I for one am glad you stayed this long," Keri said as Stone brought the Mustang to a stop in front of the Holiday Inn's main entrance. Keri stepped out of the Mustang's passenger side door. As if remembering something, she ducked her head back inside the car. "Jackson, thanks for dinner and a lovely evening," she said to him while noticing the surprised look on his face. "Yes, I'm addressing you by your first name, and I hope you do the same for me. Call me Keri. I think we know each other well enough to be on a first name basis, don't you?"

Smiling, Stone nodded. "Yes, I do, Keri. And I think we're going to make a good team against the Conigliaro Crime Family."

Martin closed the passenger side door and waved goodbye. Stone waved back as he drove out of the Holiday Inn parking lot.

Not wasting any time, he began looking for the small red compact that had been following him and Martin ever since they had left the Crow's Nest. Whoever was driving the car had kept his distance, but Stone was almost certain that they were being followed. After careful inspection he failed to see a headlight or parked car anywhere on the street. The driver must not have wanted to be seen hanging around. But where did he go? Stone asked himself, before steering the Mustang in the direction of the marina.

CHAPTER TWENTY-TWO

STONE HAD DRIVEN less than a mile when he pulled the Mustang over to the side of the road. He took out his cellphone and proceeded to punch in the numbers for Keri Martin's phone. Her voice mail popped on after the fourth ring. Stone had dropped off Martin at the Holiday Inn only minutes ago and she was not answering her cellphone. It did not make any sense to him. Especially since Martin knew as chief of police she was to be accessible both day and night. Something had to be wrong. An uneasy feeling was growing more intense in the pit of Stone's stomach. It had been plaguing him ever since he first drove the Mustang out of the Holiday Inn parking lot. What could have happened to the red compact that had been following them? The car had been behind them ever since they had left the Crow's Nest. Where did it disappear to? Could the compact's driver have doubled back? It would not have been difficult to do. He could have parked a couple blocks away and waited. Was Keri Martin the one he was after? Stone dropped the Mustang into drive and stepped on the gas. He made a U-turn heading back to the Holiday Inn.

The hotel desk clerk observed Stone entering the front door. He started to say something, but Stone stopped him. "What suite is Chief Martin in?" Stone said hurrying past the desk.

"Room 204, Lieutenant. Do you want me to ring Chief Martin's room and tell her you're coming?"

"No, get the swipe key for 204 and meet me there," Stone said not bothering with the elevator and taking the stairs. He took two stairs at a time until reaching the second floor. He immediately began checking hotel suite numbers. Stone located Martin's at the end of the hallway. He placed his right ear up against the door. Initially, there was nothing. Then the sound of a man's voice came to him.

"You'll tell nobody because if you do, it will make you a laughing stock to everyone in Pelican's Landing. I can see the newspaper headline already—*New Chief of Police Files Battery Charge against Former Boyfriend.* How do you think that will look to the fine citizens of Pelican's Landing? The people in this town would laugh themselves silly. You know that as well as I do. They sure as hell wouldn't keep you on as their chief of police for very long. No Keri, you won't say a word to anyone. You'll keep your pretty little mouth shut and take whatever I dish out and you'll like it."

Stone tried the door. It was unlocked. He opened it and stepped into the suite. Keri Martin was lying on a purple couch set against a wall on the other side of the room. Her right hand covered her mouth; tears were in Martin's eyes. A big man with a solid build and angry face stood over her. He turned to face Stone.

"Who the hell are you?" the man said displaying a disdainful look. Both his hands were clasped into tight fists. The man had broad shoulders and a muscular build. His large chest swelled after he took a deep breath. "Mister, you better get out of here if you know what's good for you."

Stone moved like an attacking cat. His right hand struck the big man's nose, breaking it. A left hook smashed into the right side of the man's face. More blows followed, piston-like in delivery, starting at the man's stomach and shifting to his face. Stone was unrelenting. The man attempted to defend himself by raising his arms to protect his face. But Stone's punches landed again and again. They were hard, punishing blows, and delivered with bone-crunching effect. The onslaught did not stop until the man fell unconscious to the floor.

"Lieutenant Stone, should I phone for an ambulance?" the wide-eyed desk clerk asked from the hallway. The young man was standing just outside the hotel suite door. He had witnessed Stone's beating of the man.

Stone took a couple of deep breaths. "No, he'll be all right. But do me a favor and call the police station and tell whoever answers the phone that I want Sergeant Potts and Officer Garcia to come here to room 204 right away. Will you do that for me?"

"Yes, sir, I will. I'll go downstairs and make the call for you. Is there anything else you need?"

"No, nothing else. Just put the call out for Potts and Garcia."

The young man hurried off. Stone turned his attention to Keri Martin who had not moved from the couch. She was looking up at him through green eyes filled with tears. He noticed the swelling to both her cheeks and the blood on her nose. There was also bruising along her wrists and arms as well a line of red marks on her throat. The upper portion of Keri's blue evening dress had been torn away. She was holding it up with her left hand to cover herself.

"Do you need to see a doctor?" Stone asked keeping his eyes trained on Martin's eyes. They appeared full of pain. He thought at any moment they would empty out. That the pain would escape. Stone knew Keri could not hold back the flow of tears much longer. The dam had to break. And then it did break. She started to cry. Keri's upper body shook. Stone put his arms around her and brought her close to him.

"It's over," he whispered into her ear. "After tonight he will never hurt you again."

"His name is Rance Stapleton," Keri said pulling away from Stone. She used her right hand to wipe the tears from her eyes. "I broke off things with him in Chicago and told him that I never wanted to see him again. But he wouldn't let go and came after me. He must have been hiding in the stairwell because after I opened my hotel suite door he came up behind me and pushed me inside. I came to Pelican's Landing to get away from him and now he's found me. He can make it so that I'll never keep my job as chief of police here. I know he can do that."

Stone told her, "He won't be coming back to Pelican's Landing again, I promise you. You won't see him anymore after tonight. Now, why don't you go in the bathroom and put on some different clothes before Potts and Garcia get here. They should be arriving any minute. While you're doing that I'll babysit Junior. It looks like he's starting to come around."

Fifteen minutes later Potts and Garcia walked into suite 204. Keri Martin was still in the bathroom. She decided to stay in the bathroom until they left. Keri did not want Potts and Garcia to see her bruised and battered face.

"Don't tell me," Potts said observing Stone standing over a bloodied Rance Stapleton who was sitting on the floor. "This joker thought it was his room and Chief Martin was one of the hospitalities that came along with it."

"Something like that," Stone said motioning for Potts to follow him outside into the hallway. Once outside Stone told Potts about how Stapleton had followed him and Martin from the Crow's Nest back to the Holiday Inn. And after dropping Martin off, he was on his way home when he got the feeling that something was not right. So he came back to the Holiday Inn and found Stapleton inside Keri Martin's room. Stapleton had beaten her. He was in the process of threatening Martin when Stone entered the hotel suite.

"And you returned the favor by beating the piss out of him," Potts said shaking his head and grinning from ear to ear. "It looks like our boy Stapleton won't take no for an answer. He wants Chief

Martin for his gal no matter how she feels about him. It makes me glad I never let my guard down and got myself involved with any particular woman. Women have the tendency to make men do the craziest things. So Jackson what do you want me and Garcia to do with this jasper? We can make it so he's never heard from again if that's what you want."

"Potts, you know I would never go along with that sort of thing. No, I was thinking more of a late night visit to that back road off alligator alley where the alligators bunch up this time of year during mating season. If you were to tie a rope around Mr. Stapleton and throw him in the water for a while that should do the trick. But just make sure he's not in the water too long. I don't want him eaten alive. I only want him scared so that he'll never want to come back to Pelican's Landing ever again. Do you think that you and Garcia can handle it?"

"I know we can. And after his bath what should we do with him?"

"Take Stapleton to the bus station and put him on the first bus back to Chicago. And Potts make it crystal clear to him that if he ever comes back to Pelican's Landing he won't be leaving next time."

"I'll do that," Potts said smiling while observing the look on Stone's face. He was surprised at what he saw. "Jackson, you must think an awful lot of this Keri Martin to be going to all this trouble. I never seen you acting like this with any other woman before."

"Just take care of Stapleton," Stone said prior to his walking back into suite 204 to check on Martin.

CHAPTER TWENTY-THREE

KERI MARTIN AWAKENED to the sound of voices outside her hotel suite's door. It was the Guatemalan cleaning ladies talking amongst themselves. There had to be a fair-sized group of them chattering away right outside her door. Don't they have any rooms to clean? Keri found herself thinking before swinging her legs over the side of the bed and coming to a sitting position. The clock on the nightstand next to her bed showed eight a.m. Keri knew that meant Stone would be knocking on her door in another thirty minutes. It certainly did not leave her much time to get ready. How do you take a shower, blow dry your hair, brush your teeth, and use makeup to cover over puffy eyes and facial bruises all in thirty minutes?

Keri went directly to the bathroom and looked in the mirror. The lid over her right eye was a dark blue color while both her cheeks were swollen with fresh bruises showing. Stapleton had grabbed Keri's cheeks with his left hand before punching her with his right. Then grabbing her by the throat, he had flung Keri bodily across the room. Luckily, she landed on the couch. That was about the time Stone entered the room. Keri could still picture in her mind Stone's beating of Stapleton. She had never seen anyone beaten in such a manner. It was both exhilarating and frightening to witness. Exhilarating in the sense that Rance Stapleton had finally gotten his comeuppance, but frightening to see Stone capable of such violence. Stone had been thorough and precise in his decimation of Stapleton. Keri was of the opinion that Stone must have fought a great deal in his life to become so good at it. The thought left her wondering about Stone.

Keri took a shower while forgoing the blow drying of her hair by putting on a shower cap. She then brushed her teeth and commenced with the tedious task of applying dabs of makeup to the dark bruises dotting her face and neck. But Keri's dark-colored, puffy right eye was another story. The makeup did little to conceal the discoloration around her eye. "I guess I'll just have to spend the rest of the week wearing sunglasses wherever I go," she said out loud to herself before slipping on a light green top and a pair of white capris. She found her beige, opened-toe sandals buried under a pile of clothes in her suitcase. Keri put the sandals on and went over to the window. She looked out for Stone's car in the parking lot. The blue Mustang was nowhere to be seen. Stone had told Keri the night before that he would be picking her up in the morning to take her out on his boat the *Roll of the Dice*. They would be spending a good part of the day on the Gulf of Mexico taking in the sun and the warm ocean breeze. Keri had been quick to accept Stone's offer. She remembered not wanting any part of showing up for work looking the way she did. She also remembered listening at the hotel room's bathroom door and overhearing Potts and Garcia discussing Rance Stapleton.

"Bob, you handcuff this jasper. I handcuffed the last guy we left in the Everglades and those damn gators ate my handcuffs right along with the guy."

"What are you talking about?" Stapleton wanted to know. His question elicited a bout of laughter from Potts.

Potts told him, "Buddy boy, we're takin' you to a dinner party and you're going to be the main course."

"Where are you taking me? I have the right to know." Stapleton began to yell. Keri heard muffled sounds coming from the room. It sounded as if something had been placed over Stapleton's mouth. A few minutes later Stone opened the bedroom door.

"He's gone," Stone said to her. "The boys are taking your Mr. Stapleton for a ride into the Everglades to scare him a little before they put him on a bus back to Chicago. Keri, he won't be stepping foot in Pelican's Landing ever again. I can assure you of that."

Keri remembered thanking Stone for helping her while keeping her eyes averted from his gaze. The shame she felt was too much. Stapleton had brought back the past life Keri Martin had been trying to escape. All the hurt and humiliation she had experienced in Chicago while being romantically linked to Rance Stapleton had returned. Stone did his best to take the hurt away. Keri recalled the feel of his hand underneath her chin, raising it up, while she stared into his blue eyes. It was as if Stone's eyes were telling her that everything was going to be all right. That she did not have to be afraid anymore. And the likes of Rance Stapleton would never enter into her life again.

Keri observed Stone's blue Mustang pulling into the hotel parking lot. There would be no more thoughts of Rance Stapleton, only the Florida sunshine and the chance for a fresh new start. Keri took the green bathing suit out of her suitcase. She put it into her handbag and hurried toward the door.

****

The *Roll of the Dice's* bow sliced easily through the calm blue waters of the Gulf of Mexico. The boat was a white-colored, 32-foot Sportcraft cabin cruiser propelled by twin Volvo 200 hp. diesels on shafts and sporting three cabins with accommodations for up to six passengers. Stone's cabin cruiser possessed all the luxuries of a land based residence including hot and cold water, cooker, fridge, toilet, 20-inch flat screen TV, and a well-stocked liquor cabinet that Stone kept replenished on a weekly basis. Stone was sitting in the captain's chair with his right hand on the boat's wheel. Keri Martin occupied the chair next to him. She was wearing a one-piece green bathing suit and dark sunglasses. Martin's red hair fluttered aimlessly in the breeze. The sensation made her feel like a bird in flight surrounded by ocean and sky without a care in the world. Keri picked up on Stone's looking at her.

"Is it always like this?" she asked him. "The sky and ocean almost touching one another and the air so clean that it makes you want to stick out your tongue so you can taste it. This has to be one of the most uplifting experiences I've ever had. Jackson, I can't thank you enough for taking me."

"It can be beautiful one moment and treacherous the next," he told her taking in Keri's trim figure and slender legs. "Just make sure your arms and legs have plenty of sunscreen on them. You're fair-skinned and could burn easy if you're not careful."

Keri reached into the handbag at her feet and removed a tube of sunscreen lotion. She held the tube up for Stone to see. "I'm covered from top to bottom. You might not be aware of it, but the sun doesn't only shine in Florida. Chicago on occasion has been known to have hot, sunny days as well."

Stone smiled. "Just wanted to be sure. I didn't want you complaining about being sunburned after a couple of hours of snorkeling. By the way we should be getting to the Islet of Tears in a few minutes. We'll drop anchor in about fifteen or twenty feet of water, put on our masks and diving fins, and jump in. You're in for a real treat. The water looks calm, which means we should have good visibility on the bottom."

"Islet of Tears? I never heard of it. Do people live on the island?"

Stone told her, "No, the Islet of Tears is just one of hundreds of small islets off the Florida coastline. Few have people living on them because there is no fresh water source other than rain water, and if you're caught by a hurricane it's curtains for you. All the islets become engulfed in water."

"How did it come by its name, Islet of Tears? It sounds so sad. Did something terrible happen to give it such a name?"

"Something terrible happened all right, but not on the island. Legend has it, about six hundred years ago when the Calusa Indians ruled this part of Florida a Spanish ship became shipwrecked after a violent storm. Some of the surviving sailors washed up on what is now the Florida coastline. The Calusa were a warlike people, but they did not kill the sailors. Instead they adopted them into their tribe. One of the young sailors caught the eye of the chief's daughter and the two of them fell in love. Well, that didn't sit too well with the Calusa chief because he had promised his daughter to the chief of another tribe so that an alliance could be forged between the two peoples."

"Don't tell me," Keri said interrupting. "The chief had the young sailor killed so that his daughter could marry the chief from the other tribe."

Stone nodded. "The chief had the young sailor beheaded, but it didn't work out the way he wanted it. His daughter was so heartbroken over the death of the sailor that she killed herself. The chief buried his daughter's body on the islet that we're going to. Ever since then the islet has been known as the Islet of Tears."

Keri said to him, "I don't want to sound too morbid but do you know how she killed herself?"

Stone looked back at Keri displaying a smile. "She took a live Cone Shell and held it up to her heart. The Cone Shell injects venom through a hollow stinger much like a hypodermic needle. The chief's daughter had placed the Cone Shell against her left breast and allowed the poisonous venom to be injected into her heart. Legend has it that she did it in front of her father and the entire tribe."

"Is that the place?" Keri asked pointing at what looked like a small mound of earth in the middle of the Gulf of Mexico. "Is that the Islet of Tears?"

"That's it," Stone said. "Here, you take the wheel while I go below and get the gear. We'll be there in a few minutes."

****

Stone dropped the *Roll of the Dice's* anchor in twenty feet of water approximately thirty yards off the Islet of Tears' sandy beach. Mangrove and gumbo limbo trees along with several varieties of vegetation covered most of the square mile island. Different species of birds were everywhere. Keri observed spotted sandpipers scurrying along the surf's edge and pink roseate spoonbills ambling beside them in search of small fish and crustaceans. A large flock of red-winged blackbirds apparently had made the island their home. The chattering birds filled the tops of the mangrove and gumbo limbo trees. Keri estimated their number to be in the thousands. But it was the bald eagle hovering high overhead that caused her the most excitement.

"Jackson, can you imagine a bald eagle way out here? I wouldn't think they would venture so far from the mainland."

Stone shaded his eyes with his right hand while peering up at the magnificent bird soaring high above them. "Bald eagles go where the food is, and there's plenty to eat for them on these tiny islets. And there's enough rain water for them as well. Besides, out here they don't have to deal with people, which is another plus. Are you ready to do some snorkeling?"

"All set," Keri said as she began putting on her snorkeling fins and face mask. At the same time she could not help but notice Stone's red trunks and well-muscled upper body. Keri appreciated the suntanned chest along with the thick, black hair covering it. He moves so effortlessly for such a big man, she thought. Stone had already secured his face mask and was in the process of stepping over the *Roll of the Dice's* side railing. Holding a black-colored snorkel, he bit down on its mouthpiece and dropped into the water. Keri did the same with her snorkel's mouthpiece and started after him.

The transformation was nothing less than exhilarating. Keri felt as though she had entered a magical world created for only her and Stone. An excellent swimmer, Martin had swum in Lake Michigan many times, but nothing could have prepared her for the clear, warm waters of the Gulf of Mexico. It was like being immersed in a clear pool of warm water that had no boundaries, no restrictions, where one had an unobstructed view of a hidden world that few people had ever seen. Stone motioned for her to follow him down deeper into the water. Keri kicked hard, propelling herself downward, and it was not long before she and Stone were swimming abreast along the Gulf's sandy bottom. They intruded upon a multitude of starfish, blue crabs, mollusks, and an assortment of other sea floor dwellers who called the sandy bottom home.

Keri marveled at the panorama unfolding before her eyes. It was absolutely beautiful. More beautiful than anything she had ever seen. Sea life seemed to abound everywhere. Varieties of species of fish swam within an easy arm's reach of her while huge limestone rock formations spiraled upward out of the sandy bottom. The limestone configurations dotted the underwater landscape appearing like so many medieval fortresses undergoing besiegement. There were schools of mackerel numbering in the thousands descending upon the limestone with more arriving all the time. The silver mackerel darted in and out amongst the rocks at lightning speed. Keri watched them as she reached out to touch a passing redfish. Stone's smiling face appeared in front of her. Keri smiled back at him while nodding yes, I am overwhelmed by it. She saw him showing a thumbs up indicating that they should head toward the surface. Together, they swam upward and after breaking the surface obtained a much needed breath of air.

"I can't believe anything could be so spectacular," Keri said removing her face mask. "It's like nothing I've ever experienced. I don't want it to end."

"Then don't let it," Stone responded heading back down.

It was a two hour snorkeling experience that Keri knew she would never forget. Schools of snook, sheepshead, cobia, and grouper were just some of the fish that she and Stone had encountered while snorkeling off the Islet of Tears. At one point a menacing-looking bull shark had made an appearance, but rapidly swam away after Stone started moving in its direction. But the highlight of the swim was the giant, green sea turtle. The hard-shelled monster was well over three hundred pounds and had swum so close to them that Stone was able to grab onto its tail. Keri watched the giant turtle pull Stone around through the water like a trained reptile in an underwater circus act.

"I loved every minute of it," Keri said after Stone helped her onto the *Roll of the Dice's* deck. "You have to promise me that we'll do it again sometime."

Stone took two beach towels off a deck chair and handed one of the towels to Keri. "I promise. We'll come back to the Islet of Tears whenever you want. Consider the place yours."

"If only it had a different name," Keri said drying herself off. Stone began to dry himself with the other towel. She watched as he rubbed the yellow beach towel across his chest dropping it down to his calves. "The Islet of Tears sounds so sad and lonely, and I don't feel that way about it. Being here leaves me feeling happy, and glad that I am able to share in the hidden beauty of the place. Even if it is only for a short period time. Jackson, do you know what I'm trying to say? I guess what I'm asking is do you feel that way, too?"

"Yes, I do," Stone said taking in Keri's wet red hair and wide-eyed look along with the tight-fitting green bathing suit that accentuated the curves of her body. It took all the self-control Stone could muster to keep from putting his arms around her. Never did he think he would feel this way about a woman again. Not after being married for five years, and his wife walking out on him the way she did. "Why else do you think I brought you here?" Stone continued. "This place has been special to me ever since I first discovered it years ago. I often come here whenever I want to get away from the craziness of the world and recharge my batteries. I was hoping you would like it."

"So it seems that I'm the only one you have brought to the Islet of Tears," Keri said setting her towel down on the deck chair and staring into Stone's dark blue eyes. "Or is that what you tell all the women you bring out for the day on your boat? Your story of the Indian girl killing herself over the death of the man she loved was so deliciously romantic. Any woman would be enthralled by it. I know I certainly was. What happens next? Do you pop the cork on a bottle of wine and invite me down to your cabin below, or are you the kind of man who likes to have his sex right here on deck?"

"Actually," Stone said smiling. "I'm the outdoor type. There's a bottle of merlot on ice down below along with the lunch I picked up this morning at the Crow's Nest. I think Fredek Lantos said it was Grouper sandwiches on French bread and German potato salad. I was planning on putting up the canopy to keep the sun off us and having an enjoyable lunch here on deck. And afterward, I intended to head back to the marina. But if you are contemplating something different, please tell me. I can be very accommodating when it comes to having a beautiful woman on my boat."

The red-faced Martin allowed a smile to surface. "So there really was an Indian girl?"

"Yes," Stone said trying not to laugh.

"And you never brought any other women here?"

"No."

"Jackson, I made a first class fool out of myself. I want to apologize."

"Don't," Stone said to her. "Let's just pop the cork on the bottle of merlot and have ourselves some lunch. I don't know about you, but after two hours of snorkeling I get mighty hungry."

CHAPTER TWENTY-FOUR

VINNIE PALERMO LOOKED at the three men seated around the coffee table. Al Ruggiero, underboss for the Conigliaro Family, was seated to Palermo's right while Alex Mallo, the family's consigliore was seated to his left. Johnny Rocco, capo of the enforcers, occupied the chair directly across the table from Palermo. The meeting was being held in the basement of Vinnie Palermo's white-pillared mansion outside of Fort Lee, New Jersey. The mansion itself was situated on three acres of heavily wooded land and enclosed by a six-foot concrete fence. Security cameras monitored the mansion's exterior while two men armed with 9mm handguns were stationed at the front entrance gate. Visitors to the Palermo mansion came by appointment only.

"We got everything we wanted from the Commission," Palermo said while making sure he looked each man squarely in the face. "I met yesterday in Lower Manhattan with the Commission's representative, 'Fat Tony' Cracchiolo.'Fat Tony' told me the Five Families and the Chicago Outfit have agreed to give the Conigliaro Family a seat on the Commission as well as control of the gambling for the southern half of Florida. The sons of bitches backed down just like I knew they would. We got everything that we wanted. Rocco, you can call off the enforcers, and tell the rest of the boys to stand down. There won't be a war. But we are going to have to fulfill our part of the bargain in order to seal the deal with the other families. That means the Florida state legislature has to pass the new gambling law, and the governor has to sign it. So what the hell is holding everything up? I dropped enough cash on Tallahassee to buy off twenty state legislators."

Al Ruggiero knew his answer would anger Vinnie Palermo. "The chairman of the senate's gambling committee wants more money before he'll allow the bill out of committee and to be put up for a vote before the general assembly."

"Who is this guy?"

"Mark Boswell. He's the most influential member of the Florida state senate and nothing passes without him first giving the okay. Boswell wants ten thousand dollars more. Vinnie, I think we should give it to him."

"Do you really, Al? You think we should give this guy, Boswell, an extra ten grand to do what he agreed to do for sixty thousand nine months ago. And what about the governor if he wants more? Do we give it to him? And how about the rest of the general assembly? If they ask for more money do we give it to them, too? Every one of those slime ball politicians have been bought and paid for. I don't pay a second time for something I've already bought. Johnny, tomorrow you and Blowtorch Charlie fly down to Tallahassee and have a talk with Senator Boswell. Make it clear to the senator that it would be in his best interest to have the gambling bill passed right away."

Rocco tapped the top of the coffee table with his right forefinger. "Vinnie, consider it done. But if the senator should prove to be stubborn, how far should we go?"

"All the way," Vinnie said staring into Rocco's black eyes and holding them. "I want him out of the picture if he doesn't get on board. The Florida state legislature can elect themselves a new chairman for their gambling committee. Then we'll deal with the new guy and have the bill passed into law."

Alex Mallo shifted in his chair. Vinnie looked over at his thirty-four year old cousin whom he had known since Mallo was first born. Alex was Whitey Gallo's youngest son. Vinnie had paid for the young man's way through Harvard Law School before setting him up in a law practice. Alex was the Conigliaro Family's consigliore and considered to be one of the best criminal trial defense attorneys in the state of New Jersey. Mallo preferred the nonviolent approach to a matter whenever possible. But with Vinnie Palermo running the family's affairs that was not often the case.

"Alex, do you have something to say?" Palermo asked not trying to hide the annoyance in his voice.

"Vinnie, as the family's attorney I advise you to move carefully here. Killing a Florida state senator could end up hurting us more than helping. It might bring down a federal investigation. And who knows where that might lead?"

"Alex, that's why you're the family's consigliore. If any federal investigation surfaces, it's up to you to take care of it. In the meantime we can't have anything or anyone getting in the way of family business. Right now it's crucial for the new Florida gambling law to be passed without further delay. If that means taking out some greedy son of a bitch to get the job done then so be it."

Palermo turned to Al Ruggerio. "What's going on in Pelican's Landing with the girl's body that was found buried there?"

"Tanner says he doesn't know anything about it. The girl was murdered and Tanner feels the police are trying to pin the girl's murder on him. He blames Lieutenant Stone for going after him. Stone is the one who arrested Tanner last year after that van load of the family's marijuana was found in his barn. I also talked to Worthington about Lieutenant Stone. He agrees with Tanner that Stone could end up causing us a big problem in Pelican's Landing. The guy can't be bought, and he won't back down. Look at what Stone did to that motorcycle gang we ended up paying fifty thousand dollars. They were supposed to keep Stone busy while we were setting up house in Pelican's Landing. He ended up running *The Satan Ramblers* out of town telling them never to come back. Stone could try the same thing with our organization once we get the gambling and narcotic operations up and running. Tanner thinks Stone should be taken out. He's asking for your okay to kill him."

"He's a police lieutenant and killing him would cause a lot of heat," Alex Mallo said not liking the prospect at all. "We don't need that kind of a spotlight put on Pelican's Landing right now. The family has too much invested to throw it all away by killing a police lieutenant."

Palermo held up his right hand for Mallo to be silent.

"Will Tanner take care of it himself?" Palermo asked while looking at Ruggiero. "I don't want a botched job. It has to be clean with nothing that can be traced back to the Conigliaro Family."

Ruggiero nodded. "Yes, Tanner will handle the hit personally. He's even looking forward to it. There will be nothing about Stone's hit that could possibly involve the family. Policemen get killed every day in this country, and the public has come to accept the fact. Most people don't think twice about a policeman getting killed anymore. To the average person out there it's just a part of the job. They'll figure Stone got wasted by some wacko who hated the police, and that'll be the end of it."

"Vinnie can I say something?" Alex Mallo asked while feeling he was wasting his breath over something that had already been decided. "What about this new police chief, this Keri Martin, who we decided on for Pelican's Landing? We went to a lot of trouble to get her appointed as chief of police so things would be easier for us. Martin's inexperienced and should be no problem to manipulate. That's what Zach Worthington said about her after he interviewed Martin for the police chief's job. Tell Worthington to have Martin rein Stone in. Make it so that Stone doesn't interfere in Conigliaro Family business. Why don't we do that instead of taking the chance on killing him and bringing a lot of heat down on us?"

Al Ruggiero was quick in responding to Mallo. "I asked the same thing of Worthington the last time I talked to him. He said Martin is going to be no help to us. Worthington won't even attempt to buy her off because he's afraid that Martin might turn on him and end up arresting him. He said that she might be inexperienced, but she backs up Stone in everything. That makes her dangerous. I don't think we have any other choice but to get rid of Stone."

"Then tell Tanner to go through with it," Palermo said standing and signaling the meeting had ended. "And let me know the minute you hear that Stone is dead."

CHAPTER TWENTY-FIVE

JOE WORTHINGTON REMOVED his sunglasses and placed them on the table next to his chair. He was seated in an old wicker chair on the front porch of his parent's beach house. The view gave him a good look of the gravel road, which connected to the main highway three-quarters of a mile away. It was half past three and still no sign of anyone. What could be keeping Sam Costello and Jack Hardin? Costello had telephoned Worthington that morning. His friend had told him that it was important that he, Hardin, and Worthington meet at the beach house around three o'clock that afternoon. Sam sounded nervous over the phone. But that was nothing out of the ordinary for Sam. Costello was the nervous sort anyway. And now that Ginny's body had been discovered he was even more uptight. Panic-stricken would probably be a better way to describe him. But Worthington could not blame his lifelong friend. The last few days had become a nightmare for him as well. Even Janet had seen the change in him. She seemed to be always questioning him wanting to know what was wrong. He would try to deflect her concern by saying that he was worried about the baby. But deep down Joe Worthington felt his wife was not buying any of it. She knew him too well.

"You've been acting strange ever since your father telephoned about that girl's body found buried on the Tanner ranch. Joe, I saw the look on your face. It actually frightened me. It was one of shock and incredible sadness all at the same time. That's why I asked if you knew her. You said the body was still unidentified. I kept asking my-self how the death of someone you didn't even know could have such an effect on you. It didn't make any sense to me then and it still doesn't."

Worthington wanted to tell his wife everything. He almost did. But after seeing the look in Janet's blue eyes and the tautness of her jaw he changed his mind. She would never be able to handle it. What woman could? Yes, your husband eighteen years ago set up a girl to be raped by his two friends, and even though he did not mean for it to happen the girl accidentally died afterward. And if the police should find out he would probably get the death penalty. But don't let any of this bother you too much. And by all means don't lose our baby over it.

"I took it hard after my father told me that it was a girl's body the police had found. It really hit home for me. We're going to have a baby girl any day now, and I could not help but think of her. The thought of our daughter someday ending up that way sent shivers through me. Ever since my father's phone call I can't seem to think about anything else. It's been driving me crazy."

Janet bought it. She reached up and kissed him. But Worthington knew that he would eventually have to tell her. He could not go on for the rest of his life living with Ginny's death. That was what he planned on saying to Costello and Hardin once they arrived. Worthington knew Jackson Stone was a fair man. After Janet had her baby, he would contact Stone and tell him about his placing the knockout drug in Ginny's drink. He would also tell him that Ginny had been raped by Costello and Hardin. He would ask his friends to accompany him to the police station and to admit their part. If they refused, he would supply Stone with bogus names, saying the men who raped Ginny were two guys he had met at school. They were spending the weekend with him. Worthington knew he had to confess his guilt. There was no other way. He could not go on living with Ginny's death haunting him every minute of every day. The finding of her body had left him with no other choice. His mind was made up. It was time to take responsibility for what he had done.

The sighting of two men walking down the gravel road caused Worthington to sit upright in the wicker chair. Apparently, the men had spotted him as well. They left the road to take cover in the high saw palmetto plants off to the side. But why? Only someone up to no good would do such a thing. Who were they? And what were they doing on a private road? The men were dark-skinned and appeared to be Mexican. Each was holding something in his right hand. Worthington could not tell for sure what it was. A gun? It certainly could have been a gun.

Worthington stood up to get a better look. He saw no sign of the two men. The saw palmetto plants were thick along the roadway. They afforded good concealment for anyone wishing to approach the beach house undetected. But what could they possibly want? What were the two Mexicans up to? Did they plan on burglarizing the cottage? If so, why did they bring guns with them? The beach house was seldom used anymore. The men would have known that if they had cased the place beforehand. And where were Costello and Hardin? His friends' arrival would most certainly frighten the intruders away. Sam had said three o'clock. And it was well past that time. Why hadn't they showed?

The hollowed-out feeling began deep in the pit of Joe Worthington's stomach. It soon consumed his entire body. The realization left him weak in the knees. Costello and Hardin were not coming. They never had intended on coming to the beach house. The nervousness in Sam Costello's voice over the phone. The look in Jack

Hardin's eyes the day Ginny's body had been found. It all became so clear to him. The two Mexicans were not looking for something to steal. They came to kill.

Worthington thought about running to his car and retrieving his cellphone to call the police. But he quickly dismissed the idea. His blue Lincoln was parked in front of the garage and a good thirty yards away. Going to the car would leave him cut off from the house and an easy target. No, he had only one chance. Worthington commanded his body to move. He directed it toward the beach house's front door. His father's gun was inside buried under a bunch of junk in a kitchen drawer. Worthington knew the gun was his only hope. He pushed open the front door. After locking it behind him, he hurried to the kitchen.

****

The Smith&Wesson 38. caliber revolver was wrapped in an oil-stained cloth. Worthington removed the cloth and opened the gun's cylinder. Five 38. caliber bullets were inside. Closer examination revealed the bullets to be old and corroded. They looked as if they had been in the gun for a long time. Worthington wondered if the bullets would still fire. He knew nothing about guns, not having ever fired one in his life. But he told himself that he had no other choice. He had to hope the bullets were still good. After closing the cylinder, Worthington observed the hunting knife. It was the one he had found years ago while hiking with the Cub Scouts in Silver State Park. He took the knife and gun with him into the living room.

The window shades were pulled down. The green drapes had been drawn. The room appeared dark. Worthington knew it would appear especially so to anyone entering from the kitchen. It would take time for the person's eyes to adjust to the change in light. Worthington realized what the change in light could mean. It could give him an edge. And he badly needed one. Both of the Mexicans were armed and undoubtedly proficient in the use of firearms. But would they anticipate that he would be armed? How could they? Hardin and Costello would have known nothing of his father's gun. That meant the assassins would know nothing as well. They would think he was defenseless. A man who would be easy to kill. The 38. caliber revolver could turn out to be the surprise he so desperately needed. But would it be enough? Could he trust the gun to fire? And if it did fire, could he hit what he was shooting at?

The cottage's front door came crashing in. A wave of panic went through Worthington. He jumped behind the living room sofa. It was the same sofa he and Ginny had sat upon so many years ago. Even now in his panicked state the realization did not escape him. But the two men speaking in Spanish brought Worthington back to the moment. The Mexicans were inside the beach house. They would begin searching for him. And he knew the living room would be the first place that they would look. He drew back on the steel hammer, training the revolver on the entryway off the kitchen. A man's figure suddenly appeared. Holding the gun with two hands, Joe Worthington pulled the trigger.

The revolver's discharge proved deafening. It filled the living room, bouncing off walls, while leaving a resonating echo. The gun had jumped inside Worthington's hands. He tried to compensate by tightening his grip. But his first shot had missed. The man was still in the doorway. So Worthington fired again. And he continued firing until he heard a loud scream. The man dropped his gun and clutched his stomach. Worthington saw him fall. A second man instantly appeared. He began firing a semi-automatic handgun. Bullets slammed into the wall behind Worthington, barely missing him. Worthington centered his aim on the second man's chest. He pulled back on the gun's trigger. A metal on metal sound came to him. The 38. caliber revolver was out of bullets.

Worthington placed the empty gun down on the floor and picked up the hunting knife. On his hands and knees he crawled the length of the sofa before stopping. The second man was no longer firing his weapon. Worthington guessed that the Mexican was coming towards him. And by now his eyes would have adjusted to the darkened room. He would have no trouble seeing his target. But where exactly was he? And how close to the sofa? Gripping the knife in his right hand, Joe Worthington raised his head. He observed the Mexican no more than twelve feet away. The man spotted Worthington as well. He started firing his gun. Bullets whizzed past Worthington's head. Worthington knew that he could not wait any longer. He had to do something. Reaching down with his left hand, he lifted up the sofa heaving it in the Mexican's direction. Both men came face to face. They stared into one another's eyes.

The Mexican's eyes were hard and cold. There was no mercy in them. He fired his gun at the same time Joe Worthington thrust forward with his knife. A burning sensation gripped Worthington's stomach. Another shot burned his chest. Worthington jerked upward with the knife. The blade ripped through the Mexican's left side. The man let out a horrible scream and fell to the floor. A weak feeling quickly took over Worthington. Thick blood oozed out of his chest and stomach. It felt as though someone had poured hot water on him. The burning sensation got only worse. Worthington knew that he was badly wounded. And there was only one hope left for him. He had to get to his cellphone and call for help. Stumbling toward the front door, he observed the blue Lincoln parked in front of the garage. Joe Worthington took a deep breath and started towards it.

CHAPTER TWENTY-SIX

Washington D.C.

FBI SPECIAL AGENT Pat Carollo did not like the expression on Randall Maxwell's face. The Assistant Director of the FBI's Criminal Investigation Division was seated behind his desk displaying what Carollo recognized as a look of annoyance. It was the kind of look someone might give a pesky fly buzzing around a plate of food. *I don't really want you here. You came on your own accord without being invited. So say whatever you have to say and get out of my office.*

Carollo stood calmly with both hands intertwined behind him. Maxwell had not bothered to offer him a seat. The obvious slight told Carollo that his boss wanted to hear nothing more about the Conigliaro Crime Family's plan to murder Stone. The FBI informant had revealed that there would soon be an attempt on Stone's life. Vinnie Palermo personally ordered the killing. Surely after being made aware of the situation, Assistant Director Maxwell would recognize the imperativeness of telling Stone. Every passing minute placed the police lieutenant that much closer to an assassin's bullet. Carollo had wanted to warn Stone about the informant's tip. But Maxwell disagreed, citing that it could serve to jeopardize the life of their informant. The assistant director gave Carollo strict orders not to warn Stone or anyone else in the Pelican's Landing Police Department. As far as Maxwell was concerned Stone was on his own.

"You are asking me to stand by while knowing that my silence could very well lead to the death of a policeman. The killing of someone who I consider a friend. I took an oath when I joined the FBI and it was to uphold the law, not to stand by and let people get murdered. I came here this morning to tell you that I can't go along with your order of silence regarding Jackson Stone. After leaving here I plan on telephoning Stone and telling him that his life is in danger."

"You will do no such thing," Randall Maxwell said coming to his feet. Tall and gray-haired, Maxwell appeared the true-blue aristocrat standing behind his oversized, well-polished desk. The facial expression of annoyance was no longer present. It had been replaced by an angry look. The look was centered on Carollo. "You are a special agent in charge working for the Federal Bureau of Investigation, and I am your superior. Therefore, Carollo, consider yourself under orders not to make a phone call or to have any contact whatsoever with Stone. You are also forbidden from contacting anyone connected to the Pelican's Landing Police Department. Do you understand the orders that I have given you?"

"Frankly, I don't. A heads up warning given to Stone would not in any way compromise our informant. I know Stone, and he would not tell anyone that the FBI had warned him about a death threat. So, Assistant Director, there has to be something else behind your orders. And if the reason is what I am thinking it is, the very thought scares the hell out of me."

Maxwell sat down and picked up a manila folder from his desktop. Opening the folder, he acted as though he were reading its contents. "So, if the welfare of our informant is not the reason for me not wanting Stone warned, what is it then?"

Carollo took both his hands and placed them on Maxwell's desk. Leaning forward, the special agent in charge waited for his boss to look up. It did not take long before Maxwell was looking into Carollo's dark brown eyes.

"Maxwell, the answer is a simple one," Carollo said. "What you really want is to nail Vinnie Palermo for the murder of a policeman. If somehow that sleaze ball gets out of all the other cases we're going after him for, including racketeering and the bribery of Florida state legislators, you know you can get him for Stone's murder. And that's what you really want. That would put you in the limelight, wouldn't it? The murder of a police lieutenant and Vinnie Palermo the head of the Conigliaro Crime Family going down for it. Every newspaper in the country would cover the story not to mention the television news coverage. Your smiling face would be right up there next to Vinnie Palermo's photograph. And following the guilty verdict, you'd probably get the Director's job. And that's what you're really after, isn't it? Randall Maxwell, Director of the FBI."

"Yes, it is. I've wanted the job ever since the first day I joined the Bureau. And don't forget as Director I could do a lot for the career of a certain special agent in charge who helped me get what I've always wanted. Come on, Carollo, you know how the world works. You help me and I help you."

"And who helps Stone?" Carollo said removing his hands from the desk and taking a step back. "Maxwell, you're everything I hate about the FBI. And unfortunately, you're not alone. There are plenty of guys in the Bureau just like you."

"Carollo, get out of my office. And remember my orders regarding Stone. If I find out you said anything to him, I'll have you kicked out of the Bureau so fast you won't know what hit you."

Carollo told him, "I won't say anything to Stone or to anybody else in Pelican's Landing. I'll keep playing the good soldier by keeping my mouth shut. But only as long as I'm working for you. Then all bets are off."

Carollo turned around and walked out Maxwell's office door. Randall Maxwell watched him go. The assistant director sat staring at the door long after Carollo had left.

CHAPTER TWENTY-SEVEN

DEPUTY LISA MOORE picked up the vase containing the red rose. There was a white card accompanying it. She looked again at the card while shaking her head. Jackson Stone's name was scribbled on it along with the Pelican's Landing police station address. The delivery man had dropped off the flower and vase less than an hour ago. It only served to perk Moore's curiosity. Who in the world would be sending Jackson Stone a single red rose? It was hopelessly romantic. Not something she would have guessed in a million years. Moore could not picture her boss being romantically linked with any woman, especially not after his former wife had walked out on him. Moore knew for a fact that Jackson Stone was still not over his former wife's death. So who sent him the rose? The deputy checked with the local florist in town and found the owner to be of little help. The woman could not supply the identity of the person who had sent in the order. She said that a party from out of state had requested that a single red rose be sent to the Pelican's Landing police station in care of Jackson Stone. A credit card listed to the Coastal Life & Casualty Insurance Company had been used for payment. Moore spent half an hour searching the computer for anything relating to the Coastal Life & Casualty Insurance Company. After her search she could not even verify the existence of such a company. It left Moore feeling not only frustrated, but even more curious. What was going on in Jackson Stone's life? And who was the person sending him a single red rose?

"Lisa, why do you keep staring at that damn blasted rose? It's none of your business who sent it. Sometimes I think you got a crush on Jackson and that's why you're always pokin' your nose in his affairs."

"Potts, don't be silly," Moore said before placing the vase and rose back onto the counter. "It's just that I don't want him getting hurt, that's all. I can still remember what he went through after his wife killed herself, and I don't want him going through anything like that again. Everybody in town saw what it did to him. Jackson Stone is my friend, and I don't want some woman hurting him all over again."

Cliff Potts got out of his desk chair and walked over to Moore. He placed his right hand on Lisa's left shoulder. Smiling, he said to her, "I know Jackson helped you out when you were in trouble and needed a job to support both you and the baby. He got you hired on as deputy here in town and you're grateful to him. I can understand that. But you got to believe me when I tell you Jackson can take care of himself. And he doesn't need you getting involved in his personal life, especially when it might lead to rustling up some other woman's feathers and causin' him all kinds of feminine mishap. Hell, that's my job anyway. Instead of me retiring and takin' it easy every day like I should be doing, I spend my days watchin' out for the boy. Makin' sure he doesn't get himself into a mess that he can't get out of. Sometimes I feel like a mother hen watchin' over a baby chick. But then I always tell myself, why shouldn't I look out for him? With Jackson being my dead sister's son and all. Besides, he's the only nephew I got."

"Well, I still can't wait to hear what Jackson has to say after I tell him someone sent him a red rose," Lisa Moore said while going over to her desk and sitting down. "He should be phoning into the office within the next half hour or so, and I can hardly wait to tell him."

"Is Jackson and Chief Martin still at the hospital waitin' on Joe Worthington?"

"Yes, they are. The last time Jackson checked in he told me Worthington was still in surgery and it was a tossup whether he would live or not. When you think about it Worthington's really lucky to be alive at all. He was shot twice and nearly bled to death. How he was able to reach his car and call for help on his cellphone had to be a miracle in itself. The ambulance crew said they found him lying unconscious on the ground with the cellphone still in his hand."

"And the two Mexicans were dead inside the beach house," Potts said, shaking his head. "Both of them had semi-automatic 9mm. handguns and shot the shit out of the place. Joe killed one of the Mexicans with an old gun that had been in the house for years while the other jasper he stabbed to death with a hunting knife. I've known Joe Worthington just about his entire life and never considered him to be a tough guy. But today he proved me wrong. It took a hell of a lot of moxie for him to take those two guys out. What I don't understand is what were they doing there in the first place? You wouldn't think there would be anything of value in the beach house for them to steal. And those two Mexicans being armed with 9mm. semi-automatics doesn't seem to fit at all. It's been my experience that most burglars don't take guns with them on house break-ins. They usually pick places where nobody is at home."

"Well, these two guys were different," Lisa Moore said while looking at the two photographs displayed on her computer screen. "Both were in this country illegally and they have criminal records going back for years in Mexico. One of them is wanted for a murder committed in Mexico City six months ago, and the other one is out on bond for an armed robbery of a gas station that took place last month in Tampa. But as far as I can determine neither of them is what you would call your typical burglar. Their past arrests are all for violent crimes making them bad guys for sure. It appears as though Joe Worthington did everyone a favor by killing them."

"Yes, but that still doesn't answer the question as to what brought those two jaspers to the Worthington family's beach house and them carrying 9mm. handguns," Cliff Potts said as he walked over to Moore's desk to check out the photographs on her computer screen. "Something doesn't feel quite right about all this. Especially with the two of them having no ties to Pelican's Landing and showing up at such a remote section of beach. It seems rather odd to me. What do you think?"

Lisa Moore's desk phone rang preventing her from answering Potts's question. "That'll be Jackson checking in," Moore said quickly reaching for the phone. Potts knew immediately that it was not Jackson Stone. He could tell by the look on Moore's face.

"What kind of information?" Potts heard her say to the person on the other end of the line. "But Lieutenant Stone is not presently in the office. Couldn't someone else from our department meet with you? But I already told you that he isn't here right now. All right, I expect Lieutenant Stone to be phoning in at any moment, and when he does I will be sure to give him your message. Yes, he knows where the old creamery is located. I can't be sure of the exact time, but definitely within the hour."

"What was that all about?" Potts asked Moore after seeing her put down the phone.

Lisa told him, "I'm not exactly sure. The woman caller said she had information regarding the dead body found on the Tanner ranch, but she will only tell what she knows to Lieutenant Stone and to no one else. She said that she would be at the abandoned creamery building outside of town in thirty minutes and for Jackson to meet her there. She wants him to blink the headlights on his car three times. Then she'll come over to talk to him."

"It's too cloak and dagger for me," Potts said while running his hands through a head of thick, gray hair. "I don't like it one bit. Did she say for him to come alone, and if he wasn't alone she wouldn't come out to meet him?"

Moore nodded. "That's exactly what she said, and if she saw anyone accompanying Jackson that would be the end of it. The lieutenant is the only person that she wants to share her information with. Potts, I didn't care for the woman's tone at all. It was too much like take it or leave it. I think Jackson could be heading into a trap and the phone call just a ruse to get him out to the abandoned creamery where there could be people waiting there to kill him."

"Whose car did Jackson and Chief Martin take to the hospital to check up on Joe Worthington?"

"Chief Martin's car. Why?"

"Because I'm going to take Jackson's blue sedan out to the old creamery building and find out what this is all about. It'll be dark and no one will be able to tell who's driving the blue sedan. When Jackson calls tell him I'll be at the creamery building and for him and Chief Martin to meet me there."

A frightened look took over Lisa Moore's face. Potts immediately recognized it. He placed his right arm around the deputy's waist and kissed her on the forehead. "Lisa, don't worry about me, I wouldn't have gotten this old if I didn't know how to take care of myself."

Moore watched as Potts headed toward the station's back door and the blue sedan parked outside.

CHAPTER TWENTY-EIGHT

THE HEAVY RAIN off the Gulf of Mexico was falling faster than the unmarked squad car's windshield wipers could clear it off. It left Stone hunched over the car's steering wheel barely able to make out the contours of the road ahead. There had to be four or more inches of rain water covering the road surface. It resulted in the unmarked car's tires sending wave after wave of water rushing to either side of the roadway. Stone attempted to keep the speedometer needle centered on the 40 mph mark. If he tried to go faster the vehicle would hydroplane leaving him with no steering control. More than once Stone and Martin had come close to ending up in a roadside ditch. And if that should happen what would become of Cliff Potts?

Stone was fully aware that he and Martin were Potts's only chance for survival. If his uncle was going to live beyond the next hour, they would have to arrive at the abandoned creamery before he did. And that would be difficult to do in this storm. After phoning the office Stone had learned from Lisa Moore that a woman wanted to meet with him at the abandoned creamery outside of town. The woman told Moore that she had information to give Stone regarding the girl's body found buried on the Tanner ranch. Then Moore dropped a bomb on him. She told Stone how Potts had taken Stone's blue sedan to meet with the woman. And that he was going to try and pass himself off as Stone. Another bomb quickly followed. As an afterthought Moore mentioned the single red rose that had been delivered to the Pelican's Landing police station. The face of FBI Special Agent Pat Carollo instantly appeared in Stone's mind. Back in New York City when Stone worked undercover for the FBI against the Giaccone Crime Family, Carollo had sent him a single red rose. It had been a prearranged signal between them that should Stone ever receive a single red rose it meant his cover had been blown. That the Giaccone Crime Family was on to him. And that Stone should seek a place of safety as soon as possible. Carollo was sending him just such a message once again. But this time it was not Stone's life that was in danger. It was the life of his uncle and friend, Cliff Potts.

"Did Moore try to raise Sergeant Potts on his car radio?" Chief Martin asked while seated in the unmarked car's front passenger seat. Her eyes were glued to the road ahead. Keri could barely make out any part of the road with the torrent of rain striking the car's windshield. She wondered how Stone could see well enough to drive in such a storm.

Stone told her, "Yes, she tried to get him on the radio. He either doesn't have the radio turned on or he's refusing to answer. It's just like him. Cliff is as stubborn and mule-headed like no one I've ever met in my life. Once he gets something into his head you couldn't pry it out of him with ten crowbars no matter how hard you tried. Believe me, I know what I'm talking about. Through the years I've tried to get my uncle to come around to the politics involved in a police officer's job these days, and it has gotten me nowhere. Potts has his own ideas about dishing out justice and what's right and what's wrong. His way of thinking might have worked fifty or sixty years ago, but not anymore."

It was dark inside the unmarked car and Keri could hardly make out Stone's face. But she quickly picked up on the nervousness in his voice. He was afraid for Potts. Keri knew as did Stone that their reaching the abandoned creamery before Potts was highly unlikely. And if the phone call from the anonymous woman was actually a part of a trap to kill Stone, Potts would be left in a precarious position. The odds of his surviving would be slim at best. Stone knew it. That was why there was nervousness in his voice.

"So you feel this FBI agent Carollo sent you the red rose to warn you about a planned attempt on your life," Martin said while trying to keep Stone from dwelling on Potts. "If the FBI is involved that means we're talking about organized crime, which brings us back to what you told me before about the Conigliaro Crime Family. They want to take over Pelican's Landing for their gambling operation and apparently see you as an obstacle to their plans. Do I have it right or am I missing something?"

"No, you got it right. Vinnie Palermo knows I would fight him and his scumbag organization every inch of the way to prevent the mob from getting its hooks into Pelican's Landing. But I think there's more to it than just that. I can't put my finger on it, but my gut tells me that I'm missing something in all this."

"What do you think it is?" Keri asked him.

"I don't know. Just about everything I guess. There's the girl's dead body showing up on the Tanner ranch after all these years, and then Worthington coming out to the crime scene to protect Roscoe Tanner. And then there's *The Satan Ramblers* coming all the way from California to set up a new home base here in Pelican's Landing when it's obvious that their only intention was to cause trouble for the police. They wanted us focused on them and not something else. But what? Is it only Vinnie Palermo and his gambling operation that they were trying to protect? Or was there something more?"

The rain did not seem to be falling quite as heavy as earlier. Keri could actually make out most of the road ahead. Stone started to increase the unmarked squad car's speed. Martin turned in the front seat to look at him.

"Does that something more have anything to do with Joe Worthington being shot today? Frankly, the entire thing doesn't make any sense to me. What was Worthington doing at the beach house when an hour before the shooting he told his wife that he was going to meet a client about a piece of real estate? And then two Mexicans drive down to Pelican's Landing from Tampa in a stolen car to kill him. Could Zach Worthington somehow be involved in all this? Maybe Joe knew something about his father's involvement with the Conigliaro Crime Family and Vinnie Palermo didn't like it. And Vinnie wanted to put Joe out of the picture for good."

"I don't think so," Stone said while keeping both hands gripped to the steering wheel. His eyes stayed focused on the rain-soaked road ahead. "Sending two Mexicans to kill someone isn't the way Vinnie operates. He normally uses his own people, and in this case Joe Worthington's murder would have been made to look like an accident. Vinnie Palermo has big plans for Pelican's Landing, and he wouldn't want the kind of heat Joe Worthington's murder could bring down. No, I don't think Vinnie was behind it. Joe's shooting had to do with something else. And we won't know what that something is until we get the chance to talk to our victim."

"And that's iffy at best," Keri said. "The doctor only gives Worthington a fifty/fifty chance of making it. He said Worthington was lucky to have survived the surgery and that the next twenty-hours could be crucial. I happened to see Joe Worthington's wife along with his mother and father at the hospital before we left. Two men were with them. Do you have any idea what they were doing at the hospital?"

"The dark-haired guy was Jack Hardin and the one with the blond hair was Sam Costello. They're Joe Worthington's best friends. They grew up together and the three of them attended the University of Florida at Gainesville right out of high school. I talked to both of them at the hospital. They had no idea as to why Joe Worthington was at the beach house by himself."

Keri Martin noticed that the rain was starting to fall heavy once again. It caused Stone to lighten up on the unmarked car's gas pedal. He was not at all happy about doing it. She saw him slam the palm of his right hand hard into the steering wheel.

Keri asked him, "How far is it to the abandoned creamery?"

"No more than a mile, but with this rain you could tack on an extra three miles with how slow we're going. I'm not what you would call a prayin' man, but right now I'm asking God to help Cliff Potts."

****

Jimmy Burke remained squatting underneath a metal overhang at the abandoned creamery. He was wearing a black rain slicker with the slicker's hood pulled up over his head. Burke was on ground level at the abandoned creamery's east building. The spot he had chosen allowed him an unobstructed view of the entrance way along with the open area that separated the creamery's east and west buildings. An AR-15 rifle with an attached scope rested on Burke's knees while his back was pressed against the concrete wall behind him. Sheets of heavy rain fell across the open courtyard. The rain caused an incessant pounding to the metal overhang above Burke's head. Its sound was loud and hard like a thousand fingers tapping all at once. The former U.S. Marine squinted through the heavy downpour. Burke knew the rain would make it difficult for him to pinpoint a target.

Burke also knew Roscoe Tanner was across the courtyard on the second floor of the abandoned creamery's west building. And like Burke, Tanner was waiting for Jackson Stone's arrival. But as to exactly where Tanner had positioned himself Burke could not say. He was unable to make out his boss's figure in the falling rain. But he knew Tanner was over there somewhere holding onto an AR-15 rifle with an attached scope. And that once Jackson Stone flashed the headlights on his blue sedan all hell would break loose.

"Don't fire until I do," Tanner had told his foreman prior to their coming to the abandoned creamery. "I'll be looking down on the driver's side of Stone's sedan. After I start shooting that will be your signal to open up on the front passenger side door. We'll have Stone in a crossfire. He won't have a chance of coming out of it alive."

Burke's wife, Marci, had made the phone call to the Pelican's Landing police station requesting for Stone to meet her at the abandoned creamery outside of town. It was Roscoe Tanner who had come up with the idea of an anonymous woman caller wanting to divulge information concerning the dead girl's body. Tanner felt that having a woman doing the phoning would make Stone less suspicious of a possible setup. Burke did not want his wife, Marci, involved in the affair. But Tanner had insisted upon it. And Roscoe Tanner was not the kind of man you could say no to and just walk away. After years of working for the Tanner Family, Burke knew all too well what his boss was capable of. Tonight was proof enough. Tanner hated Jackson Stone and within a few minutes Stone would be dead.

Burke observed a car's headlights on the road leading up to the abandoned creamery. The sighting took the ranch foreman somewhat by surprise. So Stone had taken the bait. He was coming to the abandoned creamery to meet with the unidentified woman. Burke found it hard to believe that Stone had actually fallen for such a trick. It did not fit his assessment of the man. But then again everyone makes mistakes. It's just that this time Stone had made a fatal one.

Burke picked up the AR-15 rifle. He brought the sniper scope up to eye level. Killing Stone was not something Burke wanted to be a part of. It went against his nature. Burke had never killed anyone in his life and did not want to start now. But after Roscoe Tanner told him that he would be assisting in Stone's murder, Burke could not refuse. To do so would have meant giving up his life and Marci's as well. No, he had to go through with the shooting. There was no other choice for him.

Burke observed the blue sedan driving into the abandoned creamery's courtyard. He shifted his body weight while keeping the AR-15 trained on the front of the car. The plan called for Tanner to shoot first. Then he was to follow suit by directing his fire on the sedan's front passenger side door. Burke hated the thought of doing it. His conscious mind screamed no. But he knew that he would.

****

Roscoe Tanner rose to his feet out of a crouched position. He began shifting his weight onto his left leg while bringing the AR-15's scope up to eye level. The black slicker's rain-soaked hood proved bothersome to him. Tanner flipped it back with his left hand. Sighting in his target, he kept the AR-15 steady with the butt firmly set against his right shoulder. The blue sedan stopped in the middle of the courtyard. It would be an easy shot for Tanner. The only drawback being the lashing rain. It caused the driver's side door to appear blurry in the scope. But it was of no real consequence. Tanner knew the AR-15's metal piercing bullets would tear apart the sedan's driver's door and strike Stone inside. And with Burke doing the same on the passenger side there would be no escape for Stone. The man that he had hated all these years would be dead. And with Stone's death there would be no more threat to Tanner's meth lab, or to the Conigliaro Family's gambling business. The blue sedan's headlights flashed three times. Tanner took a deep breath. It was time to end the life of Jackson Stone. Tanner pulled back on the rifle's trigger while slowly releasing the pent-up air inside his lungs. The AR-15 jumped in his hands.

CHAPTER TWENTY-NINE

STONE OBSERVED THE blue Sedan in the abandoned creamery's courtyard. The sight of the car caused his stomach to tighten. A wave of panic seemed bent on taking him over. Stone knew that he and Martin were too late to save Potts. His entire being told him so. Martin apparently knew it as well. Because she let out a loud gasp before placing her right hand over her mouth. Stone eased back on the unmarked car's accelerator. A person could be hiding in the dark shadows of one of the abandoned creamery's buildings. Prior to rushing in, he would have to think things out. A person or persons could be waiting for him and Martin to make a mistake. But Stone knew that he could not wait too long. Potts could still be alive. He very much doubted it, but there was the possibility. The falling rain made it difficult to see beyond the unmarked car's headlights. Stone looked over at Keri Martin.

"Get in the back seat and stay on the floor. There could be someone waiting in one of those buildings to shoot whoever's coming to help Potts. I can limit our exposure by pulling the unmarked squad next to the driver side of Potts's car. That would give us protection on both sides. It'll also give me the chance to check on Potts. Now hurry, jump in the back seat and get down on the floor. If there's no shooting and I don't see anyone, I'll open the back door for you. After the door opens crawl out and keep low to the ground. Any questions?"

"No, but please be careful," Martin said while climbing over the squad car's front seat to get in the back. "And Jackson don't forget, you're the one they want dead. So keep your head down because if they know Potts is the one they shot they'll be expecting you to be coming here to help him."

Stone told her, "You and I must think an awful lot alike because the same thought occurred to me. Here we go, I'm going to step on the gas and get alongside the blue sedan as quickly as possible. Are you ready?"

"Do it," Keri said before dropping down to the squad car's floor.

****

Stone grabbed a flashlight out of the unmarked squad's glove box and rolled out the passenger side door. He stayed flat on the wet ground while waiting for gunshots to ring out. Hearing nothing, he opened the blue sedan's driver side door. The beam from Stone's flashlight verified what he had already suspected. Potts was dead. His lower body was on the car floor while his upper torso rested on the front passenger seat. Stone took note of the bullet holes in Potts's body. Most were in his head and upper torso. But there was little blood showing. That told him Potts had died almost instantly. Stone reached over with his right hand to lay it on the back of Potts's head. It was still warm. The shooting could not have taken place too long before his and Martin's arrival. Stone shined the flashlight around the car's interior. The driver's side door and window were riddled with bullets. And so was the back passenger's side door. But no bullet holes were present in the front door on the passenger's side. It did not make any sense to Stone. Why would the second shooter have riddled the back passenger side door? He would have known Stone was in the front seat. Why then would he have directed his fire to the back seat? Feeling the touch to his right shoulder, Stone turned around.

"I thought I told you to stay in the car until I opened the door."

"And when was that supposed to be? Sometime tomorrow?" Martin said to him while wiping the rain out of her eyes. She took hold of Stone's right arm. "Jackson, tell me. Is Potts dead?"

"Yes, he is, and it didn't happen too long before we got here. I see it being two shooters one in each building. They had Potts in a crossfire, but for some reason only the shooter on the sedan's driver's side shot him. The shooter facing the passenger side restricted his firing to the back passenger door. It doesn't make sense to me. I was supposed to be driving the car. Why would the shooter deliberately fire at the back passenger door where his bullets wouldn't do any harm? I don't get it."

"Maybe the shooter thought someone was hiding in the back seat and he wanted to kill them," Keri said taking the flashlight from Stone to shine on Potts's body inside the blue sedan.

"No, they would have expected me to come alone. There's something more to it, but I can't figure it out just yet."

"Jackson, I feel so terrible about this. I can't help but blame myself for Potts's being killed. You wanted to take your car to the hospital to check on Joe Worthington, and I insisted that we go in my car. If it wasn't for me wanting to drive, none of this would have happened. Cliff Potts would be alive right now and not lying there dead. I can't tell you how sorry I am."

Keri Martin's eyes immediately filled with tears. She looked up at Stone and started to cry. Stone observed Martin's upper body starting to shake. He took her into his arms and held her. It was then that the reality of Potts's death struck home for him. It served to bowl Stone over. Previously he had been operating as a police investigator doing his job. He had tried to detach himself from the victim in the front seat of the blue sedan. But that time had passed. Cliff Potts was dead. Never again would Stone see his uncle's smile, or hear his cackling over some silly thing. The bond that they had shared was gone forever. Its realization hit Stone hard. He could not keep back the tears from his own eyes. Tightening his hold, he buried his face in Keri Martin's right shoulder.

"It's not your fault," Stone said to her. "Don't ever blame yourself again. Whoever was behind Potts's killing, they're the ones to blame."

Keri lifted his head from off her shoulder and kissed him. And after seeing the tears in Stone's eyes, she kissed him again. They then held onto one another, each liking the feel of the other. It was Stone who finally broke away.

"Call it in on the radio," Stone said to Keri before stepping back. "There's a blanket in the sedan's trunk. I'm going to get it and place it over Potts's body. I can't stand the thought of him lying there like that."

Martin told him, "Jackson, I will. I'll call it in right away. But after you cover up Potts, I want you to get back in our car. It's going to be a long night and I don't want you standing out in the rain. Will you do that for me?"

Stone did not answer. He went to the blue sedan's trunk to retrieve the blanket. And Martin went inside the unmarked car to grab the portable radio.

CHAPTER THIRTY

IT WAS WELL past midnight by the time Keri Martin arrived back at the Holiday Inn. Upon entering her hotel suite, she turned on the overhead light and let the gray slicker she had been wearing fall to the floor. A hot bubble bath was what Keri had been contemplating for the past two hours. Instead she settled on a shower and afterward the soft feel of a pink-flowered bathrobe against her skin. A couple sips of red wine and the coziness of the room helped to settle Keri down. It lent the opportunity to lean back in the lazy boy while crossing both her legs. After closing her eyes, she listened to the sound of rain falling against the room's only window.

Martin and Stone had waited for the arrival of Bob Garcia and Lisa Moore at the abandoned creamery. Shortly afterward, the county mobile crime lab and a van from the medical examiner's office showed up at the scene. Stone and Garcia removed Potts's body from the blue sedan before placing it in the ME's van. Keri did not think she would ever forget the moment. The look on Jackson Stone's face was something she had never seen on anyone's face before. Keri knew it would stay with her forever. Stone appeared as though someone had cut a hole in him and left the life inside empty out. Garcia and Moore wore distraught looks as well. Both deputies had tears in their eyes while they went about assisting the mobile crime lab technicians.

Keri had overheard Moore telling Stone, "Jackson, I told him not to go. But Potts wouldn't listen to me. He had to have known it was a setup, but he went anyway. Jackson, he knew you would go to the creamery alone once you found out someone had information about that dead girl's body. No one could have stopped you from going and Potts knew that. That's why he went in your place. He didn't want you getting killed."

Keri took another sip of wine. She was holding the wine glass with both hands. The crime lab technicians had been able to pinpoint the locations where the two shooters had waited for Potts. Caches of mud from their shoes were the giveaway. But no empty cartridge cases were found. That meant the shooters had picked up the empty cartridge cases before leaving. They had been careful, Keri thought to herself. But not careful enough. They ended up killing the wrong man. Jackson Stone was their intended target, and they killed Potts by mistake. Did they now know that they had shot the wrong man? Were they out there searching for Stone?

Keri placed the wine glass down on the coffee table in front of her. She stood up clasping both her hands together. Stone had said that he would be going to the Pelican's Landing police station after dropping Keri off at the Holiday Inn. He said that he would be spending the rest of the night there. But what if he didn't go back to the police station? What if he was on the street looking for Potts's killers? He would be all alone. There would be no one to help him.

Keri did not want to phone the police station. It would appear to Stone as though she were checking up on him. But wouldn't that be exactly what she was doing? Checking up on him. Keri sat back down on the lazy boy. She covered her face with both hands. Was she in love with Stone? Was that the reason why she could not get the thought of him out of her head? Yes, she cared about him, but caring about someone was not loving them.

After her years with Rance Stapleton, Keri never thought she would have anything to do with another man again. Too many times she had been hurt. Too often she had ended up not knowing who she was anymore. A man like Stapleton could do that to a woman. He could leave her feeling worthless, empty of everything that goes into making a person feel like a human being. She ends up becoming nothing more than a trinket. Something to be held up for everybody to see. That was why Keri had left Chicago to come to Pelican's Landing. It's just that she hadn't expected to meet someone like Jackson Stone.

Keri got up from the lazy boy and walked over to the kitchen table. Her handbag was on the chair where she had left it. Rummaging through the bag, she removed her cellphone. Keri punched in the phone number for the Pelican's Landing police station. She then waited for Stone to answer.

CHAPTER THIRTY-ONE

IT WAS ELEVEN o'clock in the morning. The temperature had already reached ninety degrees. An overnight storm had left high humidity and a cloudless sky. That meant an unrelenting sun would be beating down unmercifully on anyone who happened to venture outside. Sam Costello was one of those people. The night before he had agreed to meet Jack Hardin at the Pelican's Landing pier. And that was after the two men had spent several hours at the hospital waiting to find out if Joe Worthington would survive the bullet wounds to his chest and stomach. It had been one of the worst nights of Costello's life. Part of him wanted Joe Worthington to survive; the other part wanted his best friend to die. And after seeing Janet Worthington rushing into the hospital with a terrified look on her face, Costello got sick to his stomach. He had to find the nearest men's room to throw up. The entire evening stay at the hospital turned out to be an absolute nightmare. Most of it consisted of him sitting next to Jack Hardin with neither one saying much of anything to the other. Jackson Stone had talked to them briefly. But nothing Stone asked seemed to point any suspicion toward Costello or Hardin. And If Joe Worthington should end up dying it would probably put an end to everything. But what if he didn't die? What if Worthington should live? Where would that leave him and Hardin?

"So you got here before I did," a smiling Hardin said while walking up on Costello. "You look like somebody poured a bucket of water over your head with all the sweat dripping off you. We'll have to make this short because I don't want you melting away in this hot sun."

"It's the damn humidity more than anything," Costello said in response. He took out a red kerchief from his back pants pocket to wipe the sweat off his fat face. Costello was wearing a red polo shirt and blue shorts. Both garments were stuck to him. They revealed a protruding stomach and bulging hips. He looked across at Hardin who was still smiling. "Jack, how can you smile at a time like this?"

"What are you talking about Worthington? I stopped by the hospital before coming here and he's still unconscious and in critical condition. Odds are he won't last another day. And while at the hospital I heard that somebody shot and killed Cliff Potts last night at the abandoned creamery outside of town. That means Stone and Chief Martin are going to have their hands full for the next couple of days. Their minds for sure won't be on Joe's shooting. So for the time being we don't have anything to worry about."

"Somebody killed Potts? That is something. You're right about it helping us out with Stone. Potts was his uncle and Stone won't be interested in anything but finding out who killed Potts. That should give us some time. But what if Joe doesn't stay unconscious? And he lives long enough to tell somebody that we set him up. And then he goes and brings up the girl, and how you and me raped her. Did you ever think of that?"

Hardin scratched the back of his head with his right hand. He wiped the hand off on his green shorts. "Yes, Sam, I have thought of it. If it looks at all like Worthington is going to make it, we're going to have to kill him. We have no other choice. Like you just said, he could tell somebody. And I'm not spending the rest of my life in prison or having a needle stuck in my veins because some jury decides to give me the death penalty. I don't think you want any part of it either."

"No, I don't," Costello said looking into Hardin's dark eyes. "But I don't know if I got it in me to do it, Jack. I'm not like you. Right now I'm barely hanging on. My wife wants me to go see a doctor because she thinks I'm seriously ill. I just hope Joe dies so this whole thing finally ends."

Hardin told him, "I hope he dies, too. But if he doesn't within the next two days I'm going to make it happen. And Sam, you don't have to worry. I'll be the one who'll do it. I should have done it in the first place and not left it up to two damn Mexicans who weren't worth a shit."

Hardin watched Costello bring both his hands up to his face. His friend was hunched over and appeared to be crying. Hardin stared hard at the top of Costello's blond head. It was dripping wet with sweat. That's when Jack Hardin confirmed what had been on his mind for the last couple of days. He would have to kill Sam Costello along with Joe Worthington before the week came to an end.

"I guess there's no other way out of this for us, is there Jack?" Costello said after removing his hands from his face to look at Hardin. "We've become like animals killing to survive no matter the right or wrongness of it as long as we come out all right. I hate myself for having agreed to kill Joe. And for what I did to the girl that night at the beach house. I don't like what I've become. And I don't like what you've become either. We're both rotten inside. And after Joe dies it'll only get worse for us. We'll hate the sight of each other and everything else in life that reminds of us of what we've become."

Hardin smiled. "Sam, you might be right. But we'll still be alive, and that's all that matters to me. Just forget about Joe and the girl, and start thinking about your wife and kids. Nothing else should matter to you at this point. Now I have to get back to the office, so get a hold of yourself and remember to keep your mouth shut. Try focusing on how, after this week, it'll be all over with and you won't have anything more to worry about."

"I'll try," Costello said turning to walk away. "But I know it's not going to be easy for me."

Hardin watched Costello walk towards the parking lot. His friend looked like someone who was on the edge of a nervous breakdown. Would he say anything to his wife or to somebody else? Hardin could not be sure. There was always the possibility with Costello. That is when a change of mind came over Hardin. He could wait no longer. Tomorrow he would kill Costello before going to the hospital to kill Joe Worthington.

CHAPTER THIRTY-TWO

Spring Lake, New Jersey

VINNIE PALERMO TOOK a deep breath and let it out. The taste of the salt sea air brought back for Vinnie the memory of his native Sicily, leaving the head of the Conigliaro Family longing for the sight of white-washed buildings and narrow cobblestone streets. It was a fond memory. One that Vinnie found hard to let go of. It evoked life's simpler times. Not to mention a part of him that somehow had become lost through the years. Earlier that morning it had rained, but the skies overhead now appeared sunny and clear. Vinnie was sitting underneath a red beach umbrella that protected him from the hot afternoon sun. Leaning back in his chair, he observed the Atlantic's white, foamy waves roll onto the sandy beach in front of him. For Vinnie the waves uncased the image of two strong hands delicately caressing the white skin of a beautiful woman's back. He pictured his own hands doing the caressing. And the beautiful woman being one of the many he had been with through the years. The idea of marriage had never appealed to Vinnie. Probably because he looked upon women as nothing more than trifles. Something to be used and discarded. Power was the real prize. It was the only thing that gave meaning to Vinnie Palermo's life. It was the reason why he got out of bed each morning. And why he chose to live through another day.

A two-story, twenty million dollar mansion hovered on the rise seventy yards behind Palermo. Vinnie often referred to the structure as his summer beach house. It was a place he liked to run to whenever seeking escape from the world. But there would be no escape for him this day. The sound of someone calling his name caused Vinnie to turn around in his chair. He spotted Zach Worthington walking towards him.

"It must be nice to be able to sit on the beach and watch the rest of the world go by," Worthington said while extending his right hand to Vinnie. The broad smile on Zach Worthington's fleshy face disappeared once it became obvious Palermo was not going to shake his hand. "Yes, I remember the days when Carla and I would come to visit you here. Sometimes we would bring Joey with us and he'd run along the beach chasing the seagulls. Do you remember those days, Vinnie? They were good times, weren't they?"

"No, I haven't thought about those days for a long time," Vinnie answered motioning for Worthington to take the empty chair next to him.

Worthington took out a handkerchief from his back pants pocket and wiped the perspiration off his face before sitting down. He also took time to remove the sport coat he was wearing. He folded the coat across his lap.

"I took the first flight out after Al Ruggiero phoned and said you wanted to see me right away. I didn't even check into my hotel. I came directly here because I knew it had to be something important."

There was no escaping the nervousness in Zach Worthington. Zach had seen the look in Palermo's dark eyes. It was a cold, piercing look. Something one might witness in an animal prior to its attacking. Vinnie's stare caused Worthington's large frame to shift in the beach chair. It left him wondering if his voice would actually work.

"Vinnie, if it's Tanner's killing Potts and not Stone, I'm sorry. I had nothing to do with the wrong guy getting whacked. I wasn't even there. Tanner screwed up thinking Potts was Stone because Potts was driving Stone's car. If anyone is to blame its Tanner not me. I had nothing to do with it other than telling Tanner he had the go ahead and kill Stone. Vinnie, we've been friends for a long time. I married your niece. You're my son's godfather."

Palermo told him, "Zach, if you know what's good for you don't say another word. Because I don't want to hear it. In the past I had always made allowances for you because you weren't Italian. You didn't know any better. And besides that you married my niece. So I would let things go even though you pissed me off. Like when I found out you were cheating on Carla with that bimbo you keep outside Tampa. But everything's going to be different from now on. You and Tanner ended up killing a Pelican's Landing police sergeant and Stone's still alive. The heat is going to be coming down on the family just when our gambling operation is starting up. The New York City's Five Families and the Chicago Outfit are watching everything we're doing in Pelican's Landing. They've been just waiting for me to make a mistake, and Zach you went ahead and gave them one. You've got to be a bigger idiot than I thought you were."

"But Vinnie ..."

"Shut up Zach unless I ask you something. Don't say another word until then. Do you understand?"

Worthington nodded.

"Good, now we can talk. First I want you to start by telling me about that dead girl the police found buried on Tanner's ranch. Then I want you to give me the reason behind my godson's getting shot, and why he is now lying in a hospital bed fighting for his life. And while you're at it, I want the name of the person or persons who sent those two Mexicans to kill him. Don't leave anything out because if you do I'll eventually find out about it. And you know what will happen afterward. There won't be enough of your fat ass to stick in a pickle jar. Now start whenever you're ready. I'll just sit here and listen."

"Okay, Vinnie," Worthington said while feeling his stomach turning every which way inside him. "It all started with that girl who was found buried on Tanner's ranch. I know that I should have told you right after it happened, but I didn't think it would amount to anything."

"Tell me now," Vinnie said. "Before I lose what little patience I have left."

Worthington leaned forward in the beach chair. "Okay, I will, I'll tell you everything. And I promise not to leave anything out."

CHAPTER THIRTY-THREE

JOE WORTHINGTON SHIFTED his body to a more comfortable position in the hospital bed. The change in positions did nothing for the pain that he was experiencing in his upper torso. Both his chest and stomach held a burning ache that never seemed to go away. But the shifting around removed the pressure off his right shoulder. And that was something at least. Right now he told himself that he would have to settle for whatever relief he could get. After regaining consciousness, the doctor told Worthington that the pain in his upper torso would gradually diminish as his body began to heal. But it would take several days for that to happen. In the meantime he would have to deal with the pain the best way he could.

The heart monitor machine to the right of Worthington resonated. To his left, a steady moan came from the other side of the drawn curtain. Worthington knew it to be a female traffic accident victim. She had been brought into intensive care the night before. Members of the woman's family had been with her throughout most of the early morning hours. Worthington had heard some of them praying out loud. For the present, the woman's moans sounded muffled. It was as if she had buried her face in a pillow.

Worthington reached for the water cup on the table next to him. He brought the protruding straw up to his lips. That was when watery tears filled both his eyes and a feeling of hopelessness consumed him. Joe Worthington never remembered feeling more alone in his life. It was as if a dark shadow had eclipsed his brain, blocking out every bit of shining light. No more than an hour ago his wife, Janet, had been sitting in the chair next to his bed. Worthington could still picture Janet sitting there with the hurt look on her face. But it was the heart-wrenching sadness in her voice that had gotten to him.

"Joe, why did you tell me you were showing a property to a client when all along you were going to the beach house? You lied to me when you did that. Who were you actually going to see? It was a woman, wasn't it? Tell me how long you've been seeing her? I think I deserve at least that much from you. You've been acting strange lately, and I kept putting it off to your worrying about me and the baby. I never suspected that you would be having an affair. It just never entered my mind."

"Janet, there is no one else. The client I was supposed to meet called me on my cellphone and cancelled our appointment so I decided to stop by the beach house to check on things, that's all. There's no other woman in my life except for you. It's my getting shot that has you upset so much and you're not thinking clearly right now. But after the baby is born everything will be different. It'll be a big worry off both of us, and with me getting healthy again you'll find yourself in a better frame of mind."

"No, I won't, Joe. Something has happened to you. And it's not your getting shot that I'm talking about. It's something else. I've noticed the change in you ever since the police found that dead girl's body. You're hiding something from me, and if it's not another woman then I don't know what it is."

Worthington put the water cup back down on the table. How long could he go on without telling Janet about Ginny, and what he and Jack Hardin and Sam Costello had done to her? Right after she had the baby Janet would have to be told. And Jackson Stone would have to be told as well. No longer could he go on living with Ginny's death festering inside him. Even if it meant his going to prison for the rest of his life, or worse yet, the death penalty. Worthington knew the truth had to come out.

The two Mexicans tried to kill him at the beach house. They showed up at the same time he was supposed to meet Hardin and Costello. There was no doubt in Worthington's mind that his friends had set him up. Jack Hardin and Sam Costello had sent the two Mexicans to the beach house to kill him. They wanted him dead to protect themselves. It did not matter that he, Costello, and Hardin had been friends since grammar school.

Worthington shifted his gaze to the rows of ceiling tiles overhead. White squares with touches of gray in them shown down. While staring at the tiles, Worthington allowed his mind to race. Hardin, yes. Jack Hardin might perceive him as a threat and want him dead. Too many years of practicing law as a defense attorney had changed Hardin. A person can only grovel so long in the mud with swine before becoming one. But Sam Costello? Sam wanting him dead? That was a hard thing for Worthington to grasp. Comprehending it did not come easy. He and Sam had been friends for too many years. They had shared so much together. And now everything they had shared was gone. Like it never took place. And the good times were just figments of his imagination. This is what must happen, Worthington concluded, when someone you thought was your friend tries to kill you.

And it would only be a matter of time before Hardin and Costello tried again. Joe Worthington was certain of it. After their finding out that he had recovered from the shooting, Hardin and Costello would be worried about him telling Jackson Stone or someone else about what had happened at the beach house. Time would no longer be a luxury for them. Not with the death penalty staring each of them in the face. They would have to try again to kill him. His father, Zach Worthington, was of the same opinion. Shortly after Joe had regained consciousness, Zach visited his son in the intensive care unit. Not wanting to be overheard, his father leaned over and spoke softly.

"I left strict orders with hospital security that no one is to visit you except for family. That excludes Stone and Chief Martin from coming here to interview you. They're going to want to know what you were doing at the beach house after telling Janet that you were showing a client a piece of property. Joey believe me, Stone's nobody's fool. He's not going to believe that you stopped at the beach house the same time two Mexicans happened along with guns. Stone won't give up until he gets to the bottom of it. And he'll keep after you until he does. That's just the way the man operates. But for now let's forget about Stone and concentrate our attention on Hardin and Costello.

"I talked to your Uncle Vinnie and he's going to take care of everything. You won't have to worry about Hardin or Costello ever again. Family is what matters, Joey. Don't ever forget that. Now you've been through a lot so try and get some rest. Forget about what happened. Think about Janet and the baby and the life you're going to have together. That's the only thing that matters. Put the rest of this stuff behind you. Through the years I might not have been the perfect father, but I was always there when you needed me. Nobody can say I wasn't. And I'll be here for you through this as well. So get some sleep. Leave everything to me and your Uncle Vinnie."

Joe Worthington could still see the smile on his father's face before walking out the curtain enclosure. It was full of confidence. A smile Worthington had seen many times before. A politician's smile. Empty and worthless like the man behind it. Joe had no allusions about his father. For years now, he had known Zach Worthington fronted for the mob. That Vinnie Palermo pulled his father's strings.

Joe also knew that his father kept a mistress. And that his mother knew about it as well. Years of marriage had caused her to become bitter and sad. Like a beautiful flower kept out of the sun, she was withering away. There was no light left in her eyes, no sparkle. It was as if the zest for life had been taken from her and only an empty darkness remained. Joe blamed his father for what had happened to his mother. It was all Zach Worthington's fault. There would be no forgiving him for what he had done.

Shifting in his bed, Worthington experienced once again the spasms of pain to his upper torso. And there was more moaning from the other side of the curtain. The woman's moans had become louder, not sounding at all human. They were hard and guttural. Much like an animal in a great deal of pain. Worthington closed his eyes. He was tired. He wanted to sleep. But with the woman's moaning, he knew it would not happen.

CHAPTER THIRTY-FOUR

THE LATE MORNING sun was hot. It shone down like a burning furnace overhead. There did not seem to be any escape from it. Earlier there was the promise of rain. But that soon faded after the few remaining dark clouds moved off to the east. A Gulf breeze now rustled the palm trees and along with it came the scent of salt water and musky. seashore. The heat and humidity caused everyone to feel uncomfortable. Especially the men who wore shirts and ties, and the women dressed in buttoned up blouses and long skirts. More than one person had raised a hand to wipe perspiration from a sweating face. But for the most part people took the heat and humidity in stride. The majority were Floridians and accustomed to it. They stood clustered together with their heads bowed and hands at their sides while Father Rankin of St. Leo's Catholic Church read from an open book.

Stone stood closest to Cliff Potts's casket. Keri Martin was behind Stone. Father Rankin's strong voice drifted over the assembly. It was the voice of a man who believed in what he was reading. The priest finished the gospel passage and closed his bible. Everyone in the crowd instantly stood a little straighter. The people in the back stopped talking. And an eerie silence fell upon Resurrection Cemetery. Everyone's eyes stayed fixated on Father Rankin. He was standing next to Potts's casket with his right hand resting on top of it. Glancing to his right, Father Rankin nodded his head. Four uniformed U.S. Marines immediately snapped to attention. The noncommissioned officer barked out a command. The three marines responded by raising their rifles. They fired five quick volleys over Cliff Potts's casket before snapping back to attention.

Stone clasped Keri Martin's hand and squeezed it. The emotion swelling up inside him was overwhelming. He could not get the picture of Potts's grinning face out of his mind. Stone could only imagine what his uncle would have thought of the funeral. Hundreds of people were in attendance. Several of the town's people had turned out, not to mention the hundreds of uniform police officers from all over the United States. There were even officers from as far away as Canada. They all had come to say goodbye to one of their own.

"Jackson, are you feeling all right?" Keri asked while the two of them were walking away from the gravesite back to Keri's car.

Stone nodded while removing his sunglasses. "It's just that I can't help thinking about Potts and what must have been going through his mind the night he was killed. Keri, he went to the abandoned creamery for me. He ended up dying in my place, and I can't get that thought out of my head."

"Then maybe you shouldn't," Keri said to him. "Maybe you should remember it and love him all the more for it. Potts wouldn't have gone to the creamery alone that night unless he was worried about you. So Jackson, thank God someone like Potts had been made a part of your life. Keep his memory alive in you, and let yourself become a better person because of it."

Stone took hold of Keri Martin's right arm. Looking into her eyes, he detected the warm tenderness filling them. How did such a woman ever enter into his life? He had never thought it possible to feel what he was feeling at the moment. Stone did not know what to say. So he ended up by saying thank you and nothing more.

"For what?" Keri smiled back. "I'm only telling you the truth. You're the first one to step up for someone else whenever they're in trouble. You did it for me and through the years I'm sure you did it for Potts. By going to the creamery, Potts was only returning the favor. Jackson, I've got news for you. There are a lot of people in this town who care about you. And if you took the time to think about something other than your job once in a while, you would come to realize it."

"Who else cares about me? Name one other person."

"There are lots of people. Lisa Moore for one. I can see it in her eyes every time she looks at you."

"Okay, Lisa is one. Who else?"

"Lots of people. I'm not going to start giving you names while we're standing here in the middle of the cemetery."

Keri was quick to observe the sudden change in Stone. The smile once there had left his face. It was replaced by a concerned look. Stone was staring over her right shoulder. Keri turned around to see what had drawn his attention. A black-haired man wearing dark sunglasses and a brown sport coat was approximately thirty feet away standing by a tree. Keri did not remember seeing the man at the funeral service. But he could have come later. She turned back around to face Stone.

"Jackson, who is he? Do you know him?"

Stone told her, "Yes, I do. Keri, I am going to have to talk to him. You take the car and I'll meet you at the Crow's Nest. I shouldn't be too long. You wait there for me, and I'll get a ride from someone."

Martin watched as Stone walked away. She could not help but feel nervous with the stranger appearing out of nowhere. Keri headed toward her parked car while wondering if she was doing the right thing by leaving.

CHAPTER THIRTY-FIVE

"I DIDN'T EXPECT to see you here," Stone said while placing his sunglasses inside his front jacket pocket. "Pelican's Landing is a long way from Washington DC and the weekly cocktail parties, and all the other political crap that goes on there."

Pat Carollo smiled. The FBI special agent removed his sunglasses and extended his right hand to Stone. "Jackson, it's good to see you again, but if it could only have been under better circumstances. I'm sorry about Potts. He was a good man and a good policeman. I wish that I could have done more than just send a single red rose, but I couldn't. I had no other alternative."

Stone took back his hand. "Pat, a simple phone call from you might have been enough to save Potts's life. I don't understand any of this. The FBI had information concerning Vinnie Palermo and how he had sanctioned a hit on me. But I don't get a warning except for a single red rose delivered to the police station. What the hell is going on in Washington?"

"You know how the Bureau works," Carollo said, shaking his head. "You worked undercover for the FBI in New York City and saw how things are done. Nothing matters except for the Bureau, and the morning press release that shows the FBI coming out on top. That's so the upper echelon can pat themselves on the back and go around telling each other how much smarter they are than everybody else. It makes you sick I know, but nobody hates it more than I do. Some of us in the Bureau try to do the right thing by working within the system. That's why I sent you the single red rose."

"Who stopped you from making the phone call?" Stone asked while noting the grimace forming on Pat Carollo's face.

"Randall Maxwell, the assistant director of the criminal investigation division. He ordered me not to call you or anyone else on the Pelican's Landing Police Department. Maxwell said his reason was because he wanted to protect our informant who is close to the Conigliaro Crime Family. But I know that wasn't true. Jackson, he wanted you to get killed so he could later pin your murder on Vinnie Palermo. There's nothing that Maxwell wants more than to be the next Director of the FBI. He was hoping to arrest Palermo for your murder and land himself the Director's job."

Stone's face flushed red. He did not attempt to conceal the anger in his voice. "So now he has Cliff Potts's murder to launch his career. If you were ordered not to talk to me then what are you doing here in Pelican's Landing?"

"Maxwell sent me to monitor what's going on. That means I've been assigned to field operations and technically no longer under his direct command. I told him once before that I would never speak to you regarding the Conigliaro Crime Family as long as I worked for him. Well, I no longer work for Randall Maxwell. That's why I'm here talking to you now."

Stone felt his anger begin to subside. He and Carollo had been friends for a long time. Pat Carollo had saved his life on more than one occasion while Stone was working undercover in New York City. Carollo would never lie to him. Stone was certain of it.

"All right Pat, I believe you. It's just that for the past few days I've been taking Potts's murder pretty hard. So tell me, why did Vinnie Palermo sanction the hit on me? I have to assume it had something to do with the Conigliaro Family setting up business here in Pelican's Landing. They must have seen me as a threat to their plans and wanted me out of the way. But who did Vinnie Palermo actually commission to do the shooting? I want their names and everything else you got on them. Including how you came by your information. That means giving up your informant's name. I have to know everything you know if we're going to be working together."

Carollo did not answer immediately. He instead looked at Stone who was looking back at him. There did not appear to be any give in Stone. Carollo knew that he would have to tell Stone everything if he expected to get his help in bringing down Vinnie Palermo and the Conigliaro Crime Family. But would his friend play ball and not try to even up the score for Potts's murder? Carollo could not be certain. He did not know if Stone would be working with him or against him.

"Jackson, I'll tell you on one condition. You have to first give me your word that you'll not do anything until we both agree it's the right move to make. I can't jeopardize a federal investigation by having you jumping the gun because of some personal vendetta."

"You got it," Stone said while allowing his tensed body to relax. He knew Carollo was sticking his neck out by sharing confidential information with him. And if it ever got back to Washington, the FBI special agent in charge would surely be fired on the spot. It only made Stone like Pat Carollo all the more.

"All right Jackson, I'll tell you what you want to know," Carollo said moving closer to Stone. "Roscoe Tanner and his foreman, Jimmy Burke, were the ones who killed Potts. Burke's wife, Marci, phoned the Pelican's Landing Police station using the ruse of wanting to supply you with information about the dead girl found buried on Tanner's ranch. The actual order for the hit came directly from Vinnie Palermo and was passed on to Tanner by Zach Worthington. Jackson, you were right when you said the Conigliaro Family looked upon you as a threat. And Potts's murder hasn't changed that. They still see you as being dangerous to their gambling operation in Pelican's Landing. They also see your Chief Martin as being a threat as well."

"Tanner," Stone said before slamming the palm of his right hand against the tree behind him. "I should've guessed it the way Potts was set up. It's the kind of thing Tanner would do. He finally got back at me after my arresting him last year for that load of marijuana. And Pat, you can forget about Jimmy Burke. It was Tanner alone who killed Potts."

Stone explained to Carollo how one of the shooters had intentionally fired into the blue sedan's back passenger door. It was the shooter on the driver's side who actually killed Potts. And that shooter was Roscoe Tanner.

"So Jackson, you think Burke wanted no part of the murder. And he only went along with Tanner to make himself look like an accomplice. If that's true, we might be able to later use Burke against Tanner and Worthington. Who knows, eventually it could lead us to Vinnie Palermo's ordering the hit on you."

"But that doesn't tell me anything about the case you have right now," Stone said to him. "Who is this informant that's passing along information to the FBI about the Conigliaro Family's operation?"

"Jackson, I hope you're ready for this," Carollo said appreciating the look of anticipation in his friend's eyes. "As hard as it might be for you to believe, our informant is Carla Worthington. The mayor's wife has been feeding us information for the past year relative to Diamond Systems, Inc. and the Conigliaro Family. We haven't enough evidence to indict Vinnie Palermo or any of his most trusted advisors as of yet, but we're close."

Stone appeared as if he had been hit with a solid punch to the chin. He stared hard at Carollo in disbelief. "You mean to tell me Zach Worthington's wife and Palermo's own niece is supplying you with information to bring down the Conigliaro Crime Family. I can't believe it. Why would she ever do it?"

Carollo told him, "Carla has allowed her hate for Worthington to override everything, including any affection she might have for her Uncle Vinnie. She obtained the password to Worthington's personal computer, which gave the FBI access to Diamond Systems, Inc.'s software. There was a gold mine of information discovered in those files. The information will allow the Bureau to show how Zach Worthington and Diamond Systems, Inc. have been laundering dirty money for the Conigliaro Crime Family these past thirty years. Everything from extortion to prostitution is laid out in the minutest detail. Right now, we've got enough evidence to put Worthington away for the rest of his life."

"How about Palermo?" Stone asked. "Can you connect the head of the Conigliaro Crime Family to Diamond Systems, Inc.?"

Carollo smiled. "Vinnie has been careful to keep himself well insulated. You'd have to go through ten to fifteen people before ever getting close to him. Worthington could be the exception. He and Palermo must have had several one on one discussions concerning family business. But to get Zach Worthington to testify in open court against Vinnie Palermo would take a lot more leverage than we have at this point."

"But if you could connect Worthington to Potts's murder that might change things for you. And Pat, that's the real reason why you've come to Pelican's Landing, isn't it? You want to get the leverage on Worthington, so he'll testify in court against Palermo."

"You got it," Carollo said. "They give the death penalty in the state of Florida for murdering a policeman. And with Worthington facing a charge of murder, he just might become receptive to a deal. Especially if his life is on the line and he's found guilty."

Stone could not help but feel something was missing. That the entire puzzle was not complete. It was Carla Worthington that bothered him. "But I can't see Zach Worthington sharing anything with his wife. Everyone in town knows Zach and Carla's marriage has been on the rocks for years. Worthington wouldn't be stupid enough to tell Carla about Vinnie Palermo sanctioning a hit on me."

"He didn't. Carla meets Marci Burke every week for a martini lunch. Over dry martinis and cheese dip, she pumps Jimmy Burke's wife for information about the Conigliaro Family. That's how the FBI came to find out about Vinnie Palermo ordering the hit on you. And how Tanner and Burke were to be the two shooters. After Marci downs a few martinis, she tells Carla everything."

"Did she ever tell her where Tanner hides his meth lab?" Stone asked while hoping to pinpoint the location of the meth lab and get Roscoe Tanner charged for the manufacturing of meth crystal.

"No, the meth lab had been down by the river but Tanner moved it. And Marci doesn't know where he moved it to. Jackson, I know you want to nail Tanner, but right now I think you should be watching out for Vinnie Palermo. His number one hit man, Johnny Rocco, left New York City three days ago and we don't know where he is right now. A good guess is that he's in Florida. That means you and your Chief Martin better be careful."

Stone took out his sunglasses and put them on. "That reminds me. I have a luncheon date and I'm already late. Pat, it's been nice seeing you again. Stay in touch and keep me updated on everything. Especially anything you might find out from Carla. I'll do the same for you on my end."

"I'm staying at the Ramada Inn in town if you want to get a hold of me," Carollo yelled as he watched Stone run to catch a ride from a car that had stopped on the roadway to pick him up.

CHAPTER THIRTY-SIX

EVERY TABLE WAS occupied by the time Stone arrived at the Crow's Nest. The restaurant was receiving the after flow from Potts's funeral. It was alive with chattering people, not to mention the waitresses hurrying with plates of food and pots of steaming hot coffee. Ada and Fredek Lantos hurried over to Stone the moment they saw him enter the front door. Each gave him a hug while saying how sorry they were about Potts.

"It won't be the same with Potts gone," Ada said wiping the tears from her eyes. "He always made me laugh. Even when something was bothering me, I could always count on Potts to bring a smile to my face. He made whatever was bothering me go away."

Stone thanked them before heading toward the back of the restaurant. He spotted Keri Martin sitting at a small table in the corner. She was waving a white napkin to get his attention. Stone raised his right hand and waved back. Smiling, Martin watched as Stone came over to take the chair opposite her at the table.

"The place is a madhouse today. We're lucky to even get a table. I ordered coffee fifteen minutes ago and I'm still waiting."

"That's what happens when you bury a guy like Cliff Potts and afterward go to the best restaurant in town. You have to assume it's going to be crowded."

Stone observed Fredek Lantos heading toward their table with a steaming pot of black coffee. The owner of the Crow's Nest quickly filled both Stone and Martin's coffee mugs before rushing off to another table. Keri stared after him, shaking her head.

"Jackson, I hope you're not too hungry because I think we're going to have a considerable wait before getting any lunch today."

"Well, you can have lunch, I'm going for breakfast. Three or four eggs over easy with some ham and hash browns, and maybe an order of grits on the side. That sounds pretty good to me. I'll put the order in with Ada. We shouldn't have to wait too long. What can I order for you?"

Keri laughed. "I could probably get filled up just watching you eating your breakfast. But a tuna fish on wheat bread should do me. And a small glass of orange juice to go along with it."

"One tuna fish on wheat bread and a small glass of orange juice coming up," Stone said getting out of his chair and starting off toward the restaurant's kitchen. He was back in his chair grinning at Keri Martin in less time that it would have taken him to walk outside and walk back in again.

"I'm impressed," Keri said to him. "Now can you tell me about the man at the cemetery? The one you went over to talk to."

"You mean the guy with the dark sunglasses?"

"Yes," Martin said. "The man with the dark sunglasses, who is he?"

Stone took in the clenched mouth and button chin. He also noted the hint of fire in Martin's green eyes. A strand of red hair had fallen across her forehead. She was leaning forward and looking absolutely gorgeous. Stone wondered what life would be like with such a woman. He smiled while pulling his chair closer to the table.

"His name is Pat Carollo, and he's a special agent with the FBI. We've been friends ever since I worked undercover against the Giaccone Crime Family in New York City. Pat was both my handler and contact man back then. If it wasn't for him, I wouldn't be sitting here talking to you right now."

"Why was he at Potts's funeral? Did he come out of friendship for you or did he know Potts?"

Stone shook his head. "No, the FBI sent him to Pelican's Landing to get the goods on Vinnie Palermo and the Conigliaro Crime Family."

Stone informed Martin of everything Carollo had passed on to him. He left nothing out, including that it was Tanner and Jimmy Burke who had set up Potts's murder with help from Burke's wife, Marci. And it was Vinnie Palermo who had ordered that Stone be killed. Keri Martin stared across the table at him while Stone told her about Carla Worthington, and how the mayor's wife had been supplying information to the FBI concerning the Conigliaro Family. He went on to explain Diamond Systems, Inc. and the FBI's obtaining Zach Worthington's computer password through Carla.

"She hated her husband that much that she would give the FBI his computer password, and then go and squeeze whatever information she could get out of Burke's wife? Carla must have an awful lot of hate inside her to do all that. So what is Carollo planning on doing? Did he come here to help us with Potts's murder? You said Palermo ordered the hit on you, and Worthington passed it along to Tanner. Do we have enough to charge both of them for killing Potts?"

Stone told her, "Right now, all we've got is knowing who killed Potts and why it was done. There's no hard evidence to connect anyone to the shooting. I promised Carollo that I wouldn't make a move unless both he and I agreed that it was the right move to make. Keri, I'm bound by that promise. We're going to have to sit back and see what pans out. The Conigliaro Family knows it made a mistake in killing Potts instead of me. That should make everyone in the family nervous. If there's one thing that I've learned through the years, it is nervous people make mistakes. And that's what I'm counting on."

"But what if they try again?" Keri asked contemplating another attempt on Stone's life. "You said they will be nervous. Maybe they'll try and ambush you again when you least expect it. Did you ever think of that?"

"Yes, I have. But I don't think Vinnie Palermo is stupid enough to ambush me right after Potts's murder. The heat over a second policeman's murder would be too much for him. Any plans he might have for his gambling operation would go right out the window. No, for the time being I don't see that happening."

"Jackson, there has to be something that we can do. Just sitting and waiting for something to happen doesn't go well with me. You said Jimmy Burke could be the key that we're looking for. He didn't fire his gun at Potts. Maybe we could get him to give up Tanner, and who knows, even Worthington."

Stone appreciated the intense look on Keri Martin's face. It reminded him of the look that she had showed Zach Worthington after the mayor told Martin she could not interview Tanner regarding the dead girl found buried on Tanner's ranch. Keri was frustrated then and she was frustrated now. Stone was feeling the frustration, too. But there was nothing either of them could do about it.

Stone said to her, "And if he doesn't implicate Tanner in Potts's murder, where will that leave us? Vinnie Palermo will know then that we're onto him, and he'll close up shop so fast our heads will be left spinning. For now, we have no other choice but to be patient, and wait for them to make the next move."

"How about Joe Worthington?" Keri asked while still displaying the same intense look. "His doctor said that he can be interviewed, but Zach Worthington has left orders for no one, including the police, to see his son. I think that's highly unusual. I can't shake the feeling that something weird is going on here. First the girl's body shows up on the Tanner ranch, then Joe Worthington is shot by two criminals from Mexico, and then right afterward, Potts is murdered by Roscoe Tanner in an ambush meant for you."

Stone did not have the chance to respond. Ada Lantos had arrived at their table carrying a large tray. She immediately placed Stone's food down in front of him and then did the same for Keri Martin. Stone and Martin thanked her and Ada hurried off with the empty tray.

"This is what I call a breakfast," Stone said just before sticking a forkful of eggs into his mouth. He followed it up by taking a drink of black coffee out of a red mug. "If you want any of these grits, help yourself," Stone told Keri as he scooped up another forkful of eggs.

"No thanks," Martin said, wincing. "I'm not sure I will be able to finish my tuna fish sandwich, let alone any of your grits."

CHAPTER THIRTY-SEVEN

JACK HARDIN GLANCED up at the set of chains binding both his wrists. He quickly took note of the fact that the opposite ends were fastened to a metal beam high above his head. The pain in Hardin's shoulders was excruciating. It felt as though both rotator cuffs had been ripped from their sockets. While the incessant pounding inside his head seemed to be only increasing. What could have happened to him? What was he doing here? Why was he hanging naked with a set of steel chains wrapped around both his wrists? The last thing Hardin remembered was walking out his front law office door to go home when something hard had struck him on the back of his head. And only moments ago he had regained consciousness to find himself suspended in the air in what appeared to be an abandoned warehouse. It was dark and damp with the only light source being a single propane lamp. The squared-shaped lamp was resting on a wooden crate set off to Hardin's right. A strange sound caused Hardin to turn his head. Sam Costello was hanging naked next to him.

"Sam, can you hear me?" Hardin shouted with his voice echoing through the nearly empty warehouse. "Open your eyes and look at me. We're in a world of shit, and I don't know what's going on."

Costello blinked twice before opening his eyes. He tried raising his head, but it fell back onto his chest. He saw that Hardin was staring at him waiting for a response. Costello took a deep breath. He desperately wanted to say something. The words finally came out. "Jack, I woke up about an hour ago and you were hanging there unconscious. I tried talking to you, but it didn't do any good. Right now, my head and shoulders are killing me, and I don't even know how I got here. I was at work getting into my truck when somebody came up behind me and whacked me on the back of the head. For the past hour I've been asking myself, 'why would someone do this to us? What possible reason could they have'?"

Hardin told him, "I've got a good idea. It sure looks like somebody is paying us back for what we did to Joe Worthington. And if I'm right, we better not panic. We're going to have to stay cool and think this thing through."

"Are you talkin' about Zach Worthington? And his figuring we sent the two Mexicans to the beach house to kill Joe?"

"That's exactly what I'm talking about. But it wasn't Zach who hit us on the head and strung us up with these chains. It was his mafia friends. And they're going to come back here and want to know everything we know about Joe's getting shot. We're going to have to play dumb if we want to live. So don't tell them anything, no matter what they do to you. If they knew for sure that we set up Joe, they'd have killed us by now."

Costello grimaced. The extra poundage he was carrying added more stress to his arms and shoulders. Even though the temperature in the warehouse was cool, Costello was perspiring heavily. His naked body glistened in the propane lamp's soft light. He fought back the pain to speak to Hardin.

"I just thought of something. They never showed us their faces. They never let us see what they looked like. That means we can't identify them. Jack, you could be right about them not knowing for sure what happened to Joe. If they don't show us their faces, they'll probably let us go. All we have to do is keep telling them that we don't know anything about Joe's getting shot. I'm sure it'll work. After all, why would they want to kill us if they don't have to?"

Jack Hardin did not answer. He was too concerned about what was lying on the ground just below his feet. It looked very much like a hand-held propane torch. The kind welder's use to solder metal pipes. Hardin knew it was also used by the mafia to extract information from people who did not want to talk.

****

The two men were sitting in a leased car parked outside the empty warehouse. Their outlines were hardly discernable in the dark. It was nearly midnight. The men had been sitting for hours and were growing impatient. Johnny Rocco occupied the driver's side and was smoking an unfiltered cigarette. Routinely, Rocco blew smoke out the car's open window. The other man was smoking as well. He held a lit cigarette between two fingers, moving it in a circular motion. The cigarette's tiny glow occupied his attention. He contemplated how such a small flame could exist in the midst of so much darkness. His name was Charles Giovani Palmoli. He was thirty-two years old and a member of the Conigliaro Crime Family. In the mafia underworld he was known as Blowtorch Charlie. Palmoli was adept at getting people to talk even when they did not want to. Before becoming a member of the Conigliaro Crime Family, Palmoli had been a pipe welder on New York City's Eastside.

Rocco turned on the car's inside light. The sudden brightness caused both men to blink. Reaching under the driver's seat, Rocco unplugged the small speaker on the floor. It was time to move. He and Blowtorch Charlie had heard enough. Hardin and Costello were responsible for Joe Worthington's shooting. That's all they needed to know. Now it would just be a matter of finding out if they had told anyone else about the dead girl. But that should not take long. Not with Blowtorch Charlie doing the asking.

Rocco placed the speaker in his side coat pocket and turned to his passenger. The left side of Palmoli's face showed a concave look. It lent a permanent smile to the man's face. Rocco had heard Blowtorch Charlie came by the injury years ago when he was struck in the face with a metal pipe. An East Harlem pimp had taken exception to how the upstart Italian was treating one of his prostitutes. So he beat Blowtorch Charlie unmercifully. Besides the concave face there was a stream of saliva that constantly dripped from his mouth. Blowtorch Charlie carried a terrycloth with him wherever he went.

"So are you ready to go to work?" Rocco asked prior to turning off the inside light. Blowtorch Charlie did not answer. He opened the car's passenger side door and got out. Rocco opened his door and followed behind him.

CHAPTER THIRTY-EIGHT

THE SOUND OF a ringing phone awoke Stone from a sound sleep. It took a few seconds for him to realize that it was actually his cellphone that was ringing. Raising his head, he glanced over at the digital clock on the nightstand next to his bed. The clock's illuminated red numbers showed the time—3:00 a.m. 'Who could be calling me at this hour?' Stone asked himself before reaching for his cellphone on the nightstand. Uttering a gruff hello, he brought both his legs around to a sitting position at the edge of the bed. The caller wasted no time in identifying himself. After hearing the man's name, Stone's body stiffened.

Jerry Johnson was the Chief Investigator for Collier County and probably one of the most respected law enforcement officials in the state of Florida. Stone knew Johnson would not be phoning him at this hour unless it was important. Johnson told Stone that there had been a traffic accident thirty miles south of Pelican's Landing involving a white pickup truck on a secondary road. The truck had driven off the road into a ravine and caught on fire. Two charred bodies were discovered in the truck's front seat area. It would require dental records for a positive identification to be made.

Johnson explained that he was only phoning because the license plate attached to the pickup truck came back registered to Samuel B.

Costello of Pelican's Landing. And a computer check revealed that a missing person report had been completed on Costello the previous day with Stone's name listed as the investigating officer. Johnson gave Stone directions to the scene of the accident and said that he would wait for Stone's arrival.

As soon as he hung up with Johnson, Stone phoned Keri Martin. It took several rings before he heard Martin whisper a sleepy hello into her cellphone. Stone told Keri about Johnson's phone call and the fact that two charred bodies had been discovered in the front of Sam Costello's pickup truck.

"So you figure the bodies are Costello and Hardin?" Keri said while shaking off the few remaining cobwebs clogging her brain.

Stone told her, "Yes, I do. Their wives reported each of them missing yesterday evening. Costello's truck could not be located, and Hardin's black Lexus was still parked outside his law office. If it's not Costello and Hardin's bodies inside that pickup I'll be awfully surprised. I'll come by for you in twenty minutes and we'll go to the scene together. In the meantime I have a phone call to make."

Thirty minutes later Stone and Martin were driving in Stone's blue Mustang heading south on I-75. Stone had found Keri waiting for him outside the front door of the Holiday Inn. She was wearing a white blouse and black slacks with a 9mm Glock strapped to her right side. And like Stone, Martin had on a blue windbreaker with the words, "Pelican's Landing Police" printed on the back. Other than 'good morning' nothing else passed between them. The probability that the burnt bodies inside the pickup truck were Costello and Hardin had left both of them in shock. What possibly could have happened? Was it a traffic accident? Or was it murder? And if it was murder, who could be behind it?

Following Johnson's instructions Stone took the Wedgewood exit off I-75 and traveled east for approximately three miles. The sighting of red flashing lights and a half dozen or more police cars brought him and Martin to a gravel road in the middle of nowhere. The squad cars' spotlights were shining down into a ravine while a group of uniformed police officers stood talking in the middle of the roadway. Stone immediately spotted the tall, heavily-built Jerry Johnson among them. The gray-haired Johnson was wearing a white shirt and dark tie and had a clipboard tucked underneath his right arm. He must have spotted Stone as well because he started walking in the direction of the blue Mustang.

"Jerry is probably one of the best investigators I've ever worked with," Stone said to Keri as he was getting out of the Mustang. "I'm just glad he's handling the scene."

Johnson walked up to Stone and the two men shook hands. "Jackson, I'm sorry to have to drag you out of bed, but I knew you would want to know about this right away. There are two dead bodies down in that ravine, and there's no way in hell they're going to be identified without dental records."

"Jerry, we'll get them for you some time today, but I want to introduce Keri Martin to you. She's Pelican's Landing's new police chief."

Johnson's beefy, red face lit up after Martin put her right hand out for him to take. He took Keri's hand, holding onto it a bit longer than necessary. Having a reputation as a ladies man, Johnson took in the red hair and green eyes and the pretty smile directed toward him.

"Chief Martin, people told me you were a looker, but nothing could have prepared me for meeting you in person. I hope some time in the near future we can get together for lunch at my favorite restaurant down on Naples Beach. They have the freshest and best seafood you can get anywhere in the world. So don't be surprised if fairly soon you get a phone call from me."

"I won't be, Investigator Johnson," Keri said smiling. "And maybe Lieutenant Stone could join us. I know he loves seafood as much as I do. Now I think we should take a look at what brought us together so early in the morning."

A grinning Johnson nodded. "Of course, I'll take you down to the pickup, but be careful because it's slippery with all the runoff from the rain. There's about a foot of water in the ravine and along the water's edge there's something my tech guys found that I can hardly wait to show you."

Johnson took the lead while Stone and Martin followed him down the slope. A smoldering pickup truck awaited them at the bottom of the ravine. The responding fire personnel had extinguished the blaze, but there were still wisps of smoke emerging from the truck's frame. It mixed with the heavy mist rising from the water in the ravine. The combination of smoke and mist along with the bright lights shining down from the police cars lent an eerie feel. Keri imagined herself along with Stone descending into the lower pit of some smoking hell. The reassuring touch of Stone's hand on her right arm was most welcome. It served to strengthen Keri's resolve as she navigated the downward slope.

Johnson was the first to reach bottom and turned to help Martin onto solid ground. "The fire was nearly out by the time the first unit from the fire department arrived on the scene," he said while witnessing Stone stepping down. "One of our guys had spotted the truck on fire and radioed it in, but he didn't see any other vehicles in the vicinity. My guess is they doused the pickup truck with gasoline and set it on fire and then got the hell out of here as fast as they could. The fire eventually got to the gas tank and the whole thing went up."

"Investigator Johnson, how do you know someone set the truck on fire? There are plenty of rocks around, couldn't the truck have run off the road and struck a rock causing a spark to ignite the gas tank? I don't think that possibility should be ruled out."

"Chief Martin, normally I would agree with you," Johnson said glancing over at Stone. "But the evidence tells me otherwise. First of all, there are no skid marks on the road to indicate that the driver at any time attempted to brake his vehicle. I found that to be rather peculiar. But more importantly, I want you and Lieutenant Stone to take a look at the seven white flags sticking out of the ground there at the water's edge. It will help you understand why I feel this was a torch job and not a traffic accident."

Johnson removed a black-handled flashlight from his back pants pocket and shone it in the vicinity of the white flags. "Tell me, Chief Martin, what do you see?"

Keri bent down to check the area around each of the white flags. It did not take her long to notice. There was no mistaking the two different sets of shoeprints implanted in the sand and what their being there meant. Two individuals at some point had stood near the water's edge. Martin looked up at Stone before turning her attention to Johnson.

"Could these shoeprints have come from the fire personnel who put out the fire or perhaps some of the police officers?" Keri asked.

Johnson shook his head. "The fire personnel never came down here. They used their hoses from the road to put out the fire. As far as the police, my tech people and I were the only ones who approached anywhere close to this area. And I can assure you those footprints are not ours."

"Well, then I am sorry for questioning you, Investigator Johnson," Keri said displaying an awkward smile. "Lieutenant Stone told me you were the best investigator he has ever worked with, and I can see now why he said it. This pickup truck was deliberately set on fire with two people inside. Whoever did it murdered them."

"But not here," Stone said. "If it's Costello and Hardin's bodies inside the truck they were probably killed back in Pelican's Landing and dumped here. Then set on fire in an attempt to cover up their murders. We'll know for sure once we get a hold of both their dental records. Right now I want to take a look at the bodies."

Stone walked approximately ten feet into the water to peer into the front of the pickup truck. He observed the blackened, charred remains of two human bodies. It was a hellish sight. Stone felt someone grab his right arm. Turning, he saw Keri Martin standing next to him with a pale look on her face.

"You didn't have to see this," Stone said pulling her away. He quickly walked Martin back to where Johnson was waiting for them. "I don't know why you had to go and look," Stone whispered into Keri's ear. "Are you all right?"

Martin told him, "Yes, let's just get out of here. I can't take the stink of this place any longer."

****

Keri Martin did not think the smell of burnt flesh would ever leave her nostrils. There seemed to be no escape from the horrid smell. Stone suggested putting a dab of perfume under her nose but Keri had left her handbag back at the hotel. She asked him if there was anything else that might help.

"Try and not think about it," he told her while staring down at the burnt out pickup truck at the bottom of the ravine. Investigator Johnson and his tech people had taken casts of the shoeprint impressions and left. Only one uniformed police officer had remained behind to protect the crime scene. He was seated in his squad car with the car's high beam spotlight trained on the pickup below. It appeared to the naked eye as a sphere of light surrounded by darkness. Stone had informed Johnson that he and Martin would wait until the medical examiner's van came to remove the bodies. That was thirty minutes ago. In the meantime, the sun was starting to make an appearance. Tiny shafts of light were already forming on the eastern horizon while the melodious sound of finches filled the early morning air.

"It's going to be another hot one," Stone said turning to Keri Martin who had moved closer to him. "You can always tell it's going to be a hot day when there aren't any clouds off to the east. It means you're in for a clear morning with no break from the sun."

Martin could barely make out Stone's features in the dark. She could tell he was looking at her; his face was close to hers. But what was it that she wanted from him? Was seeing the burnt bodies causing this feeling inside her? Or maybe it was something else entirely. Keri could not be certain. But one thing she did know. She desperately wanted Stone to wrap his arms around her, and for a brief moment hold her close. But Keri knew that would not happen. Stone's mind was presently occupied with two murdered bodies. There was not room for anything else. Her feelings and the rest of the world would have to wait. Costello and Hardin's murders took precedent over everything. The sound of an approaching car drew their attention. Both Martin and Stone turned toward the gravel road.

"It's Lisa Moore," Keri said after recognizing Moore's silver jeep. "What is she doing here? How did she even know about it?"

"I told her," Stone responded. "I felt obligated to call and let Lisa know about the burnt bodies. Keri, there was no reason for me to mention this to you before, but now I think you should know. Lisa and Jack Hardin have been having an affair for the past three years. They were keeping it quiet because of his marriage, and I don't think anybody else knew about it except for Potts and me. You should also know that Hardin is the father of Lisa's baby."

"And here I thought …"

"That I was the one," Stone said showing no emotion. "A lot of people in Pelican's Landing believe the same thing. I say let people believe what they want to believe. I've known Lisa since she was a little girl and I gave her a job when she needed one. That was it. I tried to tell her back then that Jack Hardin was no good, but she wouldn't listen to me."

Keri wanted to tell Stone that she was sorry for thinking he was the father of Lisa's baby. But she did not get the chance. Moore came running up to them in a near hysterical state. Stone took her by both arms and held her tight.

"Lisa, I told you not to come here. There's nothing you can do for him. I'm not letting you go down there so get back in your jeep and go home to your baby."

"But Jackson, are you sure it's Jack? You said it was Costello's pickup, but maybe the other body is someone Costello gave a ride to. How can you be sure it's Jack Hardin when both bodies are so badly burned?"

"Because it's a double murder and not a traffic accident," Stone said in a raised voice. "And both Costello and Hardin turned up missing at the same time. Lisa, it's Sam Costello and Jack Hardin down there in that pickup truck. I don't know why somebody murdered them, but that's what happened."

Moore fell against Stone's chest. He immediately placed both his arms around her. Keri stood by watching, observing Lisa Moore's body convulsing inside Stone's embrace. It appeared as though the young woman had lost control of herself. She was crying with her sobbing growing louder. Then quite abruptly the crying stopped. Keri watched as Moore raised her head to look up at Stone.

"Jackson, I have to tell you something, and I hope you don't get angry with me. Yesterday, I checked on the court case of one of those Mexicans involved in Joe Worthington's shooting. It was an armed robbery case on the court call in Tampa. The court folder listed Jack Hardin as the man's defense attorney of record as well as the person who put up the bond money to get him released from jail. Reading it proved bothersome to me, especially since Jack has been asking me a lot of questions lately about the dead girl found buried on Tanner's ranch. He even asked me to get him a copy of the autopsy report. He said that he only wanted it because he was curious about the case, but I didn't believe him. So I decided to do some checking by going back and looking at missing case reports from around the time he and Costello and Joe Worthington were students in Gainesville at the University of Florida. A missing person report from eighteen years ago popped up and it looked promising. So I called the Gainesville P.D. and found out that the case was still open. The girl's name was Ginny Prendergast and her mother had called the police after she didn't return home from an out of town trip. This Ginny Prendergast matches up pretty well with our Jane Doe, even the part about her having had a baby. Before leaving work yesterday I sent the Gainesville Police Department a copy of Jane Doe's dental records. The sergeant I talked to said he would get back to me some time today with the comparison results."

"And when did you plan on telling Chief Martin and me about this?" Stone said prior to removing both his arms from around Lisa. There was no mistaking the tension in his voice.

"I wanted to first know if it was the same person. And if it was to confront Jack with it so I could hear what he had to say. I wanted the chance to look him in the eye and see if he was telling me the truth. Jackson, you have to believe me, I had no plan of hiding anything from you or Chief Martin. I would have told both of you right afterward."

"Lisa, you shouldn't have waited," Keri said. "You should have immediately told Lieutenant Stone or me about the possible identification of Jane Doe. But then again, I know from personal experience that sometimes we can let our emotions get in the way of our better judgment. So let's just forget about your not telling us. Jackson, I'm going to drive back to Pelican's Landing with Lisa in her car if it's all right with you. I think she could use the company."

"Good idea," Stone said while realizing that Martin's words to Lisa were meant for him as well. He knew Keri was attempting to apologize for assuming that he was the father of Lisa's baby. She had prejudged him and was not happy with herself for doing it. "Chief Martin, how about letting me buy you breakfast at the Crow's Nest this morning," Stone asked. "I can meet you there right after the medical examiner's people come and remove the bodies."

"Sounds good to me," Keri said while walking alongside Lisa Moore. "But I'll be the one doing the buying this time. It's my turn anyway."

CHAPTER THIRTY-NINE

EARLY MORNING WAS always Vinnie's Palermo's favorite time of day. The head of the Conigliaro Crime Family liked to have his boiled egg and two pieces of dry rye toast along with a strong pot of black coffee while sitting on his Fort Lee mansion's screened in terrace. The terrace overlooked a garden consisting of white and pink tulips, purple lilacs, golden zinnias, and an assortment of red and yellow roses. The variety of colors contrasted nicely with the herbaceous border delineating the garden. Palermo's personal bodyguard, Bobby Vaccaro, occupied a chair in the far left corner, while an armed man escorting a leashed German Shepherd passed by the terrace every fifteen minutes. Security around the Fort Lee, New Jersey, mansion was tight. The reason being Vinnie Palermo had called for a meeting with his top lieutenants—Al Ruggiero, the Conigliaro Family's Underboss, and Alex Mallo, the Family's Consigliore. The three men planned on discussing family business relating to Pelican's Landing. The meeting was scheduled to take place in an hour.

Palermo was pleased with the progress made so far in Florida. The state legislature had finally passed the new gambling bill, which now only awaited the governor's signature before becoming law. Vinnie knew the governor would sign the bill at the end of the month. Johnny Rocco and Blowtorch Charlie had done their job.

They had convinced the senate leader, Mark Boswell, to bring the gambling bill to the senate floor for a vote and it easily passed. That meant Pelican's Landing, within the next six months, would become the center for the Conigliaro Family's operations in the state of Florida. Hundreds of millions of dollars could be made on the gambling, prostitution, and the sale of narcotics. The other crime families would take a share in the profits as well. Eventually their capos would come, one by one, to the head of the Conigliaro Family and pay homage to the man who had made it all possible. And Vinnie Palermo would smile knowing that he had obtained what he always wanted—the title, *capo ditutti capi*—"boss of all bosses." He had successfully plucked the pearl from the oyster; he had snatched the prize from the lion's mouth. The power behind the Mafioso would be his alone. Vinnie told himself that he should be feeling jubilant and on top of the world. But that was not how he felt. Deep inside him there was a call for caution. Palermo could not escape the feeling that Pelican's Landing might easily become the end to all his plans.

Zach Worthington had told Vinnie about the girl's body found buried on the Tanner ranch. And that Joe Worthington, Vinnie's godson, and two of his friends had been responsible for her death. Zach then went on to explain that he had Tanner and Tanner's foreman remove the girl's body from the beach house and bury it in a secluded place on the Tanner ranch. Worthington said he had not told Vinnie about it because he did not want to bother the head of the Conigliaro Family over such a trivial matter.

"Everything concerning my godson I want to know about," Vinnie had said to Worthington while the two sat under the red umbrella at the Palermo summer beach house in Spring Lake, New Jersey.

Worthington agreed wholeheartedly. He then went on to tell Palermo that he suspected his son's two friends, Jack Hardin and

Sam Costello, as being the ones behind the plot to kill Joey. He also brought up Jackson Stone's name. And how he felt Stone would eventually figure out the reason why Joey had been shot. It would later help Stone to connect Vinnie's godson to the girl's murder. Worthington added that Stone was not the kind of man to let anything get in his way. He would not stop until he got Joey charged with the girl's murder.

Vinnie picked up the gold cigarette case from off the table in front of him. Removing a hand-rolled cigarette, he placed one end between his lips. Bobby Vaccaro hurried over with a match to light the other end. The bodyguard then returned to the corner of the terrace. Palermo attempted to block out everything in order to concentrate on the situation at hand. The threat to his godson had been removed. Johnny Rocco and Blowtorch Charlie had taken care of the two conspirators who wanted Joe Worthington dead. But Stone was another matter. The police lieutenant was not only a threat to his godson but to the Conigliaro Family as well. And then there was the matter of the FBI agent Carollo showing up in Pelican's Landing. Palermo knew that Carollo and Stone were friends. He was also aware of the damage the two had done to the Giaccone Family in New York City years ago. The family had nearly been destroyed. Vinnie Palermo could not let the same thing happen to the Conigliaro Family. He would have to do something.

Johnny Rocco and Blowtorch Charlie were still in Pelican's Landing. Vinnie had told them to remain there until further notice. They could easily kill Stone, and, if it became necessary, the new female police chief. But would the murder of a police lieutenant so soon after the killing of a police sergeant draw too much scrutiny? Palermo thought it would. And right now the Conigliaro Family had too much at stake to jeopardize their standing in Pelican's Landing. Stone would have to be dealt with differently. His death must appear as having nothing to do with police work. Vinnie thought he might have the right approach. The more he thought about it, the more certain he became. The idea should work to both Al Ruggiero and Alex Mallo's satisfaction as well. But it would have to wait until things died down over the police sergeant's murder. Then he would have Johnny Rocco and Blowtorch Charlie kill Jackson Stone.

Taking a drink out of his coffee cup, Palermo set the cup down. The head of the Congliaro Family felt considerably better now that the matter concerning Stone was finally settled. His godson would be protected and so would the Conigliaro Family's interest in Pelican's Landing. Palermo leaned back in his chair to take in the sunlight falling upon his garden. The array of colors was magnificent. It was a picture only he could appreciate. Smiling, Vinnie took a drag on his cigarette, blowing smoke rings into the air. The old, craggy face of the woman who rolled his cigarettes came to mind. "Old woman, may you live to roll me many more," Vinnie said out loud before getting out of his chair and going into the house.

CHAPTER FORTY

IT WAS MOSTLY out of town people who frequented the Crab Shack. Tourists liked the restaurant's thatched roof and open sides, not to mention its view of the beach where waves rolled onto white sand, and sunbathers lay quasi-naked under a hot sun. The Crab Shack was located on the south end of Treasure Island Boulevard, a good distance from the main strip. Occasionally, a few of the locals would stop in for a drink, but not very often. That was the reason why Carla Worthington opted to meet Marci Burke at the restaurant every Wednesday afternoon for lunch. It reduced the chances of one of Pelican's Landing's leading citizens seeing her having lunch with a ranch foreman's wife. A table for two in the far corner overlooking the beach was Carla and Marci's usual table. It gave them the privacy they desired along with the opportunity to observe suntanned, young men with hard, muscular bodies wearing tight briefs that left little if anything to the imagination.

The two women did not have much in common except for the fact that they were both in their early fifties and married to men associated with the Conigliaro Crime Family. Carla was black-haired, olive-skinned, and short in stature; Marci was blond-haired, fair-skinned, and thinly tall. Carla liked her hair short. She felt it accentuated her brown eyes and made her face appear less pudgy. Marci on the other hand liked her hair long. She felt it highlighted her blue eyes and gave her face a much fuller look.

The women's manner of dress was different as well. Carla was wearing a yellow blouse with white, short pants, and a pair of open-toe brown sandals and white socks. Marci preferred the more casual look. She was wearing a white tee-shirt with the motto, 'Knock, Knock, Who's there?' imprinted across her chest along with blue jean shorts and cheap sandals and no socks. A dry martini with a green olive rested on the table in front of each woman. There was a bowl of cheese nachos occupying the table's center. Marci sucked the green olive out of her glass, and Carla grabbed a handful of nachos out of the bowl.

"I have no idea when they're going to try and kill Stone," Marci said in answer to Carla Worthington's question. "Zach of all people should know. After all, he's the one Vinnie Palermo gave the order to when Tanner and my Jimmy ended up shooting Potts by mistake. Why don't you ask your husband?"

Carla took a sip of her martini and smiled. "Marci, I don't have to tell you how men can be at times. One day they're easy to get along with and the next day you can't stand being in the same room with them. That's how it gets sometimes with Zach and me, especially after Joey was shot, and the doctor doing a C-section on Janet tomorrow. There's a lot of tension in the house."

"I can see that happening," Marci said raising her right arm and showing two fingers for the waitress to bring them two more martinis. "It's just that Jimmy hasn't said anything to me. But knowing Roscoe Tanner, he won't give up on killing Stone. There's too much hate in the man for him to do that. I see him and Jimmy goin' out to the barn and spending a lot of time out there. They're planning something, that's for sure. I asked Jimmy what they talk about and he told me to mind my own business."

Carla was hoping for something new that she could take back to FBI Agent Carollo. For the past week, Carollo had been putting pressure on her to find out when Tanner and Burke were planning another attempt on Lieutenant Stone's life. But Marci did not seem to know. So there would be nothing new for Carla to tell the FBI agent. She was now sorry that she had ever become involved with the FBI. It was only her hatred for Zach Worthington that had made her do it. Carla allowed her hate to override her good sense. She had betrayed Vinnie Palermo and the entire Conigliaro Family by going to the FBI. Now there did not seem to be any way out for her.

Besides that, she had Joey to think of. Carla was fully aware of her son's involvement in the murder of the girl found buried on the Tanner ranch. Zach had told her long ago about the night he had summoned Roscoe Tanner and Jimmy Burke to the Worthington beach house. The rancher and his foreman had disposed of the dead girl's body to conceal the murder. But now everything had changed. The police knew about the girl. And to protect themselves, Hardin and Costello had put the two Mexicans up to killing Joey. It was only because of her Uncle Vinnie that Joey was no longer in danger. He had Hardin and Costello murdered so no further harm could come to her son. But what about Jackson Stone? Did he suspect Joey in the girl's murder? Had he put together the pieces of the puzzle? Carla felt a wave of panic moving through her. If so, Stone could one day arrest her son and send him away to prison for the rest of his life. It was better that Marci did not know anything. That way Tanner and Burke could follow through with their plan to kill Stone. And then her son, Joey, would have nothing more to fear.

"Hello, are you still here?" Marci asked waving her right hand in front of Carla's face. "I've been talkin' to you, and you've been staring at me with a blank look on your face. Honey, you better slow down on the martinis."

"Maybe you're right," Carla said forcing a smile. "I better stick with the cheese nachos and leave the martinis to you."

Marci laughed. "And honey, I won't let you down. Because there's nothing I like better than having Wednesday lunch with you."

CHAPTER FORTY-ONE

IT IS A four hour drive from Pelican's Landing to Gainesville, Florida. The drive encompasses the many citrus groves, cattle ranches, and sugar cane fields that were once part of the Everglades. The closer one gets to Gainesville, white stucco houses begin to show with their outdoor swimming pools and green manicured golf courses. The sun was shining bright in the sky. It allowed Stone to put down the blue Mustang's top so that he and Martin could feel the rush of wind in their hair. Both wore dark sunglasses and light-colored clothing. Stone had on a short-sleeve, green shirt and tan slacks; Martin was dressed in a white top and beige pants. Traffic was surprisingly light. It gave Stone the opportunity to press down on the Mustang's accelerator.

"I always thought Florida was sandy beaches and Disney World, and nothing much else except for maybe the Everglades," Keri said staring at the green landscape and the hundreds of cattle grazing on it. "I didn't expect to see herds of cows and sheep, and then all those citrus farms and sugar cane fields we drove by."

Stone observed the smile on Keri's face along with her red hair blowing every which way. "You're not alone," he told her. "Most people who haven't visited Florida think the same way. They see the beaches and hotels on television and think that's all there is to Florida. They couldn't be more wrong."

Stone and Martin were going to Gainesville to interview Joyce Prendergast, the mother of Ginny Prendergast who had been reported missing eighteen years earlier. The Gainesville Police Department had matched the dental records of Jane Doe with those of Ginny Prendergast. Stone and Martin were hoping to find something that could tie Joe Worthington to the girl's murder. Worthington along with Hardin and Costello had been students at the University of Florida about the time the Prendergast girl was reported missing. Perhaps one or all three had been acquainted with the girl. Stone and Martin thought the girl's mother might have the answer.

"Jackson, what possible reason could Joe Worthington have for not allowing us to interview him, other than for the fact that his getting shot had something to do with the girl's murder?"

"Nothing I can think of. He's been out of intensive care for the past three days and in a private room with a hired security guard sitting outside his door. Zach Worthington left standing orders for hospital personnel not to allow anyone, including the police, to speak to his son. It sure seems like Zach is trying to protect Joe from something. And it couldn't have anything to do with his killing the two Mexicans because that was done in self-defense. So we're left with the Prendergast girl's murder and the murders of Hardin and Costello. And with Lisa Moore connecting Jack Hardin to one of the Mexicans, I think we're right to suspect Worthington in the Prendergast girl's murder. All we need is something linking her to him."

"Well, let's hope Joyce Prendergast can give us the link we need," Keri said pointing to the roadway sign off to her right. "It looks like the Gainesville exit is coming up."

****

Twenty minutes later Stone parked the blue Mustang in front of a brick bungalow on Gainesville's Westside. The bungalow appeared to be well-kept with a green lawn and flower bed out front, and a walkway of gray flagstone leading up to the front door. Stone observed someone looking out the bungalow's window. He guessed it to be Joyce Prendergast. The Gainesville Police had contacted Prendergast about her daughter's dental records and their matching those of a murder victim in Pelican's Landing. She was also told Chief Keri Martin and Lieutenant Jackson Stone from the Pelican's Landing Police Department would be coming to ask her some questions. Stone and Martin knew it was going to be a difficult interview. Even if Joyce Prendergast had concluded that her daughter was murdered, the actual realization of it would prove distressful. And why wouldn't it? Any mother would feel the same. Especially in knowing that her murdered daughter's body was coming home soon. Stone and Martin got out of the Mustang. Bracing themselves, they walked up to the bungalow's front door.

Stone did not have to ring the doorbell. A bluish-gray-haired woman in her early seventies was there to open the door. The woman had a cordial smile on her face. There was a glint in her hazel eyes. A slight tremor seemed to be affecting the woman's chin. She tried to hide the tremor by placing her left hand over it.

"Chief Martin and Lieutenant Stone, it's nice of you to come. I'm Joyce Prendergast. Pelican's Landing is quite a distance from here, and you've driven so far to see me. Won't you please come in?"

Prendergast stepped back for Stone and Martin to enter. Keri took notice of the woman's finely-tailored, pink dress and white collar along with the silver earrings. A diamond-studded bracelet was showing on her left wrist. The woman had obviously gone out of her way to dress for the interview. It gave Keri a sense of how much their visit meant to Joyce Prendergast. Stone and Martin followed the woman into the dining room where they were offered a chair.

"Could I get you something to drink? Coffee, or an iced tea perhaps?"

Stone told her, "No thank you, Mrs. Prendergast. We stopped on our way here and got something. We just want to ask you a few questions about Ginny, especially who her friends were and why she would have come to Pelican's Landing. We don't want to take up too much of your time."

"Time? That's all I have, Lieutenant Stone," Joyce Prendergast said while sitting down across the table from Stone and Martin. The woman reached over to remove a white table napkin from its holder. She pressed the napkin between her two hands. "Nothing else is left for me. Every day for the past eighteen years I've thought of Ginny and what might have happened to her. And now that I know, it doesn't make things any easier. The sergeant from the Gainesville Police Department told me that since Ginny's body had been found I would at least have some closure, and not have to wonder about her anymore. You have no idea how much I hate the word closure. Only people who haven't lost someone very dear to them uses it. Because the pain never goes away, and the empty feeling inside stays with you forever."

Joyce Prendergast brought the table napkin up to her face. She wiped at the tears filling her eyes. Keri Martin reached across the table to touch the woman's right arm.

"Mrs. Prendergast, Lieutenant Stone and I hate to put you through this ordeal, but it is necessary. We need your help in order to catch the people who murdered your daughter. Without your help we can't move forward in this investigation, and the killers could very easily get away with murdering Ginny. You don't want that to happen anymore than we do. So please try and answer Lieutenant Stone's questions. Can you tell us about any of Ginny's friends and what would have brought her to Pelican's Landing?"

Prendergast set the napkin down on the table in front of her. She fought to control her emotions. Taking a deep breath, she looked across the table at Stone and Martin.

"Ginny didn't have many friends. She went to the university during the day and worked as a waitress at night. She was so busy all the time, I really didn't get the chance to see her hardly at all. I was working for an accounting firm downtown back then, and it took up a lot of my time. You see my husband and I divorced years before and I had custody of Ginny. As far as her friends, there were a couple of neighborhood girls she was friendly with, but I don't know if they could tell you anything. But there was a boy she met at the place where she worked. Ginny told me that she loved him and that he was the father of her baby. And I know she still loved him even after he told her that he wanted nothing more to do with her."

"What was his name?" Keri asked leaning forward. "She had to tell you the boy's name, the father of her baby."

"I asked her but she wouldn't tell me. Even after she had the baby Ginny wouldn't tell me the boy's name. I know he attended the university because she told me that much. And it was on summer break that she decided to visit him at his parent's house and tell him about his son. I told her not to go and to have nothing more to do with the boy, but she wouldn't listen to me. Ginny was in love with him, and I knew nothing I could say was going to change her mind. She told me that she wanted to marry the baby's father and spend the rest of her life with him. Chief Martin and Lieutenant Stone, eighteen years ago I watched my daughter walk out that front door and I never saw her again."

"You have no idea where she went to visit this guy?" Stone asked. "Was it somewhere in Florida? Did she ever mention names of places? Or how she was planning on getting there? Did she own a car?"

"No, Ginny didn't have a car. I don't know how she planned on getting to wherever she was going. I wish I could help you, but I just don't know. Ginny was high strung and very independent. I know that she loved me, but this boy was everything to her. All she cared about was being with him."

Stone shook his head and leaned back in his chair. He looked at Keri Martin seated next to him. Martin's face displayed a frown, which reflected Stone's mood as well. They both had been counting on Joyce Prendergast to shed some light on the men in her daughter's life. But after talking to her that did not seem possible. Stone felt he and Martin had run into a brick wall.

"Mrs. Prendergast, you said earlier that Ginny had a baby boy, and we have to assume she took the baby with her to show the boy to his father. But only Ginny's body was found in the grave. There was no baby's body. That leaves us without a clue as to what happened to your grandson. There is always the possibility that he is still alive, but we have no evidence to support it."

"Oh, I'm so sorry Lieutenant Stone. I should have told you and Chief Martin. Ginny didn't take the baby with her. She left him here with me. His name is Thomas Prendergast and I raised him. He is a fine young man and I couldn't be prouder of him."

Keri Martin moved in her chair. Stone grabbed the edge of the dining room table with both hands. There was no mistaking the look of excitement on each of their faces. Martin voiced what she knew Stone was thinking: "DNA."

"Mrs. Prendergast," Stone said while trying to keep the excitement out of his voice. "It is important that we talk to your grandson. Does he still live with you? And if he's moved, will you give us his new address and phone number? I can't stress how important it is that we get in touch with him."

"Lieutenant Stone, I wish that I could help you and Chief Martin, but I don't think that I can. You see, I don't have Thomas's address and phone number. He does phone me on occasion, but not often. He seems to be always busy."

"What state does he reside in?" Martin asked hoping that with his name and date of birth Thomas Prendergast could be located through a driver's license or tax record.

Joyce Prendergast told her, "Well, actually, this still is his residence. But ever since Thomas joined the Army, he moves around so much. Right now he's somewhere in Afghanistan fighting for his country. I mentioned before that I couldn't be more proud of him."

Smiling, Stone turned to Keri Martin. "We shouldn't have any problem contacting him through the U.S. Army. They have DNA kits so that should expedite things for us, but it will still take a few weeks before we get anything back from them. Mrs. Prendergast," Stone said returning to Joyce Prendergast. "Do you have a recent photograph of Thomas that we could borrow? I promise it will be returned to you as soon as our investigation is finished."

"Yes, I do. There is a photograph of Thomas in the living room. He is wearing his army uniform and looks so handsome. He had it taken just before he left for Afghanistan. I'll get it for you."

Stone and Martin watched Joyce Prendergast leave the dining room. The woman returned a moment later holding a black picture frame containing a photograph. She set the frame and photo down on the table in front of Stone. Keri Martin leaned over to look at it. She immediately took hold of Stone's right hand. The black hair, the straight thin nose, along with the high-cheekbones and tapered mouth were the same. The face in the photograph was that of a young Joe Worthington. It left no doubt as to the identity of Thomas Prendergast's father. The photo also explained Ginny Prendergast's coming to Pelican's Landing.

"I hope this photograph will be of help to you," Joyce Prendergast said. "And that it does some good in finding the person who killed my Ginny."

"I can assure you that it will, Mrs. Prendergast," Stone said before standing and nodding to Keri Martin that it was time to go.

CHAPTER FORTY-TWO

THE DIMLY LIT room was nothing more than a horse stall enclosed by four sheets of dry wall. A single light bulb attached to an electrical cord hung down from the ceiling, while a flat piece of wood set on top of an empty drum served as the room's only table. Roscoe Tanner and Jimmy Burke sat on bales of hay facing one another. The men's large frames swamped the small space. They left room for little else. It was hot and sticky in the room. Both men's faces were covered in sweat. The radio on the table had been turned up. Tanner ignored it while staring at Burke. The ranch foreman tried to stare back, but soon gave up. Tanner's steely-eyed look made him feel too uncomfortable.

"It's not that I'm saying I won't do it. It's just too close to our killing Potts, that's all. I think we should wait awhile until things settle down. That FBI agent Carollo is nosing around Pelican's Landing, and who knows where he might show up. Besides Zach Worthington told you to keep a low profile and don't do anything to Stone. That's not only Worthington talkin', it's Vinnie Palermo telling us to keep away from Stone until he tells us different."

"Just remember you don't work for Palermo. You work for me," Roscoe Tanner said above the loud music being played on the radio. The reason for the increased volume was to thwart any listening devices the FBI might have planted in the barn. Tanner was already aware of his ranch house being bugged. "I am going to kill Stone, and that's the way it's going to be. I don't care about Vinnie Palermo or the Conigliaro Family. I'm the one who Stone is trying to pin that girl's murder on, and I'm not going to stand by and watch him do it. We both buried the girl and we both killed Potts, so you've got as much to lose as I do. Are you with me or not?"

"It's Palermo that I'm worried about," Burke said while beads of perspiration ran down both sides of his face. "Look at what he did to Hardin and Costello. There wasn't enough left for their families to bury after Palermo's people doused them with gasoline and set them on fire. He'd do the same to you and me if we killed Stone without first getting his okay."

Tanner reached across the oil drum and grabbed Burke's right arm. "That's the beauty of my plan, we won't need Palermo's okay because Stone will be coming after us and leaving us no other choice but to kill him. Vinnie Palermo can't blame us for protecting ourselves. That's the way it will look."

"Why would Stone be coming after us?" Burke said pulling his arm out of Tanner's grasp. "Stone doesn't know anything about us burying the girl's body or our killing Potts. So what are you talking about?"

Tanner fought to control his temper. Burke was beginning to look more and more like a liability. Tanner told himself that he would have to deal with his foreman after Stone was no longer a threat. "You let it out amongst the boys that our meth lab is down at Cattail Marsh, and on Friday night after dark we're going to move a load of white crystal to Miami. Whoever told Stone last year about the marijuana we had in the barn will tell him about the meth lab. And you and me will be waiting for him. We'll take care of Stone and whoever else he brings along with him. Palermo and the Conigliaro Family can't blame us for protecting the meth lab. They'll probably even give us a big bonus because of it. But more importantly, Stone will be dead. And that will be the end of it between him and me."

Burke told him, "We'll probably have to kill that female police chief along with Stone, and that FBI agent Carollo might be with them. We'd have to kill him, too. That could end up bringing down a lot of heat. Tanner, I'll go along with you on one condition."

"And what's that?"

"Afterward, you and me are through. I get my share from the sale of the white crystal after its delivered to Miami, and then Marci and me are out of here. I want to be far away from Pelican's Landing when the shit hits the fan. I've saved enough money to last her and me for a long time. So what do you say? Do we have a deal?"

The hard glint in Tanner's gray eyes disappeared. A smile came to his face. "Sure we have a deal. And I hope you and Marci are happy together wherever you decide to go."

Tanner put out his right hand for Burke to shake. Burke took it while not at all liking Tanner's clammy feel. After taking back his hand he immediately wiped it off on his pants leg. Burke felt that he had made a mistake in saying yes to Tanner. But it was too late to tell his boss that he had changed his mind. He would have to go through with Tanner's plan to kill Stone. There was no other choice for him. Besides Tanner would kill both him and Marci if he did not go along with the plan.

"Just remember," Burke said coming to his feet. "After Friday night, you and me part company for good."

CHAPTER FORTY-THREE

KERI MARTIN'S EYES kept coming back to Stone. She tried averting them, but Stone's presence had that sort of effect on her. The Pelican's Landing police chief continued speaking to the small group assembled in front of her. Present were Jackson Stone, Lisa Moore, Bob Garcia, and FBI Special Agent Pat Carollo. Stone had felt it would be a good idea to invite Carollo to the meeting. Martin, after thinking it over, agreed with him. The meeting was taking place in Martin's office on the second floor of the Pelican's Landing police station. Keri had summoned everyone together upon her and Stone's return from Gainesville, Florida.

It was crowded and stuffy in the small office. The window air-conditioner was not even close to being up to the job. It hummed along lending little comfort if any to the room's occupants. Keeping the office door closed only added to the room's stuffiness. But people's comfort was of no importance to Martin. Confidentiality with respect to Ginny Prendergast's murder was all that mattered. Earlier Martin had instructed her civilian staff not to disturb the meeting for any reason.

"So now each of you knows what we're up against. We've established that Joe Worthington is the father of Ginny Prendergast's son, and eighteen years ago she came to Pelican's Landing to tell him about it. She also planned on telling Worthington that she loved him and wanted to marry him. The rest is speculation on our part backed up by a fair amount of circumstantial evidence. The ME's office found traces of the knockout drug, Rohypnol, in the Prendergast girl's hair. That is significant because eighteen years ago Rohypnol was routinely administered to young, unsuspecting women in and around the University of Florida Gainesville campus. The women were rendered unconscious and then raped leaving the perpetrator or perpetrators unable to be identified. We've also confirmed that Joe Worthington, Sam Costello, and Jack Hardin were registered students at the University of Florida in Gainesville at this time. And during the summer break when Ginny Prendergast came to Pelican's Landing all three were residing in town."

"But that doesn't mean they all raped her," Lisa Moore interjected, not wanting to believe Jack Hardin took part in the rape of Ginny Prendergast. "She only came to see Worthington. He gave her the knockout drug so that he could have sex with her. There's nothing to support Hardin or Costello's raping her. Joe Worthington was the only one she came to see."

Keri Martin turned to Stone for help. The last thing Martin wanted was an argument with Deputy Moore, especially over Jack Hardin, who was the father of Moore's baby. Keri breathed a sigh of relief when Stone stood up.

"If it's all right with you, Chief Martin, I'll take over from here," Stone said while turning around to face everyone in the room. He focused his attention on Moore. "There would have been no need for Joe Worthington to give Ginny Prendergast the knockout drug if he alone was going to have sex with her. She had come to Pelican's Landing for the sole purpose of seeing him. And before leaving Gainesville she had told her mother that she loved him. No, Worthington didn't have to force himself on Ginny. She was given the knockout drug so Hardin and Costello could have their good time with her. And if I had to guess, Worthington was the one who slipped the Rohypnol into Prendergast's drink when she wasn't looking. Then Hardin and Costello raped her after she became unconscious."

"No, Jackson. I don't believe it," Moore shouted coming to her feet. "Jack Hardin might have had his faults, but he was no rapist. And you can't say he was. You have no proof."

"Lisa, you gave us the proof when you discovered the court records of that Mexican who tried to kill Worthington. Hardin was the Mexican's lawyer and had bonded him out of jail. Both Hardin and Costello wanted Worthington out of the way because he was the only connection to Ginny Prendergast who could later implicate them in the girl's rape and murder. They were scared, and like scared people they did a crazy thing. They paid hired assassins to kill their friend. You know it's true, that's why you're so upset."

"And it cost both of them their lives," Pat Carollo said turning in his chair to face Moore. "We know that Zach Worthington visited Vinnie Palermo in New Jersey just two days before Hardin and Costello's bodies were found burnt to a crisp inside Costello's pickup truck. I looked at the photo scenes and talked with the lead investigator, Jerry Johnson. It had been made to look like a traffic accident, but there's no doubt in my mind that Johnny Rocco and Blowtorch Charlie first killed them and then set their bodies on fire. That means the Conigliaro Crime Family is involved in the Prendergast girl's murder. Vinnie Palermo must have sanctioned a hit on Hardin and Costello in order to protect Joe Worthington. If we can connect Worthington to the girl's murder it might lead us to Palermo."

"And how are we going to do that?" Bob Garcia asked. "All the players are dead except for Joe Worthington. You can't expect him to tell on himself."

Keri Martin tried to answer Garcia. "If we could only talk to him about the shooting incident at the beach house, maybe then we could bring up Ginny Prendergast's name. It might get a reaction out of him. And if Worthington was to look at the photograph of Thomas Prendergast, he couldn't very well deny he was the young man's father. It could be what we need to break this case wide open."

"And how is that going to happen with Zach Worthington keeping Joe under lock and key inside a private room at the hospital?" Garcia said looking around at everyone. The expression on Garcia's face showed the frustration all of them were feeling.

Martin told him, "Then we'll just have to come up with some way of getting into his hospital room to talk to him. Does anyone have any ideas? Now is not the time to hold back."

Stone started to say something but stopped. He was interrupted by a knock at the door. Martin's face turned red. She had left specific instructions for the meeting not to be disturbed. Everyone's eyes fell on the office door. A young woman with auburn hair and a pretty face poked her head inside the room. Sheepishly, she looked at Keri Martin. "Chief, I'm sorry to bother your meeting, but someone from the hospital just called. They left a message that Joe Worthington wants to talk to Lieutenant Stone as soon as possible."

CHAPTER FORTY-FOUR

THE YOUNG MAN at the hospital information desk did not want to divulge Joe Worthington's room number. It took only a few choice words from Stone to get him to change his mind. A set of elevators was located off to the right of the information desk. Stone and Martin grabbed the closest elevator and took it to the fourth floor. After exiting they observed an armed security guard sitting in a chair outside of Worthington's room. The guard saw them as well. He quickly rose to his feet. Stone recognized the flattened nose and extended chin along with the rounded shoulders topping a large frame. The name of Bulinski came to mind. It belonged to an ex-pug who made a living out of intimidating people.

"Stay in back of me," Stone whispered to Martin as they both walked toward Joe Worthington's room.

"What are you doing here, Stone? You've got no business on this floor. These are all private rooms."

"Bulinski, there's two ways we can handle this. You step to the side and let us in the room, or I make your nose flatter than it already is. Make up your mind before I start taking you apart."

"Mayor Worthington is the one who hired me," Bulinski said feeling uneasy. The security guard knew only too well Stone's reputation. It caused him concern. "You try anything, Stone, and you're going against the mayor of Pelican's Landing. You'll have to answer to him for it."

Stone took hold of Bulinski's uniform shirt and moved him to the side. He then motioned for Martin to open the door. Stone waited until Keri had entered Worthington's room before releasing his hold on Bulinski. Turning his back on the security guard, Stone stepped into the room and closed the door behind him.

Joe Worthington was sitting up in his hospital bed. His face bore a deadpan expression. Stone thought of a poker player holding a losing hand. There would be no more cards dealt. The game was over.

"Joe, you look a lot better than the last time I saw you," Martin said, smiling. "But I'm sure you don't remember me. It was the day you were brought in here by ambulance to the hospital. I'm Police Chief Keri Martin."

"I remember you," Worthington said while letting his gaze fall on Stone. "It's just as well you came along, Chief Martin. It will save me from having to tell you later. Lieutenant, I'm ready to tell you everything about the girl who was found buried on Tanner's ranch. But you have to promise me something first."

"What's that?" Stone asked while not quite believing what he had just heard.

"That the police don't ever bother my wife. I don't want anyone talkin' to her, and that includes the people from the District Attorney's Office. Janet didn't know anything about the girl's death until I told her, and that was a little more than two hours ago. So do I have your word that my wife won't be bothered?"

Stone told him, "Yes, you do. But Joe, I have to first warn you that anything you tell Chief Martin and me could later be used against you in a court of law. You also have the right to an attorney. There's a phone next to your bed. If you want to talk things over with a lawyer before talking to us go ahead and make the call. We'll wait outside in the hallway until you're finished talking with him."

Worthington shook his head. "No, I don't want a lawyer. I just want to get this over with. The girl's name was Ginny Prendergast, and I met her while attending the University of Florida in Gainesville."

Joe Worthington went on to tell Stone and Martin how he had first met Prendergast at a local restaurant where she worked as a waitress. They dated for a couple of months, but Worthington broke things off with her after he started dating someone else. He had not seen nor heard from Prendergast for more than a year when he got a letter from her over a summer break. She told him in the letter that she wanted to come to Pelican's Landing and spend the weekend with him. He wrote back and told her to come.

Stone observed Worthington's head slump forward. Both his arms started to shake. Martin apparently saw it as well by the expression on her face. Keeping his eyes downcast and voice low, Worthington started speaking in a steady monotone. He told Stone and Martin about the beach house and his putting the knockout drug in Prendergast's drink; and how Hardin and Costello had waited in the bedroom for the drug to take effect. Worthington admitted to the plan being his as well as to Hardin and Costello having sexual intercourse with Prendergast. He looked up at Stone with a strange look on his face. Worthington then went on to explain how the three of them had found the girl dead on the bedroom floor with a bloody head wound.

"After Hardin and Costello left I panicked, so I phoned my father and he came to the beach house. I told him what had happened and he called Roscoe Tanner who came to the beach house with Jimmy Burke. I watched from down the road and saw Tanner and Burke bring Ginny's body out of the beach house wrapped in a bed sheet. They put her in the back of Tanner's pickup truck and drove away. I never knew what they did with her body until I heard on the news that the skeletal remains of a human body were discovered on

Tanner's ranch. That's when the three of us started panicking all over again. Hardin must have persuaded Costello to go along with killing me. Because Sam had phoned to set up a meeting with the three of us at the beach house. But he and Hardin never showed up. Instead two Mexicans with guns came. Even after I knew what was happening, I couldn't believe Sam Costello would have gone along with having me killed. We had been friends since we were kids. He was the one person that I thought I could always count on."

"Who killed the girl?" Stone asked him.

"Both Sam and me always thought Hardin did it. He was the only one in the room alone with her. But she could have fallen and hit her head. It could've been an accident. I never wanted her to get hurt and end up dying. You've got to believe me."

"No, you just wanted her to be raped by your friends," Martin said while feeling disgusted at what she had just heard. "Do you have any idea why Ginny Prendergast came to Pelican's Landing to see you?"

"Not really. I thought it was about a weekend of sex. We had only dated for a couple months. We never had a serious relationship."

"Well, she didn't feel that way," Keri Martin said reaching into her handbag and removing the framed photograph of Thomas Prendergast. She handed it to Worthington. "This might be a strange way of doing things, but allow me to introduce you to your son."

Staring down, Worthington held the framed photograph in both hands. His dark green eyes grew larger. A look of vexation suddenly appeared on his face. Worthington brought the photograph closer. "He certainly looks like me."

"Well he should, he's your son," Martin said before reaching over and taking back the framed photograph. "Ginny Prendergast had come to Pelican's Landing to tell you that you were the father of her baby. She also wanted to tell you that she loved you. And she was hoping that the two of you would be married. But what did you do? You had sex with her and then gave her to your friends after first putting a knockout drug in her drink. And to set the matter straight, Ginny Prendergast didn't just accidentally fall down and hit her head and die. She was strangled to death."

"No," Worthington said displaying a look of disbelief. "I swear I thought she had hit her head and that's what killed her. Sure, Sam and I felt Hardin might have hit her or pushed her down, but we never figured on her being strangled. Hardin must have done it. I don't know why he did. But he had to have done it when he was alone in the bedroom with her."

Stone moved closer to Worthington. "Joe, you said you didn't tell Janet about Ginny Prendergast until a couple of hours ago. Did you ever tell anyone else? And what do you know about Hardin and Costello's deaths?"

"The three of us kept it our secret. We agreed not to tell anyone. I only told Janet because I wanted her hearing it from me and not finding out about it on the news. It nearly killed me to tell her. If you only saw the look on our face. It was like nothing I've ever seen. It was as though I took a knife and cut the very heart out of her. Janet was sitting in that chair holding our new baby when I told her. I watched her get up and walk out the door without saying anything."

Worthington started to cry. Stone could see the man was emotionally drained. Asking him about Hardin and Costello would have to wait. The important thing was to get Worthington's confession recorded. If Joe should later retract what he had said, it would only be Stone and Martin's sworn testimony that the District Attorney would be able to use in the prosecution of the case. And by that time Zach Worthington would have a team of the best criminal defense attorneys in the country defending his son.

"Joe, we would like to record your confession. Would you repeat what you just told us so Chief Martin can record it on her cellphone? I wouldn't ask you if wasn't important."

Worthington nodded. "Do whatever you want, Lieutenant. I'm beyond caring what happens to me anymore. Chief Martin tells me I have a son who before now I never even knew about. If I should meet my son someday, how am I going to tell him that I allowed his mother to be raped and murdered?"

Stone told him, "Joe, I don't know. Perhaps you could say to him that you did a stupid thing, and you did your best in trying to make up for it by telling the truth. That could be a good way to start."

"All right, I'll start trying to make up for it right now. Chief Martin are you ready to record my confession?"

"Yes, Joe, I am. You can begin with the first time you met Ginny Prendergast."

CHAPTER FORTY-FIVE

KERI MARTIN DID her best to keep the excitement from bursting forth. It was like winning a foot race after you had never one won a race before. The feeling was overwhelming. To think she and Stone had the recorded confession of Joe Worthington in the rape and murder of Ginny Prendergast. And along with it the evidence to show Zach Worthington had told Tanner and Burke to dispose of the girl's body. It was more than Martin could have ever hoped for. She glanced over at Stone. The two of them were walking out the hospital's front door. Keri hoped to witness some kind of a reaction on his face. But she saw nothing. There was only the look of a person in deep thought.

"Is something wrong?" Martin asked, not understanding why Stone didn't appear to be sharing in her excitement. "Worthington's confession will be admissible in court, won't it? I mean, we didn't miss anything, did we?"

"No, we didn't miss anything. We have Joe tied up good and tight. It's Zach I'm thinking about along with Tanner and Burke. Right now we have them on Compounding a Felony, which could get each of them five years in the penitentiary. But we'll need more leverage than that if we hope to persuade one of them to talk about Potts's murder."

"You must mean Burke when you say that. Because Worthington and Tanner would be facing the death penalty if they ever admitted to their part in Potts's murder. We know Burke only fired into the back of the unmarked car so he's someone we could deal with. Maybe we could arrange it so he pleas out to a lesser charge for his testimony against Worthington and Tanner. Is that what you're thinking?"

"Yes," Stone said while opening the blue Mustang's passenger side door for Martin. "But I don't think it will work, and I'll tell you why. Burke would have to be facing a lot more than five years in the pen before he'd ever consider testifying against Worthington and Tanner. He'd know Vinnie Palermo would have a hit out for him the minute he opened his mouth. No, we'll need something more to get Burke to talk. That's why Joe's confession couldn't have come at a better time. It's going to stir up a hornet's nest once it gets out. And right now that is exactly what we want."

Stone got in the Mustang's driver's side and started the car. He turned to Martin. "We'll have to call in some auxiliary police officers to guard Joe Worthington. It'll take one officer sitting outside his hospital room around the clock and maybe additional people if things heat up. Once Zach Worthington finds out Joe confessed, all hell is going to break loose. Vinnie Palermo is going to know all about it, and he's not going to sit still for it. We'll be getting too close to the Conigliaro Family for him to do just nothing."

"What do you think he'll do?" Martin asked as she watched Stone put the Mustang in gear and drive out of the hospital parking lot.

"I don't know, but it could mean an attempt on both our lives. Before it was just me they wanted dead, but now you're proving dangerous to them as well. They thought you'd be a pushover and look for cover once things got crazy. But like I told you that morning at the Crow's Nest. They were wrong about you."

"Yes, you did tell me that," Martin said feeling the emotion building up inside her. "After I first arrived at Pelican's Landing, you've done nothing but help me and give me your support, even when I made things difficult for you. Jackson, I can't thank you enough. The Prendergast's girl's murder would not have ended the way it did without you. The only reason Joe Worthington confessed was because he knew that he could trust you. He took you at your word when you told him his wife would never be bothered by the police or the district attorney's office. That's how much he respects you."

Keri reached over and squeezed Stone's right arm. He placed his left hand over hers, holding it for a moment. Each took a moment to look into the other's eyes. Smiling, Stone returned his gaze to the road ahead. Martin removed her hand and sat upright in the seat.

"Well, here's where I get out," Keri said after the Mustang stopped in front of the Holiday Inn's entrance doors. Stone watched Martin exit the passenger side door and enter the hotel lobby. He continued watching until her slender figure moved past the front desk only to disappear around a corner.

****

The overhead lights for the marina were brightly lit with only a few cars in the parking lot. If it were winter, things would have been quite different. Cars would have been parked everywhere, including along the roadway leading into the marina, not to mention the designated parking spaces adjacent to Treasure Island Boulevard. People from up north would be occupying every available space with their luxury boats docked at the marina's wharf. But with it being summer and most of the locals staying away from the marina at night, it was quiet and peaceful. Stone liked it that way. He preferred quiet and peaceful to the drunken parties and loud music that kept him awake all night.

Choosing a parking space close to the guard shack, Stone switched off the Mustang's ignition and got out of the car. He immediately felt the warm breeze coming off the Gulf of Mexico and along with it the pungent smell of sea water and brown kelp. Stone drank it in. Not wanting to let it go, he savored the overpowering scent before exhaling and closing the Mustang's door.

"Jackson, did you bring me the cigars you promised?"

Laughing, Stone held up a turquoise-colored box for Mike Pesky to see. "I told you that I wouldn't forget you three days in a row. I tied a rubber band around my baby finger so that I would remember."

Pesky hurried out of the guard shack toward Stone. A big smile instantly took over the security guard's chubby face. It caused his cheeks to puff out, leaving his black mustache to appear as a dark spot underneath his large nose. Pesky wiped a right hand across his sweaty forehead before taking the box of cigars from Stone.

"I smoked my last cigar two hours ago and was sure hopin' you'd remember tonight. Cuban Imperial Masters are the best cigars in the world. I can't afford 'em on my salary. If it wasn't for you, Jackson, I'd be smokin' those cheap cigars they sell at the flea market. The ones that fall apart almost as soon as you start smokin' 'em. I swear they're made out of dried seaweed that someone picked up off the beach. I can't thank you enough."

"Mike, you don't have to thank me," Stone said while watching Pesky tear the seal off the cigar box and remove one of the cigars. "Just keep a good eye on the *Roll of the Dice* for me. I'm working on something that could bring strangers down here looking to cause me some problems. If you see anybody hanging around the marina that you don't recognize make sure and call me right way. You still have my cellphone number, don't you?"

Pesky patted his front shirt pocket with his right hand. "I keep it close just in case I might need it. Jackson, don't you worry about the

Roll of the Dice. I'll look after her like she's my own daughter, and that means nobody gets near her. She's as safe as a girl kneeling in church with Mike Pesky standin' guard."

"Thanks Mike," Stone said before tapping Pesky on his left shoulder and walking away. Stone looked back to observe the security guard lighting the cigar with a match prior to stepping into the guard shack. It would prove difficult for anyone to get by Pesky without being seen. The thought brought some comfort to Stone as he headed down the marina's wharf toward the *Roll of the Dice*.

There were relatively few boats docked at the wharf. Stone knew most of the owners by name, and if not by name, then by sight. But nobody was present on any of the boats or along the wharf. It was a dark night. Darker than usual with an overcast sky and only the standing lights of the wharf giving off any light. Stone walked up onto the *Roll of the Dice* and adhering to his usual protocol removed the Beretta 9mm from his waistband. He stepped onto the deck and began checking for anyone who might be hidden among the shadows. Discovering no one, Stone flipped on the light switch for below deck. He proceeded down the ladder, holding the Beretta in his right hand. Stone nearly pulled the Beretta's trigger after spotting a person seated in one of the chairs at the table.

"What are you doing here?"

"Lieutenant Stone, I heard somethin' today that I knew you'd want to know about so I swam the channel and waited for you. I hope you're not mad at me."

Billy Turlop was seated with his arms around his knees in a ball. He had on only a pair of jean cutoffs and looked as if he were freezing. His brown hair was wet and his upper body shaking. Stone took a wool blanket off the counter top to cover the boy.

"Billy, I haven't seen you since you and Josh killed that snake on Tanner's ranch and discovered the dead body. What was so important to make you swim a fifty yard channel at night to come and see me? Couldn't it have waited until tomorrow morning?"

"I wanted you to know right away that I heard Jimmy Burke tellin' a guy this afternoon that Mr. Tanner has a meth lab down at Cattail Marsh, and he plans on movin' a shipment of white crystal to Miami tomorrow night once it gets dark. Lieutenant Stone, you told me to keep my eyes and ears open and to let you know the minute I knew somethin'. So that's why I'm here."

"So you heard Burke say to the guy Cattail Marsh tomorrow night. And you're sure he mentioned the meth lab and that a load of white crystal was being moved to Miami after it got dark?"

Billy Turlop nodded. "That's what I heard Jimmy Burke tell the guy. And he didn't seem to care who might've heard it either. Josh was there and so were some of the other guys. We were all sittin' around waitin' for our pay."

Stone popped open a can of soda. He handed the can to Turlop. Stone had known Billy Turlop since the boy was eight years old. Billy's mother had phoned the Pelican Landing's Police Department one day about a live-in boyfriend who knocked her almost senseless in a drunken rage. Hiding behind a couch, Billy had watched Stone pick up his mother's boyfriend and throw him out the front door of the trailer home they were living in. Stone told the man to never come back if he did not want to spend a month or two in the hospital thinking over the mistake he had made. Ever since then Turlop looked upon Stone as the father that he always wished he had, someone he could be like once he became a man. A bond had formed over the years between them. Billy wanted nothing more than to become a Pelican's Landing police officer. Stone promised him that one day he would.

"Let's get going," Stone said. "Your mother is probably wondering where you are and I don't want her getting mad at me. And if you're right about Tanner moving the meth crystal tomorrow night, I have a lot of work to do."

Stone put his right arm around Billy Turlop and directed the boy to the ladder leading to the *Roll of the Dice's* upper deck.

CHAPTER FORTY-SIX

ZACH WORTHINGTON CHANGED taxis three times before walking the last two blocks to the restaurant. He did not want to take the chance on being followed. Luigi's Ristorante was located on Mulberry Street in New York's Lower Manhattan. Worthington knew the FBI would be aware of his early morning flight from Fort Myers, Florida, to LaGuardia Airport. There might even have been federal agents in New York waiting to follow him. But Worthington did not waste any time trying to find out. He had grabbed the first available taxi and left the airport. Luckily for Zach the ex-pug Bulinski had placed his ear up to the hospital room door while Stone and Martin were inside talking to Joey. Bulinski heard everything. He telephoned Zack the minute Stone and Martin had left the room.

"That's right, Mayor. Your son just told them two cops all about how the girl was raped and killed, and how you had Tanner and Burke get rid of the body. If I were you, Mayor, I'd get out of town for a while. You know, until you figure out which way the wind is blowin'. But before you do, leave a thousand dollars inside a sealed white envelope for me at your downtown office. That way no one else will find out about this conversation we're having."

Worthington entered Luigi's through the front door. He quickly walked to the back of the restaurant where a burly hulk of a man stopped him. The man looked formidable dressed in a dark suit and tie with no expression showing. He had black, curly hair, which hung down past his shoulders. His eyes were cold and gray. Worthington found it hard to look into them. The man placed his right hand against Worthington's chest; the smell of garlic came off his breath. Worthington knew the drill, so he raised both arms above his head. The man ran two large hands up and down Worthington's body before stepping back. There was a closed door off to the right. The man pointed to it. Worthington turned the door's handle and walked into a room.

"I expected to be meeting with Vinnie. Did he get tied up with something?"

"No, he sent me instead. Did you make sure that you weren't being followed?" Al Ruggiero asked pointing to a chair. "I don't want the FBI busting through the door and you sitting here like we were friends. I don't need that kind of trouble."

"Why did you have to say that? Is Vinnie mad at me for coming to New York? What else was I supposed to do? My own son gave me up to the police. Al, you and me have been friends for years. If I can't count on you and Vinnie, then I might as well turn myself in and take my chances in court."

Ruggiero smiled and shook his head. "Vinnie and me aren't turning our backs on you, Zach. You're family. It's just that with the gambling operation starting up and the other families waiting for a reason to come down on us, Vinnie doesn't want any rat hair getting in the marinara sauce right about now. You can understand that."

"Rat hair? Is that how Vinnie looks at me? I married into his family and built up Diamond Systems, Inc. into the company it is today. I've been loyal to him all these years. Five years ago the feds put me before a grand jury and tried to get me to testify against Vinnie. They threatened me with perjury, income tax evasion, you name it.

And I kept my trap shut. Now I'm rat hair as far as Vinnie is concerned?"

"Zach, what do you want Vinnie to do? Do you want Joey whacked? Is that why you came here to New York? You tell me and I'll tell Vinnie. What do you want the family to do for you?"

"I don't know exactly. I've never been in a fix like this before. Joey told Chief Martin and Stone that I had Tanner and Burke take the girl's body out of the beach house. That puts me right in the middle of the girl's murder. I wouldn't have a chance in court with my own son's confession in evidence against me. I'll go to jail for sure."

"What are we talkin' about? A few years on a plea? You had nothing to do with the girl's murder, only getting rid of her body to protect your son. What father wouldn't have done the same for his kid? You're makin' too much out of this. Go back to Pelican's Landing and let them arrest you. We'll hire the best lawyers in the country, and you'll get nothing but the minimum sentence. They might even get you probation where you won't have to go to jail."

"But what about Diamond Systems, Inc.? And my being mayor of Pelican's Landing? I'd be a convicted felon once I got out. I could no longer be mayor, and the feds would be watching every move I made. I'd no longer be any use to the Conigliaro Family. Vinnie would see me as a liability and want me far away from everything. No, he has to do something about this right away. Al, you've got to tell Vinnie that I can't go to jail."

"Are you talkin' about having Joey whacked? Is that what you're asking me to tell Vinnie?"

"Who knows what Tanner and Burke might do. They took the girl's body out of the beach house and buried it. Stone will be arresting them, too. They could say anything about me. I wouldn't have a chance in court with the two of them and Joey testifying against me."

"So you do want Joey whacked. Aren't you somethin'. But I'll have to hear you say it before I pass it on to Vinnie. Tell me you want your own son whacked."

"Al, I'm sorry, but I can't see any other way out of this. Tell Vinnie that I want Joey taken out before he leaves the hospital."

CHAPTER FORTY-SEVEN

THE HUMIDITY WAS almost unbearable. The heavy night air made it difficult to breathe. Keri Martin felt as though she were taking in cotton balls with each breath she took. The sky was dark and overcast. That was good. They would not be standing out like silhouettes under a moonlit sky. Stone seemed tenser than usual. It had been evident in his voice prior to their leaving the police station; that was when he told Keri to stay close to him, not to take any chances. Even now she could sense it in him. The touch of his fingers on her bare hand. The way his head stayed rigid without moving. Carollo, Moore, and Garcia must have picked up on it as well. They stood huddled close to him. Closer than normal. Their bodies brushing against his body. Like a pack closing in on its alpha member. Keri could barely make out Stone's face. It was hidden in the shadow of the cypress tree.

"Everyone knows their assignment," he said to them. "Moore and Garcia will take the back of the trailer. Chief Martin, Carollo, and I will take the front. I'll knock twice on the trailer door and identify us as police officers and tell them that we have a search warrant. If there is no immediate response from Tanner or Burke, I'll use the sledge hammer on the door. Carollo goes in first and I follow him in. Chief Martin will be behind me. Remember no one fires their gun unless they're fired upon, and they've got a definite target. Are there any questions?"

Stone knew it was past the time for questions. They had been over the plan numerous times since he and Carollo first walked the barely passable road leading into Cattail Marsh. Billy Turlop had been right about the meth lab. Tanner and Burke occupied a small trailer parked on a grassy spot near the edge of the Everglades. There was only one way in by car or truck. But escape could be possible if they had a boat tied up somewhere close to the water. Cypress, pine, and elm trees encircled the trailer along with thickets of tall, large-leafed, saw palmetto plants. Tanner's red pickup was parked close to the road. It had a load on its back covered over with a black tarp. There were lights on inside the trailer and an outside spotlight illuminating the front door. Stone was about to give the order to move out when he stopped himself. Something did not seem right. A hollowed-out feeling seized his stomach. If the truck was loaded, what were Tanner and Burke waiting for? It was almost midnight. The trailer had been under surveillance for hours and nothing had changed. Billy Turlop said they would be moving the white crystal once it got dark. And then there was the outside spotlight. It meant that he, Carollo, and Martin would be sitting targets for anyone hiding among the trees and saw palmetto plants. Tanner had set up Potts using the abandoned creamery. Was he now attempting a similar ruse with the meth lab? The words uttered by Turlop came back to Stone. "That's what I heard Jimmy Burke tell the guy. And he didn't seem to care who might've heard it either."

"There's a switch in plans," Stone abruptly said. The tone in his voice caught the four of them off guard. "I'm sure this is a trap Tanner has laid for us. The two of them aren't inside the trailer. They're waiting somewhere outside in the saw palmetto plants. They want us to walk up to the front door as big as you please with that light shining down. Well, we're going to disappoint them. Lisa and

Bob, I want you guys to take the stand of saw palmetto plants along the water. Carollo and I will take the ones closest to the road. Chief Martin will stay here and keep an eye on the pickup. We don't want Tanner and Burke jumping into the truck and taking off with a load of white crystal."

Keri started to object, but Stone stopped her. "You're the best shot out of all of us, that's why I'm asking you to stay right here. If Tanner and Burke should make it to the pickup, I want you to use your Glock and shoot out the truck's front tires. They won't get far on two flat tires. Besides that, the four of us have 12 gauge shotguns. We're better armed for crawling through the saw palmetto plants. And as for the rest of you, it's going to be close quarter shooting so be careful you don't shoot your partner. Tanner and Burke will likely be carrying submachine guns. Probably the Koch MP5. It's the most common and effective submachine on the market today. So be ready for it. After the 9mm bursts start up, don't go into a panic. Just keep your heads down and shoot at the flashes. And whatever you do, don't take any unnecessary chances. I want everyone going home tonight. Are we ready?"

"Yes," they whispered in one voice. Moore and Garcia quickly headed toward the water. Stone and Carollo turned in the direction of the road. Martin grabbed Stone's right arm. No matter how much she tried to shake the feeling it would not leave her. Stone would not be coming back. Tanner was going to kill him. 'Don't go,' Martin wanted to say but she didn't. "Jackson, good luck," Keri said before releasing Stone's arm and stepping back under the cypress tree.

****

Roscoe Tanner fought to keep his rage from consuming him. The heat and humidity were like nothing he had ever experienced. The mosquitoes were unrelenting, and the closeness of the saw palmetto plants made breathing problematic. Prior to entering the thicket, Tanner and Burke had doused themselves with insect repellant. But that was hours ago. Since then the repellent had washed away by their heavy, merciless perspiration. They were both soaking wet, dark shirts sticking to chests and backs. The men's sweat continued to draw throngs of mosquitoes. Little devils with wings. Creatures unremitting in their attack, especially for anyone foolish enough to enter their domain.

It was becoming too much for Tanner. The unbearable heat and the effort needed just to take a breath. Not to mention the constant buzzing of mosquitoes along with the slew of stinging bites. Where the hell was Stone? Why hadn't he and his deputies approached the trailer? It had turned dark hours ago. What were they waiting for? Surely Stone's informant had heard Burke spreading the news about the meth lab, and the shipment of white crystal going to Miami. But maybe Stone didn't know? Maybe Stone no longer had an informant secreted on the Tanner ranch. And he and Burke were sitting in a thicket of saw palmetto plants being chewed alive by mosquitoes and sweating their asses off.

"They should've been here by now," Tanner said to Burke who was resting on his knees next to him. "Are you sure that you spread the word around to everybody about the meth lab? You told them that it was at Cattail Marsh, didn't you? And you said it was right after dark that we were movin' the shipment to Miami?"

"Yeah, I made sure everybody knew about it," Burke said in reply. It was the third time he had answered the same questions in the last two hours. Between Tanner and the mosquitoes and the lousy air Burke was more than ready to jump out of his skin. He didn't know how much more of this sitting around with Tanner he could take. Where was Stone, and why hadn't he shown up? If there were an informant on the Tanner ranch, Stone would be aware of the meth lab and that a load of white crystal was being transported to Miami. Why then hadn't he shown? Where was he?

Burke tilted back on his knees and sat down. Picking up the Koch MP5 from off the ground next to him, he rested the submachine gun on his lap. There was a buzzing around his right ear. Burke swatted at it with an open hand. Tanner had to be out of his mind following through with his plan to kill Stone. It was something only a crazy man would do. Murdering Stone and a bunch of his deputies on Tanner's own property was absolutely insane. Burke wanted no part of it. He even told Tanner that he wanted out. He told him that morning after breakfast when the two of them were heading to the barn to break out the Koch MP5s. They were going to test fire the guns behind the barn. Tanner had grabbed Burke by the throat.

"You'll do exactly what I tell you to do and nothin' different. Your ass is in the same sling mine is in. We killed Potts, and Stone won't rest until he finds out who did it. Remember that tonight when you see him walking up to the trailer's front door. You need him dead as much as I do. If given half a chance, he'll put each of us on death row, and that includes your precious little Marci. That's why we have to get him first. Don't ever mention to me again about your backing out. I'll kill you if you do."

Burke could still feel Tanner's hands squeezing his throat. It was not something he would forget anytime soon. He told Marci that he would have to go through with it. There was nothing else he could do. Besides, his share for delivering the white crystal to Miami would be worth at least twenty thousand. That along with the rest of the money they had saved should take care of the two of them for a long time. Burke had sent Marci ahead to Miami to purchase two one-way tickets to Mexico City. Once in Mexico they could obtain false passports, which would help them travel to South America. Brazil or Argentina sounded good. Any place where Stone and the FBI would not find them. Tanner slapped Burke on his left shoulder.

"Two of them with shotguns down by the water. Did you see 'em?"

"Yeah, I saw 'em. It doesn't look like Stone fell for your trap, now does it?"

"And there's two more. They're coming on our side. And they have shotguns, too. The tall one looks like Stone. He must've figured we're hiding in the saw palmetto plants."

"But he doesn't know where," Burke said.

"No, he doesn't. And that's our ace in the hole. We'll wait for the two of 'em here. Once I start firing, you do the same, and don't stop until I do. This is going to be the last time in this life Stone comes lookin' for me."

****

Stone and Carollo dropped to their knees. They immediately began crawling into the large thicket of saw palmetto plants. The plants proved to be dense and unyielding. Unforgiving as well. The tall stalks were covered in sharp, prickly needles that scratched Stone and Carollo's exposed arms and cheeks. Hungry mosquitoes driven mad by the scent of blood swarmed the two men. It caused Stone and Carollo to quicken their pace. They continued to move forward, dragging the 12 gauge shotguns with them. Stone abruptly came to a halt. Reaching over, he touched Carollo on his right arm. It was dark inside the thicket. Stone could barely make out Carollo's face. If this was how it was going to be, how would they ever see Tanner and Burke in this maze?

"We could crawl up on them and not even know it," Stone said taking a deep breath. "We're going to have to spread out more, and hopefully hear them before they hear us. What do you think?"

Carollo slapped at the buzzing mosquitoes around his face. "I quit thinking the minute we crawled into this hell-hole. Both of us are going to need a blood transfusion by the time we get out here. All right, I'll veer to the left while you go straight ahead. But don't forget I'm to the left of you. I don't want a round of double-ought buckshot hitting me in the ass."

"Don't worry, I'll remember," Stone said before pushing forward through the dense saw palmetto.

The sound of a shotgun blast stopped him. It came from somewhere on the other side of the house trailer near the water. Moore and Garcia. One of them had discharged their shotgun. But there was no automatic fire preceding or following the blast. Lisa Moore's face appeared in Stone's mind. It had to have been Lisa. Earlier Stone had witnessed the nervousness in her. Besides, Garcia had military service. He was a combat veteran. Lisa, don't let it bother you, Stone found himself thinking. No harm done. Get on with the task at hand.

Stone resumed crawling. He tried to keep the point of his chin tucked tight against his chest. But the sharp needles scratched his face anyway. And then he heard them. Two voices off to his right. Did Carollo hear them? Probably not. The FBI agent was too far left. Stone wondered what to do? Should he move closer, or start firing at the sound of the voices? Stone chose the former. Releasing the shotgun's safety, he proceeded slowly to his right.

"Damn it, where are they?" There was no mistaking the voice. It belonged to Tanner. The rancher and his foreman were no more than 10 to 15 yards in front of him. The sound of an open hand slapping bare skin came to Stone. One of them killed a pesky mosquito. Should he move closer? Stone knew that he would be taking a chance. Tanner or Burke might hear him moving through the saw palmetto plants. No, the time was now, he told himself. Shoot before they know where you are. Coming to a standing position, Stone cut loose with the 12 gauge shotgun.

He directed his fire 10 to 15 yards in front of him. Round after round of double-ought buck tore through the saw palmetto plants. A man screamed. Another swore. Stone dropped to the ground. He flattened his body against the sandy soil. It was fortunate that he did because a barrage of machine gunfire erupted. The gun flashes lit up the dark field. A spray of bullets flew all around Stone. Relinquishing his hold on the shotgun, Stone took the Beretta 9mm from his waistband.

A shotgun blast to Stone's left sounded. More blasts followed. Carollo was firing at the machine gun flashes. Tanner and Burke directed their gunfire at Carollo. Seeing the opportunity, Stone quickly came to his feet. He repeatedly fired the Beretta at the flashes in front of him. Then there were no more flashes. It became quiet. Someone stood upright and ran toward the pickup truck.

Stone observed Keri Martin hurrying out from the cypress tree. She dropped to a shooting position and fired two rounds in the direction of the pickup. Shifting her aim, Martin fired three more rounds at the ground in front of the man running. The man stopped and raised his hands. Earlier he had discarded his weapon. Moving closer, Stone recognized Burke. Martin was in the process of forcing the ranch foreman to his knees. She ordered him to place both hands behind his back. Stone glanced over at the pickup truck. The front tires were flat. Martin had shot out the tires from more than forty yards away.

"Stone, don't shoot," Burke said staring up at Stone. "Tanner's dead and I give up. You've got to believe me, I wanted no part of this. It was all Tanner's doing. He made me do it."

"Just like he made you shoot Potts?" Stone said slapping handcuffs on both of Burke's wrists. "I don't buy any of it."

"But you have to. Tanner killed Potts. I only fired into the back seat of the car."

"You were there. That's enough for me."

"But I didn't kill him. You can't put a man on death row for somethin' he didn't do."

Carollo walked up to Stone. "Tanner's dead. I was really hoping that we could take him alive. But unfortunately things didn't work out. So much for getting him to flip on Zach Worthington."

"Worthington? Is that who you want?" Burke said while struggling to get himself to a standing position. "I can help you get Worthington."

"Did you hear Worthington give the order to kill Potts?" Carollo asked him.

"No, he only told Tanner. And I wasn't there. But Tanner said Worthington got the okay to kill Potts from Al Ruggiero, Vinnie Palermo's underboss. I'll swear to that in court if it would help me out."

"Hearsay isn't admissible. Your testimony wouldn't do us any good."

"But then how about another murder? I can give you Worthington on a different murder."

Stone moved closer to Burke. He brought his face within inches of Burke's face. "What murder would that be?"

"The girl buried on Tanner's ranch," Burke said. "Zach Worthington strangled her and I saw him do it."

CHAPTER FORTY-EIGHT

THE POLICE INTERROGATION room was 10 feet by 12 feet. It had a steel bench with handcuff rings attached to one wall and a table with two chairs in its center. There were no windows. A ceiling light illuminated the room. Visible over the only door was a video camera. It allowed for police interrogations to be recorded and used later in court. The camera was connected to a TV monitor in Chief Martin's office. The room temperature remained a steady seventy degrees Fahrenheit. Jimmy Burke found the room a bit warm. He was sweating profusely.

"How many times do I have to tell you guys? Worthington strangled her and I saw him do it. We've been over it so many times I'm startin' to lose my voice. I can't testify in court against Worthington if I can't talk. How many more times do you guys have to hear it?"

"Until we tell you to stop," Stone said coming out his chair. Stone looked over at Carollo who was standing in a corner of the room. Carollo nodded his head. The FBI special agent was more than satisfied. Stone nodded back. He, too, was satisfied. They had all that they needed to charge Zach Worthington with first degree murder. Burke's recounting of the strangulation death of Ginny Prendergast had exceeded all their expectations. His court testimony alone would put Worthington on Florida's death row. Burke was sitting at the table with his hands folded. Stone came back around to face him. "Jimmy, start from the beginning where Tanner gets the phone call from Worthington. And he wants you and Tanner to come to the beach house right away."

Stone kept an extra white shirt in his office in case of an emergency. Earlier he had given the shirt to Burke. The ranch foreman's black shirt had been stained by Tanner's blood. Staring back at Stone, Burke now ran the shirt's right sleeve across his sweaty face.

"After Worthington's phone call, Tanner and me drove to the beach house in Tanner's pickup. Worthington came out to meet us. He said there was a dead woman inside the beach house and he wanted us to get rid of the body. Tanner asked him what happened, but Worthington just shook his head and started back toward the beach house. We followed him and he took us to a bedroom where a girl about eighteen or nineteen was sitting on a bed with her hands covering her face. She was crying and didn't have any clothes on. I could tell Worthington was surprised by how he looked at her. He grabbed one of the girl's arms and she started screaming saying that she had been raped and wanted the police to be called. That's when Worthington slapped her and pushed her down onto the bed. Tanner and me just stood there watching, not quite believing what was happening. Worthington then got on top of the girl and started choking her. She didn't put up much of a fight with him straddling her. It was over in less than a minute. He got off her and told us to wrap the girl's body in the bed sheet, and dump it some place where nobody would find it. And that's what Tanner and me done. We buried the body at the spot where the police found it on Tanner's ranch."

"And what about her clothes?" Stone asked him. "And her suitcase with her other belongings? She had to have had a purse. Did you and Tanner take them along with the body?"

"No, like I told you before. We just wrapped her in the bed sheet. We didn't touch her clothes or anything else. Worthington must've got rid of everything after we left."

Carollo came out of the corner and placed both his hands on the table. "Did you see anybody else besides Tanner and Zach Worthington there? Do you know Joe Worthington? Was he anywhere around during the time you and Tanner were at the beach house?"

"No, just Zach Worthington. There was nobody else. Now I told you everything I know. What happens to me after this? You'll give me and my wife protection, won't ya? You're not goin' to put us in jail so they can kill us?"

Stone told him, "You will be going before a grand jury tomorrow morning and testify to everything. About how you and Tanner went to the beach house to meet Worthington and how he killed the girl. Afterwards, U.S. Marshals will put you on a plane to Miami where your wife, Marci, will be waiting. The FBI has arranged for the two of you to be taken out of state and placed in the federal witness protection program. If you have any other questions save them for the FBI because I'm through talking to you."

Carollo's cellphone rang. The FBI special agent answered it before leaving the room. Stone quickly followed him out the door. Keri Martin and Lisa Moore were waiting outside in the hallway. They wore matching smiles, and a sparkle appeared in each of their eyes. Keri grabbed Stone by his right arm.

"Jackson, Lisa and I saw and heard everything on the TV monitor in my office. We can now get Zach Worthington charged with the Prendergast girl's murder, and who knows where that might lead us. Worthington might even give us Vinnie Palermo for killing Potts. I can't tell you how happy I am. It has worked out far better than I ever thought it would."

"It'll all depend on Worthington," Stone said appreciating the happy smile on Martin's face. "We have to arrest him before we can talk to him. He's left town and, who knows where he's at right now."

"LaGuardia Airport in New York," Carollo said while placing his cellphone back into his coat pocket. "I phoned the FBI field office in New York City right after Burke implicated Worthington in the Prendergast girl's murder. Federal agents took Worthington into custody a little over an hour ago. He was getting on a flight to take him back to Florida. After being told Burke fingered him for the girl's murder, Worthington started asking about a deal. He knows Burke's eyewitness testimony against him and his son, Joe, placing him on the scene wouldn't give him a chance in court. He'd end up getting the death penalty for sure. They told me that Worthington's asking for a life sentence and protection. In exchange, he'll give us Vinnie Palermo and Al Ruggiero for Potts's murder along with the murders of Hardin and Costello. He'll also testify to the money laundering scheme the Conigliaro Family used with Diamond Systems, Inc. That should bring down the entire organization."

"What are you going to do with Zach?" Stone asked after seeing the pieces finally coming together. "Palermo will have a hit out for him the minute he hears Worthington was charged with murder. Vinnie won't take a chance on Worthington making a deal like the one he's making now. How are you going to protect him?"

Carollo smiled before answering. "As we speak, Zach Worthington is being transported to the Jacksonville Federal Penitentiary in Jacksonville, Florida, where he is going to have 24 hour protection. Let Vinnie Palermo try and get to him there."

****

The Crow's Nest was just opening up when Stone and Martin arrived for breakfast. After turning on the inside lights, Fredek Lantos hurried out of the kitchen to greet them. Lantos was wearing a chef's white smock and a black nylon hair net. Both his hands were covered in white flour. Fredek had been making the dough for apple strudel when he observed Stone and Martin coming through the front door. As far as he was concerned nothing was too good for Jackson Stone, or for that matter the new police chief, Keri Martin. Fredek's wife, Ada, had noticed how Stone and Martin would look at one another whenever they were together. Especially while seated at their favorite table in the far corner of the Crow's Nest.

"Fredek, they look at each other like we once did," Ada had said to her husband on a day Stone and Martin came to the restaurant for breakfast. "Remember before we were married. And we hid in the old church in Budapest dreaming of coming to America to start a new life. We had the same look in our eyes that they have now. You just don't remember."

"Do you really think so?" Fredek said while wondering if what Ada was saying could be true. But then she would know, he told himself. Women see things that men don't often take notice of.

"A plate of eggs over easy and a slab of ham to go with it," Stone said to Fredek before patting the Crow's Nest owner on the back. "And a pot of black coffee to wash it all down."

"And Chief Martin, what would you like?" Lantos asked peering into Keri Martin's green eyes. Fredek tried but he could not detect anything in them. The woman's eyes were beautiful, for sure, but he could only see their color. What was he missing? Lantos told himself that he would have to speak to Ada about it.

"Just a poached egg and rye toast for me, Fredek. And black coffee sounds good. Jackson and I have had a long night at work."

Lantos rushed off to the kitchen. Stone and Martin went to the rear of the restaurant to their usual table. Keri sat down. Stone removed his sport coat and placed it on the back of his chair. Keri watched as he sat down opposite her. Scratch marks from the saw palmetto plants were visible on Stone's face and arms. He looked as if he had been attacked by a wild animal. Smiling, Keri ran her index finger over the marks on his right arm.

"Do they hurt?" she asked him.

Stone looked down. "No, not anymore," he said taking hold of her finger. "Not after getting Burke's videotaped confession and having Zach Worthington in federal custody. Nothing could hurt me after that. Maybe nothing ever will again. I can't remember feeling this good. It reminds me of what Potts used to say whenever he was drunk and feeling no pain. 'Jackson, there's nothin' like tellin' the world to stick its head up its ass to get rid of whatever's botherin' ya.'"

Keri laughed. "You miss him, don't you?"

"Every day. It's always nice to have someone who knows the real you and not the person you're trying to make yourself out to be. I didn't have to be Lieutenant Jackson Stone with Potts. The tough cop no one ever gets one over on. I could be myself. It's nice when you have someone like that. Somebody you can really talk to. And yes, I do miss him."

Keri moved forward in her chair. She could feel the emotion building inside her. Did he know that she was in love with him? God, he should know. Didn't he see it in her every time she was with him? "You can be yourself with me, can't you?" she finally got up the nerve to ask him. Keri hoped Stone would say something. Something about how he felt about her. After all, he was holding onto her finger. "I mean, we're friends, aren't we?"

Stone brought Keri's finger up to his lips. "Yes, and hopefully a great deal more," he said to her. "Because I'm in love with you. I think it all started that first day you arrived in Pelican's Landing. We met at the gravesite on Tanner's ranch and Zach Worthington told me that I wasn't to talk to Tanner about the girl's body. You came between us and told him you were the chief of police and he wasn't giving orders to your people. And then later you jumped in front of

Tanner and me when we were nose to nose. Keri, there was a fire in you that I'd never seen in any other woman. And that same fire showed itself at the Blue Marlin when you put three bullet holes an inch apart in the dart board on the wall. You stopped the *Satan's Ramblers* before they could even get started. But it was the night we found Potts dead, and we were standing in the rain. I was hurting and you kissed me. That's when I knew for sure that I was in love with you."

"Jackson," Keri said with tears filling her eyes. "You have no idea how happy you've made me. Let's go somewhere together. Let's find a place where we can be alone. And for a little while forget about Zach Worthington and Vinnie Palermo and all the other evil in this world that we've had to deal with these past weeks. Just you and me, and no one else. How does that sound?"

"It's like you read my mind," Stone said while taking Keri's hand inside his two hands. "There's a month long festival going on down in South Padre Island off the coast of Texas. I try to make it every year if possible. We can take the *Roll of the Dice* and be there in no time. You'll absolutely love it. There's a party atmosphere that I haven't experienced anywhere else. What do you think? Say yes and we'll go."

"Yes," Keri said overcome with excitement. "Let's go right now. We'll pack a few things and tell Lisa Moore to take charge until we get back. I was going to talk to you about promoting her to sergeant anyway. I can be ready in half an hour."

"No, we'll have to wait until everything is squared away with Burke and Worthington first. It should only take a couple of days. Once Burke testifies at the grand jury and Worthington is charged with Potts's murder and all the other charges against him, we'll pack up and go. Is that okay with you?"

"As long as you promise that you won't change your mind. Because I'm going to hold you to it. I'm even going out later today to buy a new bathing suit for the trip so you better not come up with some other reason two days from now."

Stone laughed. "No, we'll be going, and we'll take our time getting there. There's a lot of beautiful coastline to see between here and South Padre Island."

Fredek Lantos approached Stone and Martin's table carrying a large metal tray. He set a plate of food down in front of each of them. A pot of steaming, black coffee was placed in the center of the table. While preparing to leave, Lantos happened to look over at Keri Martin. What he saw in her eyes caused him to glance at Stone. Instantly, a smile appeared on Lantos's face. As usual, his wife had been right. Stone and Martin were in love. Not wasting any time, the owner of the Crow's Nest hurried off to the kitchen. He could hardly wait to tell Ada what he had seen.

CHAPTER FORTY-NINE

Spring Lake, New Jersey

A GRIM-FACED VINNIE Palermo looked out over the Atlantic Ocean. It was an overcast afternoon, almost dismal compared to other days. Three-foot white caps streamed across the water's surface while a cool northeast wind blew, unimpeded, in Vinnie's face. It was not a good day to be on the water. Too choppy and cool for Vinnie's taste. But then, circumstances made it necessary. The head of the Conigliaro Family was left with no other choice. He, along with Al Ruggiero, the family's underboss, and Alex Mallo, the family's consigliore, were on Palermo's luxury ocean yacht, *The Predator,* cruising off the New Jersey coastline. Vinnie estimated *The Predator* to be about twenty miles out. Far enough distance from land to escape the FBI's eavesdropping capabilities.

"Where do the feds have Worthington?" Palermo asked staring into Al Ruggiero's eyes. Vinnie was surprised at his friend's frightened look. It was the first time he had witnessed such a look in Ruggiero.

"The federal prison at Jacksonville. It's maximum security and probably the safest place they could find for him. Vinnie, it'll be tough getting to Worthington. We've got people on the inside working on it, but time is running out for us. Worthington has to be whacked right away. And it has to be done prior to his testifying before a federal grand jury or we're all going down for murder and everything else they can throw at us."

"Vinnie, you have to do something," Alex Mallo said grabbing Palermo's left arm. "You've got to have Worthington killed before he can testify. We wouldn't have a chance in hell of beating a RICO charge if he takes the stand. Worthington can connect all three of us to Diamond Systems, Inc. and the money laundering behind the shakedowns, gambling, prostitution and the rest of the family's business. The news media would have a field day. Vinnie, what are you going to do?"

Palermo shook loose Mallo's hand. "So now you want to dirty your hands with a killing. Before you wanted no part of it because whacking somebody was beneath you. It was the part of the family business that you chose to ignore. But with your ass on the line you can't wait for Worthington to get whacked. Alex, if you weren't such a good lawyer I'd kill you right now, cousin or no cousin of mine."

"But Vinnie, this is different. Worthington can put all of us …"

"Shut up. If you open your mouth again, I'm going to knock you out of your chair." Palermo turned to face Ruggiero. "Al, what are the odds of us getting to Worthington before the feds have him in front of a grand jury?"

"I figure thirty percent if the guys on the inside move within the next two days. After that, who knows? They might move Worthington to a different prison or some safe house we don't know about. No, our best chance is within the next two days."

"Then tell our people on the inside to go ahead with it. And at the same time Worthington is getting whacked, I want Johnny Rocco and Blowtorch Charlie to move on Stone and Chief Martin. Coordinate it so the hits take place simultaneously. If Stone and Martin should hear that Worthington got taken out, it would put them on guard. They'd be extra careful. So get a hold of Rocco right away and tell him what I want."

"Will do, Vinnie," Ruggiero said looking into Palermo's dark eyes and gathering strength from them. "It will be done just as you say."

Alex Mallo raised his right hand. Vinnie stared hard at him. After seeing Palermo nod his head, Mallo lowered his hand and came erect in his chair. The family's consigliore found it difficult to meet Palermo's gaze.

"As the family's attorney I have to advise caution with respect to killing Chief Martin and Lieutenant Stone. Are we not in enough trouble as it is with Worthington testifying against us? Killing Martin and Stone could end up landing us in even more trouble. It could give the feds and the news media a national platform to focus on the Conigliaro Family, and not letting up until we were all charged with murder. I advise that we take care of Worthington first and then turn our attention, if need be, to Martin and Stone later."

"So that's what you advise?" Palermo asked him.

"Yes, it is. Caution should be our number one priority."

Vinnie Palermo wanted to tell Alex the real reason for his wanting Martin and Stone killed. They had gotten Joe Worthington to implicate his father, Zach, in the girl's murder at Pelican's Landing. And afterward they had arrested Tanner's foreman, Burke, and obtained his confession, which had further implicated Zach Worthington in the girl's murder. Martin and Stone, by their actions, had placed the Conigliaro Family in jeopardy. What they had done was unforgiveable in Vinnie's eyes. But Alex would not understand any of it. The same way he would not have understood why Palermo had killed his father, Whitey Mallo, twenty-five years ago on a fishing trip to Canada. Vinnie had come back to New York with the story of how his Uncle Whitey had fallen into a fast-moving river and drowned, when actually, Palermo had stabbed Mallo to death and buried his body. It was payback for all the times Whitey had slapped him while Palermo was working at his uncle's tavern in Lower Manhattan. The ultimate price had been paid. The head of the Conigliaro Family would not be insulted. Alex Mallo failed to understand Vinnie Palermo's mind.

"Let me know the minute you hear anything," Palermo told Al Ruggiero before getting out of his chair and going below deck. "I don't want to be disturbed until then. I have other family business to attend to."

CHAPTER FIFTY

Jackson Federal Penitentiary
Jacksonville, Florida

TOMMY BURNS WAS playing a game of checkers with Charcoal in the prison yard when he observed Snake Eyes walking towards him. Burns cleared his throat so Charcoal would know. A white-tooth grin appeared on Charcoal's face. He brought his huge head up to look at Burns. Nothing had to be said between the two men. They were both lifers. Each knew the other's mind. It got that way after sharing a cell with someone for more than thirty years. Doing time had bonded them, along with the thousands of games of checkers and countless conversations, not to mention the baring of souls late at night when the prison walls started closing in to choke the life out of a man.

"Have you made up your mind? Are you goin' to do it?" Charcoal asked.

"Yeah. I'll tell him when he gets here."

"I guessed as much. You haven't said shit all morning."

"Man, I'm not in the talkin' mood. They're goin' to beat my ass after I stick the guy, and that'll be it for me. But I keep asking myself 'what've I got to lose'? With this bum heart I'll be dead in six months anyway. Better to go out kickin' and screamin' than lyin' on your back in some prison hospital bed like a busted out whore with no one givin' a shit. Besides the money will help out my daughter in Chicago. She and her two kids live in a hole of an apartment on the Southside. And the kicker is I haven't seen her since the day she was born. She doesn't even know I exist. At least her getting the two hundred thousand will be somethin'."

"Here comes Snake eyes. I don't want to be around when he gets here. I'm goin' to disappear. I might as well take the checkerboard and checkers with me."

"Yeah, and keep them," Burns said. "After tomorrow I won't be around to play checkers anymore."

Snake Eyes waited for Charcoal to leave before taking his place on the ground opposite Burns. Two gray eyes peered through the narrow slits in Snake Eyes' face. His cheeks and forehead appeared red and bumpy. He wore a passive look like someone who was detached from the business at hand. Burns knew Snake Eyes was mob-connected and doing 15-20 for extortion. But he had never talked to the man before. And it came as a surprise to hear him speak. His voice did not fit his face. It was low and soft, not much louder than a whisper.

"Checkers, you heard the deal yesterday. What's it going to be?"

"I'll do it on one condition."

"What's that?"

"If, for some reason, the guy survives, my daughter still gets the money."

Burns thought he saw Snakes Eyes make an attempt at a smile. But he could not be sure.

"She'll get the money. But we want the guy dead. Remember that. Tomorrow Doughboy will be sick and you'll be taking his place on the food cart for C-Wing during dinner time. There'll be a knife hidden in one of the meal cartons. They'll search you before going in so don't pick up the knife until you get through security. Chief Calloway heads the security for C-Wing. Nothing much gets past him. So you're going to have to be sharp and don't act nervous no matter what he says to you. Do you got that?"

"Yeah, I got it."

"Stall once you get inside. The guards always bring the guy his meals, so he should be just about finished eating by the time you get there. Two of them will escort the guy from his cell to C-Wing's exercise area. They have to walk past you to get there. Don't look at them until they walk by you. That's important. Don't pay any attention to them. The guard on the guy's left will glance back to see that you're still putting meal cartons in the cell portholes. Once he turns back around, you take the knife out of the meal carton and make your move on the guy. Stab him in his back on the left side. Bury the knife blade deep. You've got to get his heart. Make sure you do. And be ready for a beating afterward. The two guards will have nightsticks. Do you have anything to ask me?"

Burns stared at Snake Eyes. "Yeah, who is this guy?"

Snake Eyes told him, "A rat who needs to be whacked. And that's all you've got to know."

****

It was not like Tommy Burns hadn't killed before. He was currently doing a life sentence for the 1978 robbery/murder of a mailman in South Boston. It took place on Pilsudski Way in the Old Colony Projects. Burns was running with the Winter Hill Gang back then, and a lot of money could be had in the stealing of social security checks. So killing the guy in C-Wing did not bother him. The guy had to be cooperating with the feds. He was a rat and deserved whatever he got. It was just that Burns knew it would be the end of the line for him as well. The chest pains seemed to be getting worse. He just hoped that he could make it to C-Wing and get the job done. Burns pushed the meal cart through the prison kitchen's double swinging doors. Without looking back, he directed the meal cart toward C-Wing.

"Checkers, what are you doing here? What happened to Doughboy?"

"He's sick and they told me to deliver the meal cartons."

Chief Calloway pushed the red button to electronically open the steel bar door. He stood in the open space staring at Burns. The fifty-three-year-old Calloway had worked nearly his entire adult life in the federal prison system. He worked his way up to wing chief while exhibiting a no-nonsense reputation. His hard-eyed stare had caused more than one prisoner to crumble beneath its weight. Burns was now feeling it. It was like the man could see into his mind and know what he was thinking. Burns could not look into Calloway's eyes any longer. He lowered his head.

"Raise both arms and spread your legs," Calloway said before running his hands up and down Burns's body. "Checkers, you bother me. This is your first time delivering meal cartons to C-Wing, and on top of it you're late. And I don't like what I see in your eyes. You're hiding something. Now tell me what is it about you that makes the back of my neck itch? What are you hiding?"

"Nuthin' Chief Calloway. I'm not hidin' nuthin'. They told me to bring the meal cartons to C-Wing and that's what I done."

Burns felt the burning sensation in his chest getting stronger. He did not have much time. The previous two heart attacks started out the same way. The increased burning in the chest followed by the weak feeling and then unconsciousness. But he would not wake up from this one. It was the end of the line for him. Tommy Burns knew it.

"Do you want me to bring this shit back to the kitchen, all right I will. It's no hair off my ass. I ate before they sent me over here. If you don't want these bastards to eat, I could give a shit."

Burns observed two uniformed guards at the end of the tier. A cell door opened and a big guy in orange prisoner garb stepped out. They started walking in Burns's direction. In less than a minute they would be on him.

"Go ahead and deliver the meals," Calloway said with a wave of his hand. The C-Wing supervisor was satisfied. Checkers had passed the test. He could now go ahead and do his job. Burns entered C-wing with the meal cart. Chief Calloway pushed the red button closing the steel bar door behind him.

The big guy was talking to the guards. He had a smile on his face. Forty feet away or maybe less. Both guards were staring at Burns. He opened the first cell door's porthole and shoved a meal carton inside. The guards couldn't keep their eyes off him. Did they suspect something? Burns felt a paralyzing pain in his left arm. His chest was on fire. Don't pass out, he told himself. They were nearly on him. The big guy was still smiling. Burns turned his head so as not to look at them. He opened the meal carton containing the knife. They walked past him. He put his right hand in the hot dogs and beans; he grabbed the knife. The guard on the guy's left glanced back. It was only for a second. Burns nearly fell down moving toward the guy. Regaining his balance, he lunged with the knife. The blade went into the guy's back on the left side. Burns heard him scream. He pushed down, driving the knife deeper. The guards hit Burns with their nightsticks. He felt the first blow to his head, but none of the others.

Chief Calloway hurried over to them. He looked down to observe Zach Worthington lying on the cement floor. Tommy Burns was lying next to him.

"Worthington's dead," one of the guards yelled.

"And so is Checkers," Calloway said after witnessing the blank stare in Tommy Burns's eyes.

CHAPTER FIFTY-ONE

A GULF BREEZE rustled Keri Martin's hair. It caused her to brush away the few loose strands of red that had fallen across her eyes. She told herself that she would have to get her hair cut soon. Shorter hair was more manageable, especially during the summer. Stone was looking at her from across the table. He had a smile on his face. The *Roll of the Dice's* deck lights lit up his blue eyes, making them appear bluer than normal. And the Gulf breeze served to rearrange his black hair where it now covered his forehead. Yes, she loved him, Keri confirmed in her mind, and she would go on loving him. And tomorrow at first light they would be heading to South Padre Island. They would start their new life together. Keri could hardly wait.

Stone had cooked salmon smothered in his own garlic sauce for dinner. He served it on saw palmetto leaves with steamed vegetables and buttered mushrooms. He and Keri sipped glasses of merlot and talked about their upcoming trip to South Padre Island and the things they would see along the way. They had decided upon stopping off at Tampa for dinner. Stone knew of a restaurant called—*The Irishman's Daughter*—where they could watch the chef grill extra-large Delmonico steaks covered in onions and mushrooms. And afterwards eat their dinner while seated on a wooden deck overlooking the Gulf of Mexico. They would be able to wave at people in boats passing by. It would be a delightful experience. Keri could not remember feeling so happy. She matched Stone's smile with one of her own. An overwhelming joy consumed her. Keri could not keep it bottled up any longer.

"Jackson, I can't tell you how happy I am. Everything has turned out so perfect. We're leaving for South Padre Island tomorrow morning while knowing Burke testified before the grand jury, and Zach Worthington has been indicted for the murder of Ginny Prendergast. Pat Carollo feels we could eventually get Vinnie Palermo and Al Ruggiero charged in Potts's murder. I know that has to make you happy."

"It does. Getting those two charged in Potts's murder would cap everything for me. And the fact that Zach Worthington will never see the light of day again is another plus. The three of them can go to hell as far as I'm concerned."

"What about Joe Worthington? What will happen to him? I still can't quite understand how he and Hardin and Costello thought the Prendergast girl was dead when she had only hit her head. Surely they would have felt for a pulse to see if she was alive."

"I asked Dr. Snyder from the medical examiner's office about that. He told me it would have been difficult to obtain a pulse. The knockout drug, Rohypnol, lowers the heartbeat to the point where a pulse is barely discernable. They probably tried to get one but couldn't. And it's too bad because none of this would have happened if Joe hadn't panicked. He made a terrible mistake in phoning his father for help."

"Jackson, that reminds me. This morning I talked to Lisa Moore and she told me that Janet Worthington is going to stand by her husband and not leave him. She knows that Joe did a terrible wrong, but she still loves him and is going to support him. Janet has even encouraged Joe to contact his son in Afghanistan. How much time do you think the judge will sentence him to? He did give up Zach

Worthington in his confession. And he is willing to testify against him in court. That should mean something."

"But Joe's the one who put the Rohypnol in Ginny Prendergast's drink. It was all his idea in the first place. No, he's going to do some heavy prison time. I'd say the DA's Office will be recommending anywhere from 10-20 years. Joe's baby girl should just about be starting high school by the time he gets out of jail. Anyway, that's enough about Joe Worthington and the rest of them. Let's talk about you and me. We were a good team working this case. And I'm sure if your father were alive he'd be proud of you. In fact I'd like to hear you say it. Tell me, Keri. Tell me Jack Martin would be proud of his only daughter."

Warm tears instantly sprung up in Keri's eyes. She attempted to wipe them away with a napkin from the table. Stone was staring at her. He was waiting for an answer. How did he know? Keri asked herself. Was it something she had once said? Could it have been that obvious? That she had spent her life seeking the approval of a dead man? Her father. Sergeant Jack Martin. Trying to find it in other men. But always coming up empty. Two and three month affairs. Two years with Rance Stapleton. Then coming to Florida. And her meeting Jackson Stone. Keri questioned herself. Was she still seeking her father's approval? Or had she found it?

"Yes, he would," Keri said while placing the napkin back down on the table. "I can actually say it out loud and believe it. I never thought this day would ever come."

"Well, this calls for a special toast," Stone said coming out of his chair. "I have a bottle of champagne tucked away below deck. I'll go and get it. Hold on to whatever you're thinking about until I get back."

Stone hurried below deck. The bottle of champagne was in a storage bin located in his bedroom. Wasting no time, he went directly to the bin and opened it while setting aside the rain gear on top. A black plastic bag that he could not recall seeing before was next to the bottle of champagne. Where did this come from? Stone asked himself. It wasn't here two days ago. He opened the bag and took a step back. A wave of panic hit him. Inside the black bag were several clear plastic packets of what looked like white crystal methamphetamine. In addition to the white crystal were thousands of dollars. A classic setup if he had ever seen one. Stone reached into his front pants pocket for his cellphone. He had to notify Pat Carollo right away. DEA agents could descend upon the *Roll of the Dice* at any moment to arrest him and Martin. Stone's cellphone rang before he had time to punch in Carollo's phone number. Carollo was phoning him.

"Pat, I was just going to call you. You won't believe …"

"Jackson, don't say anything just listen. I am at the Jacksonville Penitentiary where we were holding Zach Worthington. Palermo's people were able to get to him. He's dead."

"But how?"

"It doesn't matter how. It's already been done. And I think you and Keri Martin might be next. Is she with you?"

Stone told Carollo that he and Martin were on the *Roll of the Dice*. He then told him about the black bag and the packets of white crystal along with the thousands of dollars in drug money. Carollo did not seem surprised.

"That just goes to confirm my hunch. Palermo is going to have you and Keri taken out sooner than later. Maybe even tonight. Dirty cops don't get good press, and that's probably what Vinnie is counting on. Jackson, as soon as I get off the phone with you, I'll be sending FBI agents down from Tampa to assist you. But it'll take them at least three hours to get there. How about your people? Can you get anyone to back you up?"

"No. Bob Garcia is off for the weekend visiting his parents in Miami. That leaves Lisa Moore as the only one on duty. And she's handling a house break-in on the other side of town. She phoned me a little while ago and told me about it. It looks like, for the time being, it's going to be just Keri and me. Pat, I got to go. I'm below deck and Keri is by herself topside."

"Jackson, one more thing before you go. Johnny Rocco and Blowtorch Charlie will be the hit men coming after you and Keri. They were spotted in Port Charlotte yesterday with another thug by the name of Carl Rossi. Rossi carries a 9mm Uzi and walks with a limp. Shoot the three of them on sight if you get the chance. They'll do the same to you."

Stone put his cellphone back in his front pants pocket. Prior to taking the stairs up to the deck, he grabbed the Beretta 9mm and extra magazine off the nightstand next to his bed. Martin was waiting for him when he got back on deck. She had a questioning look on her face. She's probably wondering what took me so long, Stone thought. He decided to check out the pier before joining her.

Earlier, Stone had seen a guy still fishing near the pier's entrance. The guy was no longer there. And someone had been standing on the houseboat further down from the *Roll of the Dice*. He, too, was gone. Quickly, Stone turned his attention to the guard shack forty yards away. A uniformed Mike Pesky was sitting inside. There was a lit cigarette dangling from the security guard's mouth. Everything seemed all right. Stone started towards Keri when he abruptly stopped. Mike Pesky didn't smoke cigarettes. He smoked cigars. It could not have been Pesky. Stone looked back at the guard shack. It was now empty. Whoever had been in it was gone. Without hesitating, Stone switched off the *Roll of the Dice's* deck lights and ran to Martin.

"Keri, do you have your Glock with you?"

"Yes, it's in my handbag," Martin said reaching down to remove the Glock. "Why? What's wrong?"

Stone told her, including the fact that Worthington was dead and Carollo felt they could be next. He also told her about the men he had seen earlier. And about someone taking Mike Pesky's place in the guard shack.

Keri asked him, "What happened to Pesky?"

"My guess is they killed him. And in a few minutes they're going to do their best to kill us as well. They're probably waiting until it's completely dark. That shouldn't be long now. Then they'll come at us from both sides. They'll try to pin us down in a crossfire. Keri, I don't have to tell you about Johnny Rocco. Not only is he an excellent shooter, he's as cunning as they come. We have to expect the unexpected with Rocco. Once things kick off, don't let your guard down for a second."

Stone could see the worried look in Keri's eyes. She was afraid. But he did not see any panic, and that was what he was looking for. Fear was a good thing. It could keep a person alive. He bent down and kissed her.

"Like I said before, you and me make a good team. And we're not going to let three thugs ruin our plans for going to South Padre Island. So pick your target, and when you fire use three round bursts. They'll be shooting back at you, so you'll have to keep your head down. Now slowly slide out of your chair until your knees touch the deck. They should be coming at us any minute."

Martin did as Stone instructed. Kneeling down, she removed the extra magazine from her handbag and placed it in her front pants pocket. Keri was glad she had on a long-sleeved top and long pants. It would be easier on her arms and knees should she have to slink across the deck. Stone had moved to the middle of the *Roll of the Dice* on the pier side. Keri knew that the position would give him a better view of the pier. She decided to join him.

"Those wooden pilings should make for good concealment," Keri said while taking note of the line of pilings along both sides of the pier. "They could work their way from either direction and be on top of us in no time. Jackson, I wish there was more light. I can barely make out the pilings let along anyone hiding behind them."

Stone told her, "They'll have the same problem in seeing us. Just shoot at their gun flashes once they open up. But remember to move to either side after firing because they'll be aiming at your gun flashes as well. Keri, I just saw some movement down by the houseboat. I think someone is on the pier. He's probably making his way toward the *Roll of the Dice*. It looks like it finally got dark enough for them. They'll be coming now, so get ready."

A loud burst of automatic fire erupted from the right of the *Roll of the Dice*. It was followed by another burst of fire from the left. Both Stone and Martin ducked down as a spray of bullets cascaded all around them. Keri looked at Stone next to her. He was curled up in a ball looking back at her.

"They're right on top of us," he yelled. "Keri, we have to separate. Crawl towards the bow and don't come up until you see me firing. Shoot at their flashes. They should be directing their fire at me. Hurry. We don't have much time."

Keri crawled to the bow of the boat. She looked back to see Stone. He was holding the Beretta with two hands. After a pause in the shooting, he rose up to fire three bursts. Instantly, the automatic firing became focused on Stone. The sound of gunfire was deafening. Keri raised her head to peer over the side of the boat. There was a flash of gunfire approximately thirty yards away. A shadowy figure. He was firing an automatic weapon. Martin leveled her Glock. She aimed at the gun flashes, pulling three times on the Glock's trigger. The man dropped his gun and fell face down onto the pier.

"Get down," Keri heard Stone yell just before a barrage of automatic rounds struck the *Roll of the Dice* to the right of her. Stone stood and fired his Beretta. Someone on the pier screamed; Stone continued firing. Keri peeked over the side. A dark figure was lying in the center of the pier. He did not appear to be moving. Keri heard her name being called. It was Stone. He was shouting for her to come to him. Keri hurried over as fast as she could.

"Jackson, you've been shot," Martin shrieked after seeing Stone holding a white handkerchief against the right side of his chest. "How bad is it? I'll phone for an ambulance."

"No, there's not time. Rocco. He's got to be close. The other two were just a diversion. I told you with Rocco it was the unexpected that you had to look for. We didn't figure on the water. Keri, he has a boat. Rocco is going to try to board the *Roll of the Dice* from the water."

Two bullets splintered the deck next to them. Keri looked up to see a human shadow at the boat's stern. She pointed the Glock, firing two rounds. But Rocco had moved. He was no longer there. Where did he go? Keri asked herself. She glanced down at Stone. Both Stone's eyes were closed; he appeared to be unconscious. Keri knew that she was on her own. Stone would be of no help to her. The very thought left her gasping for air. What to do? Think, she told herself. You've got to do something. What wouldn't Rocco expect? That's what you have to do. And then it came to her. Keri moved swiftly to the *Roll of the Dice's* portside. She looked for the main light switch. Keri knew the switch controlled the deck lights. Finding it, she pressed the button.

There was instant brightness. The deck lights proved momentarily blinding. Keri brought up her left hand to lessen the glare. Rocco was doing the same less than twenty-five feet away. Keri saw him pointing the barrel of the 38. caliber revolver in her direction. It was like slow motion. She observed everything. The dark look on Rocco's face. Mike Pesky's uniform that Rocco was wearing. Even the bloodstain on the left shirt pocket of the uniform. Pesky's blood. Keri centered her aim on the bloodstain. She squeezed the Glock's trigger. The first bullet hit the center of the uniform shirt pocket. The second and third bullets struck an inch above the first. Rocco dropped his gun. He fell forward collapsing onto the *Roll of the Dice's* deck. Keri wasted no time in getting back to Stone. He was conscious when she got to him.

"Did you get Rocco?" Stone asked her.

"Yes."

"I knew that you would. Keri, I just want to say …"

"Jackson, don't say anything," Martin told him before sitting down and placing Stone's head on her lap. "You don't have to. I know you love me."

Keri reached into her front pants pocket for her cellphone and called for an ambulance.

CHAPTER FIFTY-TWO

Fort Lee, New Jersey

"OUR GAMBLING OPERATION in Florida is in jeopardy. The feds are all over Pelican's Landing and there's talk of a federal grand jury. It's being called to investigate the Florida State Legislature for accepting bribes. Besides that we have the Five Families movin' in on our territory more each day. With Johnny Rocco dead, they're not so much afraid of us anymore. Vinnie, I don't know what to do. The boys are nervous and I can't blame them."

Vinnie Palermo and Al Ruggiero were huddled together in the back seat of Vinnie's black limousine. The limo was parked with the motor running in a vacant lot three miles from Palermo's Fort Lee, New Jersey mansion. The driver and bodyguard, Bobby Vaccaro, was standing outside the limo smoking a cigarette. Inside the limo a car radio was blaring. The volume had been turned up to keep Palermo and Ruggiero's conversation private. There was always a chance the FBI could have a listening device planted somewhere inside the limo.

"Let them be nervous. It'll keep them on their toes. I have more to think about than their being nervous. Worthington is dead and no longer a problem, but there's still Carla to be dealt with. You're sure about her meeting the FBI Agent Carollo on two separate occasions. There's no mistake?"

"No. I personally saw her meeting with him the second time. Vinnie, I'm sorry. I know Carla has always meant a lot to you. She's your favorite niece. And besides that, her son, Joe, is your godson."

"Not anymore," Palermo said. "Carla doesn't mean a thing to me. I want her taken out before the end of the week. Make it look like an accident for her mother's sake."

"Vinnie are you sure?"

"Yes. And I don't want her name mentioned ever again."

The two men's heads were so close Palermo could smell the calamari Ruggiero had eaten for lunch. Vinnie looked into his friend's dark brown eyes and shook his head. He and Al Ruggiero had been friends since the early days. The two men were like brothers with how each felt about the other. And after all that time Ruggiero still didn't really know him. Maybe that was good, Vinnie thought. Don't let anyone get too close. The day might come when you have to fix it so that they never see the light of day again.

"How about Stone and Martin? Are you still keeping tabs on them? It's too soon to take them out now. We'll have to wait for the right time. But I don't care if its next year or the year after, it's going to happen. Just don't lose track of them."

"I won't, Vinnie. I promise. But what are we goin' to do about the other families? We couldn't survive a full scale war right now. But if we don't do somethin' they're goin' to keep nibblin' away at our territory."

"Al, let them. All I want you to do is to buy me some time. With Zach Worthington out of the way the feds got nothing on us. It's only the other families we have to deal with. I've got to find me another Johnny Rocco. And once I do we'll get everything back and then some. I'm leaving for Sicily in the morning. If you need me, you know how to get hold of me."

"Okay Vinnie, I'll buy us some time. But I don't think it's a good idea to take out Stone and Chief Martin. Can't you just forget about them?"

"No," Palermo said, moving his face even closer to Ruggiero's. Their noses were almost touching. "No, I can't forget about them. No one does what they did to me and gets away with it. There'll come a day when I'll see both Stone and Martin dead. It won't be anytime soon, but the day will come."

EPILOGUE

Six Weeks Later

THE DAY WAS sunny with a breeze out of the west. Keri Martin adjusted her sunglasses before looking over at Stone. He was standing at the *Roll of the Dice's* helm staring straight ahead. It was early morning. Heavy rain had fallen overnight; overcast skies opened up to make everything clean. The fresh rain scent was still in the air. Keri took a deep breath. She held it in for as long as she could before letting it out. It was so good to be alive, she thought. There was a time when Keri did not think this moment possible. That she and Stone would be taking the *Roll of the Dice* to South Padre Island. Almost nobody had expected him to survive the surgery. The doctors had given Stone little chance of living out the night. The 9mm bullet had perforated his right lung, causing it to collapse. And a great deal of blood had been lost, which put additional strain on his heart. But Keri knew Stone would survive. He had to survive. She had searched too long for him. He could not die after she had finally found him.

"I've been thinking," Stone said turning to Keri. "We'll be going by New Orleans on our way to South Padre Island. She's a great town New Orleans. I thought we might stop and spend a night or two there. There are plenty of things to see and do."

"I think it's a fantastic idea," Keri said, smiling. "I've heard a lot about New Orleans, but I've never been there. Jackson, I can't tell you how excited I am about this trip. After all those days I spent worrying about you. Now, just to get away and not have to worry anymore. It's such a good feeling. I don't think I would have made it through your being shot if it weren't for Lisa Moore and Bob Garcia. And Pat Carollo. He was there as well. They waited at the hospital with me until you were out of danger. I'll never forget them for it."

"How does the saying go? A man isn't rich if he doesn't have friends."

"And that goes for a woman, too. I am rich. Richer than I ever thought I would be."

A smile formed on Stone's face. He reached with his right hand to remove Keri's sunglasses. He had a sudden need to see her eyes. Two pools of green looked back at him.

"A good friend of mine lives in New Orleans," Stone told her. "His name is Father Anthony. He was my chaplain back when I was stationed in Iraq. He's the pastor at Our Lady of Perpetual Help Parish, and I know if I ask him to marry us, he will. You can pick out your own wedding ring in New Orleans and have a church wedding to go along with it. What do you think? All you have to do is say yes."

A sparkling wetness pervaded Martin's eyes. A bright smile quickly followed. Keri rose up to kiss Stone on the mouth. "Yes," she said to him while wrapping both her arms around his neck. "Yes, yes, yes."

"Hold on now. Don't put me back in the hospital with a broken neck. Besides that, we have to put our heads together to figure out how our getting married is going to go over with the Pelican's Landing Town Council."

"What do you mean?" Keri asked before removing her arms from around Stone. "What does the town council have to do with our getting married?"

"Everything. They're not going to go for a husband and wife team running their police department. One or both of us will be out of job once they find out. No, we're going to have to keep it to ourselves, and tell no one that we're married. That's the only way it will work."

"You mean I can't wear my wedding ring? I can't tell anyone that you're my husband? Jackson, I don't care for that at all. Is there anything we can do? Maybe if we talked to them."

"No, we're going to have to keep it to ourselves. You will only be able to wear your wedding ring when we're alone together. It'll have to be that way for a while. But we'll still be married. And that's all that matters, isn't it?"

"Yes," Keri said, "That's all that matters."

"And one other thing you should be aware of," Stone said while hoping not to spoil the moment for her. "Vinnie Palermo is not going to let us get away with what we did to him and the Conigliaro Family. Someday he'll be sending people to kill us. I don't know when, but one day they'll show up. We have to always remember it. Keri, I wish things could be different, for your sake."

"Jackson, you're not telling me anything that I don't already know," Keri said taking back her sunglasses and putting them on. "If Vinnie Palermo wants to send people to kill us, let them come. I'll be watching your back and you'll be watching mine."

ABOUT THE AUTHOR

J.C. Quinn resides in Florida and is a member of the Gulf Coast Writer's Association. Besides *Secret Murder*, he has written *Dead Priest at Gator's Pond, To Kill a Fox, Triple Murder*, and *Heroes: Stories, Letters, and Thoughts of a Catholic Man.*

CPSIA information can be obtained
at www.ICGtesting.com
Printed in the USA
FFOW02n0033280215
11373FF

9 781941 536247